Claudia Silver to the Rescue

Claudia Silver
to the Rescue

A NOVEL

Kathy Ebel

HOUGHTON MIFFLIN HARCOURT
BOSTON   NEW YORK   2013

Copyright © 2013 by Kathy Ebel

For information about permission to reproduce selections from this book,
write to Permissions, Houghton Mifflin Harcourt Publishing Company,
215 Park Avenue South, New York, New York 10003.

www.hmhbooks.com

Library of Congress Cataloging-in-Publication Data
Ebel, Kathy.
Claudia Silver to the rescue : a novel / Kathy Ebel.
p. cm.
ISBN 978-0-547-98557-2
1. Young women—New York (State)—New York—Fiction.
2. Self-realization in women—Fiction. I. Title.
PS3605.B445C57 2013
813'.6—dc23
2012039062

Printed in the United States of America
DOC 10 9 8 7 6 5 4 3 2 1

Dedicated with deepest gratitude to
Jessica Vitkus,
my first *first reader,*
who told me so

Contents

Claudia Silver to the Rescue

Fast & Sloppy

CLAUDIA SILVER, the production assistant, ordered lunch for the ladies of Georgica Films every day. The all-female staff ate family-style, around a large oak table that their employer, executive producer Ricky Green, had purchased at considerable expense for just this purpose. While the daily lunch order at the little production company was perhaps her chief duty, Claudia had other key responsibilities, including the speedy typing of contact sheets for different production jobs on the Selectric in the corner. She handed the documents to her bosses Faye, Tamara, or Kim to review, and invariably trudged back to the typewriter, taunted by the crop of typos that only minutes before were nowhere to be seen and now required immediate correction.

Claudia ran errands and picked up giant brown-paper-wrapped bunches of flowers from the wholesaler on Twenty-

Seventh Street. Ricky, who'd gotten into the business of producing television commercials because he wanted to wear jeans to work and considered restaurants and a place in Idaho important, arranged the flowers himself in various Depression-era pottery vases from his sprawling collection. Claudia FedExed gift certificates from day spas and salons to clients whose birthdays had almost been forgotten. She called the messenger service for pickups and drop-offs around town. She greeted, with a wink, the various rangy, ripe, dreadlocked, tattooed, gold-toothed, knit-capped dude-bros whose cycling cleats clattered on the parquet and whose Public Enemy pounded through their Walkman headphones as they waited for a signature, while her bosses tensed, silently calculating the degree of sexual threat the messengers posed.

Claudia carefully observed and pitied the ladies of Georgica Films. She was determined to perform her daily tasks with an ever-so-slight yet palpable indifference, which, when paired with her charisma, would keep her pointedly on the fringe of the operation and protect her from ever turning out like them.

Her idiosyncratic work ethic had earned Claudia the nickname Fast & Sloppy.

Every day at Georgica Films there were fights, usually over the phone. They typically began with first-date nervousness, rocketed into cocky aggression punctuated with gales of ballsy laughter, and ended with a pounding of the receiver into its cradle, followed by loud analysis, frustrated tears, and a cigarette on the fire escape. Faye, Tamara, and Kim screamed at production managers and casting directors on the phone: hours later they would call back and laugh it off, comrades once again. This style of conflict resolution was a new one for Claudia.

In the home of Claudia's mother, Edith Mendelssohn, fireworks had always been followed, swiftly, by cataclysmic ice ages. Only once, when she was eleven, on a long, cranky car trip, Claudia told Edith that she hated her:

"I HATE YOU."

Hearing the hot syllables leap from her throat had been satisfying. She'd heard other children rage at their parents similarly with negligible consequences, and telling her mother she hated her made young Claudia feel, briefly, normal. But she soon regretted it. Edith didn't react suddenly. Her hand didn't fly into the backseat to box an ear. She kept driving, under a remarkable silence that Claudia soon realized Edith planned to keep up. As it turned out, Edith neither spoke to nor looked at her child for three straight days. Finally, when Claudia couldn't take it anymore, she dropped to her knees and begged for forgiveness at her mother's lap. This method was successful. Edith accepted her child's apology, recognized her once again, and life resumed.

Ten years later, Claudia was a senior in college, sitting on the floor of her dorm room on Manhattan's far Upper West Side, on the phone with Edith. In one week, Claudia would graduate and set out to seek God knows what. She was afraid. Over the last month, she'd visited several of her favorite professors at their office hours to ask what *they* thought, but none of them had a particular plan of action in mind for her. Recognizing that she was utterly unprepared to depart the snug little campus, Claudia was tempted to demand a refund from the bursar, despite the fact that her education had been financed largely on credit.

Claudia had called her mother to discuss the upcoming summer. Graduation ceremonies would be held in a few days, and Claudia's various friends would be going home to catered graduation parties held in leafy backyards, professional internships killing time before graduate school, or bright new backpacks that would soon be hauled off on wine-dark European tours. Claudia had the weekend waitressing job in SoHo she'd held on to since her senior year in high school. Plus a hangover.

"I'm afraid I'm unable to offer you accommodation at this time," Edith explained. Edith, who spoke more languages than she owned bras and trusted poetry more than people, might have been known for her slim but stunning volumes of sestinas in multiple translations, had circumstances far beyond her control not required her to become a business-school librarian at Baruch College. She spoke in calligraphy.

"*Accommodation?*" Claudia echoed, disbelievingly. "Are you my mother, or Howard Johnson's?"

Claudia's best friend, Bronwyn Tate, had just come downstairs from her own nearby single to visit. Theirs was the druggy dorm, now in a wistful state of dismantling as its residents prepared to scatter. Good-quality museum posters had been stuffed, ignominiously, in trash cans, as a general scorn for the Impressionists was required as an exit visa, and futon frames, broken by one too many threesomes, were piled on 114th Street to dry their particleboard bones in the hot May sun. Bronwyn joined Claudia on the floor, pulling the shredded cuffs of her faded Nantucket Reds up over her bony knees and folding her long legs Indian-style.

"Quarters have become close," Edith continued, "and I'm afraid I just don't have the space."

"And would those close quarters by any chance go by the name of Robbie Burns?" Claudia accused, as she and Bronwyn exchanged a look. Bronwyn communicated her focus and sympathy by tucking a long, loose strand of blond hair behind her ear.

Edith's gentleman friend was Robbie Burns, although Claudia knew he was neither. Edith had become involved with Robbie a decade before, when she'd still been married to her second husband, Mr. Goldberg, the father of her younger child, Claudia's half sister, Phoebe, who was eight years Claudia's junior. Neither Claudia's father, a hotshot émigré professor with a penchant for psilocybin mushrooms and primal scream therapy, nor Phoebe's father, a Jewish playboy with a sixth-grade education and a velour wardrobe, had remained in the picture. But each girl resembled her own father as well as the brunt of Edith's humiliation, embodying separate failed chapters of her fragmented life. Edith had kept her maiden name.

The family was shaped like a triangle.

Edith and Robbie Burns had met at Baruch. She'd been thirsty and flagging, en route to a Hillel Club event, a lecture on Malamud and Roth presented by a darling widower of the English department who would have been a suitable mate for Edith, if only he'd been fifteen years her junior, tall, ponytailed, spottily educated, occasionally incarcerated, wearing a canvas coverall provided by the beverage distribution company that had disregarded considerable doubts upon hiring him, and stocking the soda machine, like Robbie was. Robbie handed her a cold one, on the house, with a saucy comment that made Edith feel wanted, dangerous, and armed. She'd divorced Goldberg a few years later, and kept Robbie as her poison: he was the Little Debbie Oatmeal Creme Pie of paramours, and like bodega pastry was best consumed in the dark. Edith's solution to managing the shame of Robbie's presence, alongside motherhood and her respectable profession, was to pretend to Claudia that he didn't exist.

Edith, erudite and accomplished in certain realms, was very, very bad at her chosen ruse, dropping endless extravagant clues over the ensuing years for Claudia to pick up. Edith was either whispering to Robbie in the bathroom, the long cord of the kitchen phone dragged across the dinner table, or she was visiting Robbie, first in rehab, then in prison, then in rehab, and bringing Phoebe along, who would later report to Claudia exactly where they'd been. Or she was pulling the car

5

into every available rest stop between the city and the beach to "call a friend" on the pay phone, while the sisters waited in the hot, old Karmann Ghia and made up spoof lyrics to movie theme songs. Skipping over introductions or explanation, Edith finally moved Robbie into her home with her two daughters the dreadful summer before Claudia had left for college. Claudia didn't know whether to act surprised or not. But she knew from precedent that she wasn't supposed to act *angry*. Which made Claudia exponentially ripshit, enough for all of them.

"I'm not sure where it is written that a grown woman continues to live with her mother," Edith was saying.

I'm not a grown woman, Claudia was tempted to counter.

"When people graduate from college, they go home," Claudia argued instead. "They at least have it as an *option*. I'm not saying forever. Or even for the whole summer. But literally. You know, I come home for a week or two, regroup, and then I'm outta there." Bronwyn had reached out to give Claudia's knee a caring squeeze with her long fingers.

"I'm afraid," Edith countered, firmly, "that you'll need to revise that agenda."

"You realize that what you're saying is that your fucking junkie boyfriend is more important to you than I am," Claudia croaked. It wasn't even that Claudia was so eager to return. Or that she thought of Edith's domicile as *home*, particularly. It was simply the *injustice* of it all.

"What I realize is that you're very angry right now."

"Do you wonder at all where I'm going to sleep once the dorms close?" Claudia asked her mother. Bronwyn had now dipped her head to rest her cheek on Claudia's shoulder. She smelled familiarly of Chanel and cigarettes.

"I think you might inquire with the housing office," Edith suggested. "You may be able to secure suitable campus housing for the summer, and perhaps beyond."

"You're saying I am not welcome in your home."

"There comes a time," Edith declared, "for a young person to be, simply, on her own. Do you think *I* ever went home, quote unquote? By the time I was your age, my childhood home was a mass graveyard, and we had lost everything. And not just tea services and dowry linens, I assure you."

Edith's Hitler card, Claudia knew, was her mother's prerogative and impossible to trump. She promised herself she would not cry until she had hung up the phone, which would be soon. "We should have talked about this," she said, plaintive. "Before it was too late."

"No one put a gun to your head and forced you to ignore your own next steps until the eleventh hour, as they did us."

"Oh my God!" Claudia cried, hot tears of rage making her break her promise. "You know what? You are a terrible fucking mother."

"And you, my dear," Edith replied, "aren't so hot as a daughter."

Claudia hung up the phone, shifted into Bronwyn's bony embrace, and wept.

"It's okay," said Bronwyn. At that very moment, forty blocks downtown, Bronwyn's own mother, Annie Tate, was sitting at her kitchen table, affixing Dinah Washington stamps to the invitations for Bronwyn's graduation party, which would be held at the Boathouse.

"No, it's not," Claudia sobbed.

Bronwyn sighed. "I know," she admitted. "Your mom is . . . who she is. But you're going to be okay."

"If you say so," Claudia managed to get out.

"You can stay in our guest room. We'll help you figure it out."

Claudia clung to Bronwyn. "Thank you," she eventually said.

"I love you, Claudia. You're my best friend." There was not

a tissue in sight. Bronwyn offered Claudia the hem of her Indian print tunic. "Do you want to blow your nose?"

"Oh *hell* no," Claudia replied, finding her ability to chuckle.

"Do you want to go with me and my dad to Corner Bistro?" Bronwyn asked. Bronwyn's dad was Paul Tate. He was what a father was supposed to be. Handsome and powerful, with a taste for both problem solving and fun, and a large collection of witty cuff links. "He's down in the Village," Bronwyn continued, "and I'm sure he'd love to see you."

"Even under dreadful fucking circumstances?" Claudia shuddered, the last of her sobs moving through her.

"Are you kidding?" said Bronwyn, rising fluidly to her feet and offering Claudia her hand, "he eats dreadful fucking circumstances for breakfast."

It was midafternoon and midweek, but Paul Tate, a senior partner at a white-shoe law firm in midtown, was able to get away and spring for burgers, beers, and advice. He would have quarters for the jukebox, favoring Stan Getz and "Box of Rain." He was a man who would *be* there. For his kids, for his kids' friends, even for his friends' kids. He was sane, and he was buying.

"Yes," said Claudia, as Bronwyn took her hand and pulled her up to standing. "Please. Totally."

That May night at the Corner Bistro had been almost two years ago, and Claudia and Bronwyn had since become roommates. They now shared a first-floor apartment in Brooklyn, on the south side of Park Slope. During the summer, their place had been sweltering, with plastic box fans in every room. But now that it was November, a chilly draft swept in and the old windows rattled. In the last two years, Claudia had started what was apparently her adult life, complete with taxes, credit cards, birthdays, Pap smears, snowstorms, clumsy accidents involving avocados and paring knives and requiring a few stitches, and other milestones and phenomena on which, she noticed, Bronwyn regularly consulted Annie and Paul Tate.

In these two years, Claudia had not heard a single word from Edith, who lived four subway stops away.

Edith had always expected her eldest to recite poetry, write charming thank-you notes, rise when an adult came into the room, eat her pizza with a fork and knife, deftly analyze major works of art and literature, assuage her depression and counsel her heartbreaks, and otherwise promote the aristocratic values of her rightful home, a Europe that no longer existed. Claudia had been a cowed, entertaining child, aware of the chaotic sea that rose up on all sides around her mother, an atoll. But these same skills had come in terrifically handy over the last two years, during which Claudia had become an expert on soliciting temporary rescue from other people's parents, the Tates chief among them. Performing for them, projecting a confidence that belied her fear, dining for weeks on the leftovers from their Thanksgiving tables, belonging nowhere. Surviving.

Bronwyn Tate received a monthly allowance of four hundred dollars and brought her laundry home once a month for Annie's cleaning lady's loving regimen of bleach, softener, and sharp folds. With the paychecks she earned as an assistant producer on a syndicated morning talk show hosted by a former Miss USA whose girl-on-girl photos had cost her her crown but landed the front page of the *Post*, Bronwyn paid her share of the rent and utilities and put ten percent in savings. With her allowance she bought steak frites, theater tickets, first editions, and shirts from Steven Alan. When her allowance ran short, she met Paul for lunch in the partners' dining room and left with a check.

But in Claudia's case, "no money" really did mean *no money*, especially toward the end of the month. Accordingly, she had become an expert on free things in Manhattan: the exact timing of subway-to-bus transfers, the Thai tofu cubes, baked falafel, and other after-work samples at Healthy Pleasures that would do for dinner, and the listening booths at Tower Records, where she'd lose herself in Lisa Stansfield for forty seconds at a time. In the evenings, at the dive bars, Mexican restaurants, and dance clubs that she frequented, Claudia paid for shots, beers, and margaritas with the generous allowance always on offer from her new credit card. Weaving slightly in her cowboy boots, Claudia would scan the free promotional postcards that had recently popped up in display racks at her favorite haunts. The postcards boasted cheeky graphics that often referenced sadomasochistic sex and usually celebrated hard liquor. Claudia combed them for G-rated images, and sent off innocuous, Edith-proof messages to her sister, Phoebe, who had been fourteen the last time they'd seen each other. Claudia's estrangement from Edith had ushered a storybook frost into the triangular kingdom, with Snow White and Rose Red encased in separate blocks of blue ice at its center. Claudia was prepared to play all roles in the tale: the dastardly villain, the chilblained victim coughing spottily into an embroidered handkerchief—shit, she'd even be her own handsome prince.

"*Darling Feebz,*" a typical note would read, "*Today I saw a white guy with locks at Smith/9th Street reading CATCH A FIRE and I thought of you. Say hi to Barkella. I miss you and love you. Claude.*" Barkella was Phoebe's beloved terry-cloth dog, whose irises had long ago been rubbed from her plastic eyes. For all Claudia knew, Phoebe might have already relegated Barkella to a cardboard box.

At fifty-two, Edith Mendelssohn's beauty had taken on a voracious quality as it defended itself. She was anxiously fixated on Phoebe's lanky form, with its willowy limbs, her loose mane of sandy waves, and her large, sexual mouth. Phoebe's captivating appearance only fueled Edith's quiet doubts about her child's intelligence. As Edith piled and twisted her own lush, silvering mane in the mottled mirror of her tiny bathroom's medicine cabinet and grimly considered that her own refugee parents had been unable to afford braces for her teeth, she reaffirmed her belief that beauty and brilliance were mutually exclusive. Brilliant women used their minds to seduce, and as they accumulated and discarded suitors, their brilliance tended to harden, diamondlike. Beautiful women, on the other hand, had no choice but to quickly tether themselves to dull men with paunches and briefcases, and then face a lifetime of constant pregnancies and pristine living rooms devoid of a single real book.

Had Claudia brought home anything shy of an A-minus, Edith's response would have been baffled and withering. But to the simplest of Phoebe's achievements—a painting of a Thanksgiving turkey fashioned from a handprint, a B-minus on a social studies quiz—Edith responded with an overwrought gasp. The fact that this dramatic praise was actually relief was not lost on Phoebe. It made her want to fail.

Phoebe was a junior in high school now. She probably wasn't a virgin; she probably did drugs, and which ones and with whom and how often and where, Claudia knew full well, would chart her future as powerfully as what college she would attend—with the defining question of what drugs to do in college looming powerfully on a rapidly approaching horizon.

Of course, Phoebe never wrote back.

She would have needed Claudia's address to do that.

Every day at noon, it went something like this.

A loaded silence would choke the sunny, stifling, open-plan work space at Georgica Films as Claudia headed for the menu drawer.

Everybody lived for lunch. Everybody was worried that Claudia was going to forget about it. Everybody bragged to their cubicle-dwelling friends about the homey, civilized rituals of Georgica Films. Everybody was worried about the restaurant choice. Everybody was starving, struggling with a bottomless hunger that had been stuffed every which way. Everybody was wondering if they would go to the gym that night and if so, how that would inform the sandwich-versus-salad dilemma. Everybody loathed one another, wishing to God they could just eat at their desks or duck out for a god-damned slice like the rest of New York City.

Claudia grabbed a handful of menus. Her bosses' ears were satellite dishes scanning the universe for anything resembling a side order of fruit. She'd return to the work space and take her customary place at its center, as the daily debate would commence.

On this November day it went exactly like this.

"So where are we ordering?"

"Oh, I don't know," Faye sighed, thrusting her arm toward Claudia and wriggling her fingers and thumbs, stacked with silver and turquoise rings, in an excited bid for a menu. A nobody from nowhere, as Edith would say, Faye was Georgica Films' senior producer, Ricky's second in command. In a bid for eternal youth, Faye colored her hair a rich shade of egg-plant and wore matching lip liner, unaware that these choices broadcast her spot as the oldest woman in the room. Ricky, a Jewish American Prince from Great Neck who admired and scorned the artistic life, grudgingly appreciated that Faye's collection of squash-blossom necklaces and conch belts com-plemented his design scheme.

"Where did we order yesterday?" Faye inquired.

"Around the Clock diner," Claudia reminded.

"Right. Grilled chicken caesar," Faye reminisced, cupping her chin.

"Dressing and Parmesan toasts on the side," Claudia elaborated.

"Mm." Faye nodded contemplatively, deflated by the memory.

Kim put her call to a Miami production designer on hold. She was the only *married*-married woman at Georgica Films, and emphasized her status by facing the framed, drunken candid from her wedding night into the room. "Sushi?" she offered hopefully, having perfected the art of milking her job for expensive perks.

Nearby, Tamara pushed a wall of angry air through her wide nostrils. "Hello, parasites?" she threatened rhetorically. She was a tall, curvaceous woman with fluffy, multicolored hair. In her daily costume of leggings, cowl-necked knit tunics, and floppy, jewel-toned Arche boots, she still managed to swagger.

Kim cupped her fingers toward the ceiling and, with a wink to Claudia, ever so subtly flipped Tamara the bird. "How about Thai," Tamara suggested.

"How about I get a tattoo that says *I'm allergic to peanuts*," countered Kim.

"I'm good with Around the Clock," came a timid voice from another corner, belonging to Gwen, the morbidly obese production accountant, who commuted from Staten Island and who had just signed the contract on a new townhome in which she'd continue to live with her mother and Fabio, her adored cat. Gwen was actually raising her hand.

Claudia looked around the room. "Going once, going twice, sold," she determined, calling on Gwen as the other women quickly absorbed their respective disappointment and returned to their phones. "Yes, Gwen."

"I'll have a grilled chicken caesar," said Gwen. "Dressing and Parmesan toasts on the side."

"Me, too," said Kim.

"Me three," sang Faye.

"Me four," whined Ricky, his nasal voice floating over the glass-brick walls that encased his office, where he was hunched over on a bark-cloth couch, rolling a joint on a book of Bruce Weber photographs, well aware that someone had been dipping into his stash again.

Tamara snapped her fingers at Claudia. "Let me see the menu."

While she waited for lunch to arrive, Claudia tidied up the mess of stems and leaves left from Ricky's flower arranging and set the table with Fiestaware and thick cotton napkins. She made visits to the bathroom mirror, where she pushed her bangs this way and that way across her forehead and fidgeted with the thick ropes of ceramic African beads that formed a tangled breastplate over her vintage cardigan.

Her whole body was prickling hot and cold.

She was not thinking about lunch.

The house phone by the loft's front door rang and she dove on it.

She tried to make herself sound distracted and offhand. "Georgica," she said.

"Hey, girl," said a voice like gravel and velour. It was Ruben Hyacinth, the rock-and-roll doorman. Claudia leaned against the wall. "Eat or be eaten," Ruben growled, then exploded in laughter. Claudia hung up and caught her breath, remembering exactly how she came to know that Ruben had pierced nipples. Tamara was staring at her from behind her desk.

"Getting lunch, be right back," she chirped, breaking a strict office rule as she let the heavy door slam behind her.

In the elevator, Claudia pulled up her textured tights, tucked her T-shirt into the denim skirt she'd made from a pair of jeans, and jittered the pointy toe of her black cowboy boot. As the elevator doors opened, she pushed the sleeves of her cardigan up above her elbows, jammed her hands in her pockets, sucked in her stomach, and casually ambled toward the front desk, behind which Ruben sat. He unfolded his legs and propped them on his desk, his large hands clasped behind his shaved brown head. The better to watch Claudia with.

"What's up?" Claudia offered coolly.

"Not much, little girl," Ruben replied, grinning. He was part peacock, part pit bull, with gorgeous teeth, real choppers, framed by full, bow-shaped lips that shone coppery behind their veil of Carmex, inside a handsome face that was ravaged, despite a clear complexion. Ruben had about nine hundred silver earrings piercing each of his ears, tiny hoops where the cartilage neared the skull, growing larger as they marched toward the lobes, which were embedded with thick silver thorns. He had Chinese characters tattooed along each forearm, the dark navy of the designs camouflaged against his skin. He wore a P. Funk T-shirt stretched taut, leather jeans, motorcycle boots, and smelled expensively of Guerlain. He had a very long, very skinny scarf, black and silver stripes, looped once around his neck, its fringes trailing his thighs. Claudia had no idea how she was managing to walk toward him. What she wanted to do was surrender, to let him see the truth—that Ruben put her in a depraved state. She should be crawling toward him across the marble of the lobby.

Claudia signed for the delivery and the anonymous little man in the stained white apron scurried away.

"What's for lunch?" Ruben asked, blocking the takeout bags with his saucy pose.

"The usual. Salads for fat girls."

"Except for you," Ruben chuckled. "You ordered the dark meat."

Claudia rolled her eyes and shook her head. "You need some new material," she said, burning red at the same time.

She knew that Ruben was a tragic cartoon, and she wondered why he'd decided to dress himself up as a big black cock and bounce his way toward destiny on his balls. She knew that he lured her by chipping away at her dignity, having forfeited his own. But also, she didn't give a shit, he was *beyond* beyond mad hot—that was the twisted magic of Ruben Hyacinth.

"What you doing tonight?" he asked her, indifferently.

"I don't know." Claudia pushed Ruben's heavy leather legs out of her way and reached for the takeout bags.

"Playing paper dolls?"

"Yeah," Claudia replied, "And then I'm going to whip up some killer stumble biscuits with my Easy-Bake oven and start an empire."

Ruben frowned. "Come see my show."

"Puppets?" Claudia made one out of her hand and flapped its fingertip gums. "It's the Ruben show!" her hand announced in a squeak as Ruben's grin vanished. "Starring me, Ruben Hyacinth, as Ruben! Special guest star . . . Ruben!" Teasing Ruben frightened Claudia, but she made her puppet hand kiss Ruben's cheek with a *mmmmwWAAH!*

Ruben whipped his legs back under the desk in a gesture of disgust. "Shut the fuck up."

Claudia's heart pounded. "Sorry, Angry," she said lightly.

"Yeah, well, don't mess with my shit," Ruben warned.

Claudia raised her right hand in a solemn oath. "I hereby will not mess with your shit," she intoned. "Where's the show?"

Ruben made a petulant display of rearranging the papers on his clipboard. "It's a JustUs thing," he said, "at Wetlands." The Ministry of JustUs, a coalition of black rock musicians, was Ruben Hyacinth's brotherhood of choice, although his fealty to the Ministry was fueled less by cultural politics and more by his desire for a starring role in an MTV music video and sexual release, in that order.

"Well, I'll pass the paper-bag test, that's *fo sho*," said Claudia.

Ruben narrowed his eyes, provoked. Claudia couldn't tell if Ruben knew what a paper-bag test was or not. "What I'm saying is," she persisted, "are white girls actually allowed at JustUs events?"

Ruben shrugged. "It's a free country, ain't it?"

"If it was a free country, you wouldn't need a Ministry of JustUs," Claudia countered. "What the hell kind of revolutionary *are* you?"

Ruben just shook his head. "I'll put you on the list," he decided.

"Cool," said Claudia.

Ruben rose from the desk, and Claudia remembered that he was never as tall as he seemed. "Lemme get you an invite," he said. The heavy ring of building keys jangled loudly as he opened the gate to the service hallway off the lobby. "C'mere." Claudia glanced guiltily at the lunch bags and followed him.

Ruben closed the gate behind them and jogged up a small flight of stairs, through a shaft of dusty sunlight that poured from a high window, to the coatrack where his jacket hung. He wore a black nylon bomber, lined in quilted orange, just like the one Claudia had recently bought.

Claudia leaned against the wall as Ruben dug in his jacket pockets. He pulled out a stack of invites, a violent font sprawled on fluorescent card stock, and turned. He shoved the invites back in his pocket and came down a step. Slowly, in a gesture evoking both the vaudevillian seduction of a male stripper and the grave ceremony of a religious rite, Ruben pulled his scarf from his neck and arranged it around Claudia's throat. The scarf was cheap, with loose, scratchy metallic threads, a find from a stall on St. Marks or from the closet floor of another conquest, yet a thrilling vapor of vetiver eau de toilette rose from it. Ruben pitched his body forward, letting his tan palms smack against the wall on either side of Claudia's head.

Claudia's body flooded with warmth.

Arousal and triumph. Coupled.

Ruben was a *man*.

She knew he felt nothing, but at least he desired the same thing she did.

Claudia could have cared less; she could have bowed down and worshipped. She felt bold, alive, removed. She pictured various people she knew watching this scene in complete horror or crushing envy; she gave them all the finger behind Ruben's broad back. He traced her cheek, her jaw, he grasped the ends of his scarf and drew her to him; he kissed her. His tongue was exquisite, ginger and peppermint, clean, tender, expertly wielded. The skin of his bare, muscled arms was baby soft, pampered, the complete opposite of the hardness he broadcast. There was no ashy dryness on Ruben Hyacinth. With their hands moving in perfect sync, they got her boots and tights off and his leather jeans lowered just enough.

When Claudia stepped off the elevator, her tights were twisted and her heart paced wildly inside her rib cage. The lunch bags she clutched contained a wilted sea of romaine. Tamara was waiting at the end of the hall, her hands on her meaty, sweatered hips.

"Hey. Fast & Sloppy," she demanded. "Where have you been?"

Claudia's voice emerged from her jangled body in a strained falsetto. "I was picking up lunch."

"It takes you forty minutes to pick up lunch? We were calling and calling the lobby, and Leonard wasn't there. We are beyond starving."

"*Ruben.*"

"Whatever, Claudia." Tamara exhaled loudly and shifted tack as she pulled the bags from Claudia's arms. "Listen to me," she tried. "You've been a little edgy these days. A little . . . unpredictable. Is everything okay?"

"Your salad's getting cold." In an attempt to staunch the smell of sex currently snaking from her pores, Claudia folded her arms tightly.

"I'm serious," Tamara insisted.

"Everything is fine, Tamara."

"Because this is a small office, and when one of us has a problem, *all* of us have a problem."

"You mean like when sorority girls get their periods simultaneously?"

"Oh *God*, no," Tamara replied, her face contorting in a disgusted grimace. Then: "Kim told me you've been dealing with some problems at home. You know, with Mom."

"*Mom?*" Claudia repeated, incredulous. Edith was *Mother*, and always had been. And home was . . . not. She inhaled through her nose to the count of seven, held her breath for four counts, and as she exhaled through her mouth for the count of eight, just like the therapist at the college's Health Services had once taught her, she processed Kim's betrayal.

Tamara's eyes glittered with a different kind of hunger, one with which Claudia was familiar. Tamara wanted to get her mitts on Claudia's fascinating drama so that with it she could recalibrate her own standing in the world and assuage her own uselessness and call it *help*. "Kim says you haven't spoken to Mom in a couple of years."

Claudia shrugged. "True dat."

"How old are you exactly, Claudia?"

"Forty."

"*Claudia.*"

"Twenty-four."

"And what about your little sister?"

"Phoebe?"

"Is she still at home with Mom?"

Claudia pictured Tamara's frosted pumpkin head smashing against the pavement, after landing with a satisfying thud, having been launched from the fire escape. Kim would catapult and perish shortly thereafter, Tamara's splayed and broken body serving as an ineffectual crash pad.

Home with Mom. Was that what they were calling Edith Mendelssohn's house these days?

Oh, the thrill when the brownstone had been purchased: the longed-for promise of respectability.

How wonderful the word *brownstone* had sounded, how Claudia had steered every conversation toward it.

The defeat when the house was first viewed: a metal gate for a front door; the back garden peppered with dead rats, used needles and condoms, and fresh cat shit.

The unfinished basement where she and Phoebe had occupied neighboring twin mattresses underneath a low canopy of exposed pipes and stapled wires, Edith's foam mattress against a nearby concrete wall.

How the clamp-on lights affixed to the pipes and rafters illuminated the view from her bed: empty cardboard boxes, broken umbrellas, rusted ironing boards, expired appliances, garbage bags stuffed with old school assignments, and piles of cracked, curled shoes forming an unsteady mountain range. How she swept her eyes across the space, renovating it in her mind as she had seen other white folks in the neighborhood do in real life, making the unfinished cellar into real rooms, with heat, and doors.

The tempera vines and flowers with which the sisters had gamely decorated the plywood floors.

The exposed-brick wall behind the fireplace on the parlor floor upstairs, which was for Claudia not just a glimmer of the battered house's possibilities, but of their own. A few house-proud square feet, visible at certain angles from the street.

How Claudia had considered finally inviting a friend or two over, or at least letting friends hang around the dining room table on the parlor floor, where, if you squinted, things seemed kind of okay. Real art on the walls, good books on the shelves.

How the beloved exposed-brick wall became the exclusive domain of Edith and Robbie Burns when they turned the front room into a bedroom. This was after Robbie ditched rehab again and moved in with them, the morning after Edith had finally confessed that he existed, after years of pretending to hide their relationship in plain sight.

The John Lennon poster that Robbie hung over the fireplace.

The alarm system that Robbie installed in the foyer of the ground floor: a plastic tub stocked with aluminum baseball bats and hand axes.

The evenings when Edith would brush Robbie's long hair and carefully wrap his braid with a leather thong as he ignored her, chain-smoking Pall Malls, glaring at Claudia as she hurried past, staring at Phoebe.

"Yup, *at home with Mom*," Claudia told Tamara, punctuating the space between them with air quotes. "And her boyfriend."

"Have you thought of contacting Mom first? Maybe sending her a card? They have some really great ones at the Open Center."

The office door flew open, and Faye appeared.

"Hallelujah, let's eat!" Faye cried, snatching the lunch bags from Tamara and disappearing inside.

Tamara cupped Claudia's chin and peered at her closely. Claudia noticed the tiny dark roots at the base of Tamara's feathery mustache: she must have devoted hours a week attempting to keep it blond. "I want you to know that I am here for you, Claudia," Tamara said. "We all are, okay?"

"Got it, chief," said Claudia. They went inside.

"Where *were* you?" Kim asked, feeling betrayed herself, despite her free discussion of Claudia's secret troubles.

"I can guess where she was," Ricky singsonged, emerging from his office. The joint in the breast pocket of his flowing shirt peeked out. He raised his sunglasses and gave Claudia a wink.

"Where? What?" Kim cried, accusingly.

"Trust me, you can't handle the truth, Kim," said Ricky. He yanked the end of Ruben's long striped scarf. Claudia had forgotten she was still wearing it.

"Oh!" Faye exclaimed, always on the hunt for an in with Ricky, glancing at the scarf as she emerged from the bathroom. "Is that from Daffy's?" Ricky rolled his eyes and headed to the fire escape for a toke.

Claudia now stood alone in the office hall. From the dining room, she heard the plastic snap of salad boxes opening.

A lumbering, backlit shape appeared.

It was Gwen, the first to order, the last to join. She avoided the awkwardness of the narrow hallway and her labored gait by holding back until the rest had been seated. Claudia breathed in Gwen's powdery scent as she approached. "Don't let the turkeys get you down, kid," Gwen said, as she made her way to the rustle and chatter of family-style lunch at Georgica Films.

Later that night, Claudia stuffed her vinyl Adidas flight bag under a bar stool and made her way to the corner of the Wetlands main stage. Of course, she wasn't going to wave, she wasn't even going to nod. But she wanted the residue of her hallway sex with Ruben to be their inside thing. Yet Ruben was fully ignoring her, really putting an effortless effort, it seemed, into confirming what she already knew: that she shouldn't mistake Ruben for anything resembling a boyfriend. And yet, watching him tweak his setup, laugh hard with his bandmate, tear out a thrilling solo during which he jutted his hips, sneered, tossed his head, and earned applause from the growing crowd as the veins in his neck popped, Claudia felt proud. Unable to hold back, she let herself picture them as a couple. Striding up Avenue A in tandem, passing a cigarette back and forth. Attending an opening at the Studio Museum in Harlem. At the baggage claim after a long return flight from Paris, a stunningly gorgeous baby on her hip, possibly named Djuna. Never *ever* lolling around on a Sunday reading the *New York Review of Books* and eating toasted bagels because, fuck it — that shit was played.

Claudia had seen the handful of ancient Kodachromes of her mother and father as newlyweds, a tan pair in tennis sweaters gunning for the Jewish Intellectual Good Life. She'd been raised in the mysterious aftermath of their joint swan dive, and knew that she would never marry well. Marrying well was a strategy instilled in eager daughters by their driven, practical mothers, and Claudia was a confirmed scrapper, not a desirable bride. At best, she would be a charity case for whatever summer associate or MBA candidate she could try for, scrambling for borrowed cocktail dresses.

A posse of gorgeous young women with big gold hoops and kohl-rimmed eyes threw daggers at Claudia. They'd probably been Tri Delts at Spelman, but were lately emboldened by their kente-cloth head wraps, motorcycle jackets, and the sustained, empowered rush that comes from getting one's law school applications in early. Still, Claudia shrank herself from the fray, moving further away from the bright stage until it became the size of a shoe box, then a Hershey bar, and finally, a Pink Pearl eraser. She returned to the bar and took her place among the three other anonymous white girls, assuming a casual pose with good posture that would telegraph a kind of badass dignity, as opposed to loneliness.

Claudia glanced at the door and considered her options. Past the mountainous bouncer who loomed in the vestibule of the club, she caught a glimpse of the dark, windswept Tribeca street. Ruben had her address and phone number, and Claudia wanted more than anything in the world to expect him. At the same time, she wanted to leave, to feel the rush of cold air off the Hudson, to stalk to the subway and make eye contact with the first hot guy with a knit beanie and headphones who landed across the aisle. But she didn't want Ruben to go home with somebody else, and if he did, Claudia wasn't sure which would be worse, Anonymous White Girl Number Two or Kente-Cloth Bitch-Rag, Esquire, so she had better stay lest he forget she existed—

No, fuck it, she decided, reaching under the bar for her flight bag, hung on the purse hook. *I'm out*. But her hand felt only hook. Ducking her head to examine the dark space where her bag should have been, she continued to grope around at nothing. Her bag was gone. Snatched. Jacked. *Fuck me dead*, she reflected, dropping her head into her hands to mourn her wallet, her keys, her Filofax, her makeup, and, as long as her head was bowed in misery, the possibility of ever actually having anybody. When she glanced up, she spotted the bag, darting in a flash through the dim club toward the door, in the grip of a fast-moving, skinny black girl with scrawny braids bouncing out from under a striped, pom-pommed acrylic ski hat.

"Here we go," Claudia muttered as she slid from her bar stool and hurried to the little thief's side. "Excuse you, Miss Thing," she declared, grabbing the strap of the stolen bag before the girl had reached the illuminated exit. "I think you have something of mine."

The girl, who had drawn both peace and anarchy signs on her green army pants in Sharpie marker, and wore pink cat's-eye glasses and white shell toes with fat laces, turned, eyes flashing. "Excuse *you*," she replied, snatching the bag closer to her side. Then: "Claudia?"

Startled, Claudia scanned the girl's face, and was shocked by its familiarity. "Ramona Parker?" she asked, incredulous, relaxing her grip on the bag strap long enough to allow the girl to yank it back. "What are you doing here?"

The Parkers had been Claudia and Phoebe's neighbors, in the days when they'd lived together, with Edith. Mrs. Parker had earned her masters at Yale Drama, but in the absence of any game-changing roles had accepted an extended run as temp, with the occasional non-union commercial and off-off-off-Broadway play. Like Edith, Mrs. Parker had two kids from two dads, but rather than add yet another sticker to her doorbell, she'd given them all her maiden name. Darleen, a tough former girls' varsity basketball player, was a grade ahead of Claudia, but the girls had never hung out in school. Instead, they'd acknowledged each other in the halls with a taciturn mutual respect born on the block, knowing better than to jeopardize their official social positions. Claudia felt a clutch of homesickness for the intimate universe of the Parkers' front stoop, Darleen shooting hoops with the boys in the lot across the street, Ramona letting Phoebe brush the turquoise hair of her My Little Pony.

"I'm writing an article for the school paper on the Ministry of JustUs," Ramona explained, unsnapping the magnetic closure of her bag and displaying its contents to Claudia: a stapled yellow paper bag from Tower Records, a thick key chain strung with squeezy-armed koala bears, a rolled up *Seventeen* magazine, a green package of Nature Valley granola bars with one bar eaten, and a pair of Guatemalan fingerless gloves. "And *this*," she added, plainly, "is my bag." Ramona nodded at Claudia's abandoned bar stool.

Claudia's own Adidas bag was right where she'd left it, not on the purse hook under the bar, but wedged behind the metal legs of her stool. It might have been an unfamiliar sensation, the jolt of dismay, on the heels of an emphatic reaction, fueled by a low thrum of suggested violence, to something that hadn't actually happened. But it wasn't. As a result, Claudia was adept at shifting gears and saving face. "Great bag, isn't it?" she remarked lightly, turning back to Ramona with a miserable smile and a mortified shrug. "Durable vinyl. Dirt wipes clean like *that*."

"I guess," Ramona said, edging toward the door.

"Did you get yours on Canal Street, too?" Claudia inquired gamely, as the younger girl fled.

Later that night, Claudia lay in bed in the pale light that somehow made its way from the air shaft outside her bedroom window and wondered if she was waiting for Ruben. Claudia pushed the button on her Indiglo alarm clock: it was twenty minutes past two in the morning. She sighed, folded her hands behind her head, and recapped the day's events. She had gone to work in the morning, and fucked Ruben Hyacinth at lunch in a stairwell, and written yet another postcard to Phoebe, and gone to Ruben's gig. She'd mistakenly almost mugged a young girl from the old neighborhood, and now, maybe, she and Ruben were going to fuck again.

She certainly was living her life to its fullest.

And yet, she had missed a crucial opportunity, the realization of which made her restless with regret. She slid from her futon bed and padded into the kitchen. She pulled the Brooklyn white pages down from the shelf on which it slumped next to her crumbling paperback *Joy of Cooking*, and thumbed through it, looking for the Parkers' phone number. There were about four million Parkers in Brooklyn. And she should have asked one Miss Ramona Parker if she'd seen Phoebe recently, and if so, how Phoebe was doing.

Just then, the buzzer rang. It was a terrible noise, a rusty, disturbed shriek. Claudia looked up from the phone book, stuck a chopstick in her place, and slammed it shut. Bronwyn appeared in her bedroom doorway, weaving on her long, skinny legs, gangly in a tie-dyed union suit, her dishwater-blond hair in two messy braids. "It's for me," Claudia quickly assured her.

"Oh, really?" Bronwyn grunted sarcastically before disappearing into her room.

The building's foyer smelled like yesterday's fried potatoes and onions. Ruben waited on the other side of the glass, at the top of the stoop, his guitar in its black case strapped across his leather jacket, a knit cap pulled over his head, and the hood of his sweatshirt pulled over that, his breath pouring from his nostrils in the cold predawn air. He was a sexy thug, the kind of man that preppy mothers in plaid coats, clutching their children's mittened hands, crossed the streets to avoid. Claudia imagined the kiss they were about to have, how Ruben's cheeks would feel cold and how one rough hand would slide into the henley placket of the long-underwear shirt she had seductively unbuttoned for the occasion as the other dove into her boxer shorts, and what his tongue would be like. But Ruben brushed past her in the vestibule and stamped the dirty slush from his feet before scrubbing at his nose. "I need to use the phone, baby girl," he growled. "Long distance."

Claudia was not about to tell Ruben that she and Bronwyn didn't *have* long-distance service, because as part of her post-collegiate Brooklyn experiment Bronwyn had determined she would split expenses with Claudia and thusly live, officially, at least, according to Claudia's resources. Claudia was not about to tell Ruben that the phone call Ruben needed to make, to his mother, no doubt, or an elderly auntie, would take Claudia weeks of paltry paychecks to pay off. Instead, she reveled in the sound that Ruben's shit-kickers made in the long, dark hallway of her apartment, and from her Bad Batz Maru address book she extracted the charge code with which Gwen from Georgica Films had entrusted her. Now she gave the charge code to Ruben, and she pointed Ruben toward her bedroom, and she followed him until he closed the door in her face.

Claudia went into the living room and fell asleep on the couch. She awoke when Ruben nudged her shoulder. Groggy, she followed him back to her room. Ruben told Claudia to take off her clothes, and she did, and he told her to turn around, and she did, and he fucked her, and it was different from their stairwell tryst. This time, while Claudia felt the coarse hairs of Ruben's lower belly scraping against her ass, and felt him enter her, she had the vague sense that Ruben was angry. She kept herself asleep enough to avoid igniting whatever was roiling inside of him, but awake enough to conjure the passionate hope that she would see him again.

A few Saturdays later, Claudia and Bronwyn strolled the Seventh Avenue flea market, held in the concrete yard of the highly rated public elementary school that Claudia and Ruben's improbable children would never attend. Claudia was looking for vintage purses for her collection. Bronwyn sipped a Diet Coke and trawled for first-edition children's books.

"So are you and Ruben going out tonight?" Bronwyn asked lightly.

Ruben had arrived at Claudia's building every night since that first one. So the affair, which Claudia felt at this point she was entitled to describe as such — *The Affair!* — had been carrying on for close to two weeks. Claudia would go to bed at her regular time and wake after midnight to the shrieking buzzer. Ruben's fierce masculinity consumed the little apartment. His leather clothes creaked with cold, his guitar scraped the walls of the narrow hallway, a fresh, warm cloud of vetiver rose from his body. He unwound his scarf and flung his knit hat on Claudia's crowded desk.

Claudia shuffled to the living room and dozed on the couch while Ruben used the phone in her bedroom. She'd wake with a start when he poked her, once, on the sole of her foot, and she followed him back to her bedroom. Ruben sat, muscled and taut, at the edge of her bed to remove his shit-kickers. Only once had Claudia made the mistake of climbing behind him and kneading his shoulders as he went about the business of disrobing. Ruben shot her such a look of flaring irritation that she recoiled as though he might bite. She crept under her duvet and waited for him to slide in and mount her.

Last night, Ruben had flung Claudia up against the wall, hoisted her leg, and as her lower back slammed repeatedly into one of the vintage evening bags hung on her bedroom wall, fucked her with a driving rhythm that brought to mind a football scrimmage. Now, amid the bright bustle of the flea market, Claudia stopped in front of a sprawling display of eight-track tapes, crumbling paperbacks, and matted stuffed animals. "We don't go out," Claudia replied. "We stay in."

"Yes, I know," said Bronwyn. "Loudly."

"Oh, can you hear us?" Claudia was unable to keep the delight from her voice. Bronwyn herself was a murmurer: she murmured to the boys she dated as she welcomed them back from volunteer stints with the teen mothers of the Ute nation. She murmured into their corduroy shoulders as they strolled, arms linked, to and from the Film Forum, she murmured as she handed them an enduring copy of *Harold and the Purple Crayon*, she murmured in her loft bed, wrapping her long, thin arms around their prominent shoulder blades and contemplating, wide-eyed, the collage of black and white postcards, iconic images of Paris, mostly, that she'd plastered to the ceiling.

"I haven't heard you, exactly," Bronwyn explained, "Just lots of crashing around."

"Yeah—Ruben's kind of a natural athlete."

"Aren't you afraid of getting hurt?"

Claudia turned her back to Bronwyn. "Look," she said, lifting the knit waistband of her jacket and the merino turtleneck under it to display the navy-blue bruise, crescent shaped and tinged with yellow, hanging low over her kidneys.

"Oh my God," Bronwyn gasped. "Why is it shaped like that?"

"Bakelite handle," Claudia explained, nonchalantly proceeding to a rack of belted leather jackets before turning to enjoy the reflection of her sex badge on her friend's face. Claudia selected a forest-green number and cocked her head, considering it for Bronwyn. "Very you," she said. "Very Ali MacGraw in *Love Story*."

Bronwyn snatched the jacket and returned it to the rack with an impatient clatter. "Ruben's a menace. He's going to kill you and I'm going to have to find your body and it's going to be completely disgusting." Claudia raised a clear Lucite bangle bracelet and cocked an eyebrow. "Are you being racist right now?"

"*Racist?!*" Bronwyn cried. "Oh my God. You're on crack."

"I've been thinking of trying it," Claudia taunted.

"Just because I don't like your boyfriend doesn't make me a racist."

"You're scared of him," Claudia accused, as she excavated two marvelous bracelets from the box.

"Not because he's African American."

"*African American*," Claudia repeated, giving a little snort.

"I love that. You realize black folks don't call themselves that, right?"

"Excuse *me*, Angela Davis," said Bronwyn, as they strolled on, "but what I am *trying* to say is that the reason Ruben is creepy has nothing to do with the melanin content of his *skin*. He's creepy because he's using you, because he's mean, and because he's old."

"He's thirty-five! Baldy MD was forty-two!" "Baldy MD" was the name they'd given to the recently separated invest- ment banker, a managing director in Mergers & Acquisitions, with whom Bronwyn had gone on exactly two dates. Bron- wyn had met Baldy MD at a benefit for the Children's Aid Society. He had taken her to dinner at Indochine, and, the following weekend, received from Bronwyn a mortifyingly brief hand job in the front seat of the Sebring he'd hired for their antiquing junket to Connecticut.

"But I didn't have violent sex with Baldy MD," Bronwyn argued. "And Ruben is thirty-five like I'm Jewish."

Claudia scowled at her friend. "What are you saying?"

"Ruben is *old*, Claude. Like *old*-old. As in Jimi Hendrix was his guitar teacher."

"You're telling me Ruben is pushing . . . ," Claudia calcu- lated and faltered, "whatever it is that Jimi Hendrix would be pushing?"

"When you're black, you don't crack," Bronwyn offered with a shrug. "I mean . . . right?" Bronwyn deferred to Clau- dia on this sort of thing.

Claudia indicated a display of folded sweaters, arranged on a card table. "Cute cashmere," she observed.

"*Listen* to me," Bronwyn implored, grabbing Claudia's el- bow. "One-quarter of Ruben's bravado is his hatred of women, the other quarter is his hatred of white people, and the rest is covering up his age."

"Now *you're* the one who's mean."

"Don't you want a nice, smart guy who will actually hold your hand walking down the street during daylight hours?" Bronwyn implored.

"That sounds like pure hell," Claudia scowled. "Come on. I'm starved. Let's go." Claudia headed for the exit, but Bronwyn stayed put.

"Is it like Robbie?"

Claudia froze. "*Excuse* me?" she said, very slowly.

"You know. Your mom has Robbie, and you have Ruben. It's the bad-boy thing. Maybe you guys can double-date."

Claudia wheeled around, her hands on her hips. All on its own, her foot stomped. "Oh my *God!*" she laughed, furious and about to cry. "Shut up!"

"Well?" Bronwyn folded her arms. Her bony elbows emerged from the whimsical holes in her cardigan.

"Seriously," said Claudia. "Stop talking now."

"Their names even sound alike. Ruben. Robbie."

On a blustery Tuesday afternoon in late November, the ladies of Georgica Films desperately longed for tuna melts and extra-crispy French fries. But because Ricky was kicking around the office in the bored rage he typically got into when he'd just submitted a bid for a job, the earlobe he'd recently pierced throbbing quietly with the infection he refused to acknowledge, they'd ordered Monster Sushi instead. Claudia had delivered the massive party platter of cut and hand rolls from the lobby with the cucumber still cool and crisp, because Ruben was off.

Not that he'd told her that.

Claudia and Ruben had left the apartment together that morning, strode to the subway stairs, and galloped their descent to the platform. With each step Ruben expertly distanced himself from her, so that while they began the brief journey to the train as lovers, they became acquaintances at the stairwell, and were complete strangers by the time they were smashed together on the rush-hour train. Ruben's hand grazed Claudia's body with the indifference of a commuter.

It was Melvin, the middle-aged Caribbean super of the building, who'd buzzed up to announce the arrival of today's lunch. Claudia's disappointment clutched as she realized she wouldn't have the chance to see Ruben, to wink at him, let alone follow him into the gated stairwell so he could "show her something." *Where was he?* Where did he go when he wasn't with her, which was most of the time, and when was he coming back? Maybe he had quit his job, maybe he had left the country, maybe he had caught his big break shortly after getting off the train at Second Avenue and become the kept man of an actual rich white woman. Maybe he was on the road with the Digable Planets.

As Claudia approached the front desk, she realized Melvin was looking at her differently. She'd slated him as a grandfatherly working man with a hepcat streak: he wore a beret and a single earring and attended jazz festivals on his vacations. But today Melvin was eyeing her—Claudia was sure of it. What had Ruben told Melvin? She toggled between hoping he hadn't said anything and hoping he had.

Claudia's anxious reverie was interrupted by Gwen, stuffed behind her spindly desk, beckoning her with a plump finger. Gwen, whose girth was mysteriously maintained, as she barely touched her food at work, had offered her typical excuse for not joining the ambivalent shuffle to the lunch table. As ever, she was wrapping up a few accounting tidbits and would be there in a minute. Claudia had her own excuse for lingering at her desk. She was tracing her hand in her journal book, in preparation for painting long fingernails with Wite-Out.

"I need to ask you about something," Gwen said, as Claudia approached her desk. "Have a seat." Claudia had never before heard this sort of commanding tone from Gwen, whose requests were usually tinged with apology. "Have you by any chance been bidding on jobs or dealing with clients from home?" she asked.

"Uh, nope," Claudia responded, genuine. Claudia didn't take work home with her. Claudia wasn't even thinking about work when she was *at* work.

"I'm just a little confused about this," Gwen said, handing Claudia the company's most recent phone bill. Businesslike, Gwen scrolled her frosted pink fingernail down a long column. Claudia's home number, with its 718 prefix, formed a solid column down one side of the page, but the numbers that corresponded were completely unfamiliar to her.

Florida.

Puerto Rico.

Panama.

Amsterdam.

Tokyo.

Thirty-seven-hundred-and-sixteen-dollars' worth of calls.

And forty-seven cents.

"We pay an astronomical surcharge for every international call that gets billed to our calling card," Gwen added.

Claudia blinked. Her face ignited, flames of mortification tearing along her cheeks and searing her eyes. She didn't want to cry at her job, or for that matter, at all. She only wanted to feed the ladies of Georgica Films crumbs enough to resemble connection and camaraderie. She only wanted to cash her crummy paychecks until she figured out where it would actually make sense for her to set her sights.

Claudia sat next to Gwen, the kind, powdery mountain who lived with her mother, dropped her face in her hands, and wept.

Gwen reached out across her Stickley desktop, and she took Claudia's hand. Claudia grabbed it and held on, feeling the snot cascading down her left palm, which was still clamped to her face. She squeezed Gwen's hand like a hurricane victim who has stubbornly resisted the evacuation until now. She felt Gwen's hand squeezing back. The hand was warm and dry, the pads of Gwen's joints plumped around the bands of the delicate twelve-karat rings that Claudia could picture from behind her closed eyes: a claddagh and a gold, filigreed heart.

How could Ruben . . . ?

Easy as pie, you stupid little motherless punk-ass bitch. All sorts of bullshit goes on right in your own house, and you have no fucking idea.

How am I ever going to pay . . . ?

You're not.

Oh my God.

Slowly, Claudia raised her face to look at Gwen, still gripping her hand tightly, and shuddered. Gwen handed Claudia a tissue and gave her an understanding smile with her sad eyes, decorated with the glimmery, pale-green eye shadow she'd probably purchased at Duane Reade. Claudia blew, and suddenly realized that Gwen might have known heartache in her life, this exact kind. Maybe she wasn't the devoted virgin, as Claudia had assumed, the ardent devourer of romance novels who had considered taking her vows but seized on a calculator instead. Maybe Gwen knew the rocket launch of desire and its cruel plummet. Or maybe it was just that everything about Claudia was obvious. She had been as fast and sloppy with her secret affair as she'd been with everything else.

"Gwen," Claudia said quietly, "I did not make those calls." Gwen nodded, diplomatically. "What am I going to *do?*"

Gwen sighed, figuring she could do a lot with this question. "Don't worry," she said. "I'll just call the phone company and straighten it out with them. We'll change our calling card number and—"

"Does everyone else know?"

Gwen's reply was a pained grimace. Claudia's tears crawled silently. In the dining room, Faye, Tamara, and Kim's whispers exploded into shrieking laughter.

"I fucking hate family-style lunch," said Claudia.

"Me three," Gwen agreed.

"Fast & Sloppy!" Ricky Green's tense, nasal twang floated over the green glass bricks that formed a half wall around his office. "I need to speak with you, please."

"He came in early today," Gwen whispered, with a miserable shrug, "and opened the mail." Claudia rose. It was a long walk to where Ricky sat, sprawled on his bark-cloth settee. The stereo cabinet was open, and a large ziplock Baggie of Humboldt County's finest had come to rest on the cover of his Bruce Weber coffee-table book, next to which lay a copy of the incendiary phone bill. Ruben's stolen calls had been highlighted, and Gwen's elegant question marks, written in mechanical pencil, decorated the margin.

"Have a seat," Ricky said, patting the space he had made next to him. Despite his fresh juice, the purple-tinted glasses nestled in his Jewfro, and his Arche boots propped casually on the coffee table, he had the gleam of an executioner. Claudia chose the leather African pouf, aware that silence had now overtaken the dining room. Ricky took a loud, final pull on his carrot ginger juice and set the sweating takeout cup on a cork coaster. "So let me get this straight," he said. "You come in here, and you eat my food, and you smoke my pot." Ricky reached for the Baggie, once much fuller, and waved it. A few large buds crouched in the corner of the bag, surrounded by shake and a handful of roaches. The crumbs that Claudia had pinched on bold occasion were easily dwarfed by spliffs the size of thumbs that Kim regularly rolled on Friday afternoons in summer, when Ricky had long departed for the Hamptons jitney, but this didn't seem to Claudia like the moment to provide clarification.

"And answer your phones and arrange your flowers, right?" she reminded hopefully.

With his soft-booted foot, Ricky pushed the phone bill across the coffee table. "Speaking of phones," he said.

Claudia shifted on her pouf, but made no move to touch the bill. "Yeah."

"I've gotta say, Claude. Pretty fucking shocking."

Could she and Ricky by any chance find themselves on the same side of this debacle? "I have a theory," Ricky said, with a sadistic twinkle.

"Actually," Claudia managed, hating the quaver that betrayed her voice, "I did not make those calls."

"Oh, I don't doubt it," Ricky agreed. "Who the hell would you know in Amsterdam? What *I* think," he said, shifting forward in his seat with a hungry smirk, "is that you 'accidentally' gave our company card to your thug *shvartze* boyfriend."

Claudia inhaled sharply. Here was her out, as simple as drop-kicking Ruben under the bus. But she had already been overtaken by a passionate surge of fealty, what the white girl at the SNCC meeting might have felt for Stokely Carmichael. Her position in the revolution was prone, yet she would not sell out to the Man. "He's not my boyfriend," Claudia said, her voice finding a grim, determined register.

"Okay," Ricky snorted, "so he's just a thug *shvartze*."

"You shouldn't say that word," she warned.

"And *you* shouldn't be doing a lot of things." Ricky shifted in his seat and produced an envelope. "Look. I have something for you, okay?" He leaned forward and handed it to Claudia. "Open it," he said, letting his knees sprawl open.

Inside the envelope was a check for one thousand dollars. *Two weeks*, Ricky had printed in block letters on the MEMO line. "I'm letting you go, Claudia. Effective immediately."

There was a pause, during which Claudia fixated on Ricky's handwriting. She scorned the ballpoint pen and his malformed little *w*'s. One thousand bucks. A hefty pile of ching. She owed something like that on her MasterCard. A mound of dust. "You," Claudia repeated slowly, "are letting me go."

"*Effective immediately*," Ricky repeated.

"But it's the most passive-aggressive phrase in the English language," Claudia declared, having not even considered the possibility of pleading. Ricky donned a small, bothered smile. "*You're* going to let *me* go. Like you're doing something I'm asking for. And it's a favor. Born of politesse. As opposed to just straightforwardly firing me."

"You're fired, Claudia."

"No, I get it." She rose from the pouf and folded the check in half. It was done.

"Look in the envelope."

Camouflaged along its bottom fold was a tightly rolled joint, assembled on a roller. It was the only way Ricky knew how to roll them. Claudia would have liked to see him fuss with that shit while riding in between cars on the G train.

"I don't want you to work for me," Ricky continued, "but I still hope we can be friends."

Friends. Claudia plucked the joint from the envelope. "Effective immediately?" she asked, tucking it away with the check. Honestly, she wasn't sure it was even legal, what Ricky was doing. Firing someone without warning. Drugs as a parting gift. "Is this like when you break up with someone," she asked Ricky, rising from her seat, "and they say 'let's be friends'? I never saw friendship as a default setting when some other status implodes. It's like its own thing, right? But maybe we can work on that." Ricky cocked his fluffy head with the air of a threatened Shih Tzu. "You know," Claudia continued, "hang out and listen to ska records. Eat icing from the can." She extended her hand and he shook it, baffled. "Thank you for the opportunity," she concluded.

Claudia circled the glass-brick wall and entered the larger

work space. She took a parting scan of the worn, expensive pastel rugs at odd angles, zealously evoking Georgia O'Keeffe according to Ralph Lauren, or something, and the tall windows with the view of cold lavender sky, water towers, and steam pipes, the dust motes dancing in the last, low shafts of today's sunlight. There *was* such a thing as a free lunch, and Claudia had known it at Georgica Films.

From the dining room, Claudia heard the scrape of chairs. "Don't drag the Stickley!" Ricky hollered from his office. He had gone back to his magazine. Faye emerged in the hall with Kim behind her, then stumbled to Claudia and hugged her tightly, smelling of China Rain and pinning Claudia's arms to her sides before letting a sob fly. "Don't leave till I tinkle," she choked, and hurried off to the bathroom.

"You know what they say," Kim began. "When one door closes . . ."

"It's closed," Claudia concluded brightly. The first thing she needed to do was deposit Ricky's check. The next thing, she had no real idea.

"Take me with you," Gwen joked, as a few tears spilled over the rims of her pale eyes. "We're really going to miss you around here." She thrust a neon sticky into Claudia's palm, on which she'd written her phone number. "You can call me at home anytime if you need anything, or just to say hi."

"Thanks, Gwen," Claudia said. She was gone before anyone noticed she'd forgotten to request low-sodium soy sauce.

In the two long years she'd worked at Georgica Films, Claudia had never once left the building during lunch. Now, as a newly former employee, she walked south, toward the Village, adopting an appreciative daze as the city rushed around her with the bustle and purpose of midday.

Lunchtime out in the world was a revelation. Claudia waited in the long line at the window counter of John's Pizza, among the UPS guys, NYU students, slim gay men with

39

teacup breeds tucked under their arms, and young mothers grabbing a slice as they wearily eyed their nearby toddlers, muzzled with sippy cups and strapped into flimsy umbrella strollers laden with Korean-grocery bags. Claudia threw away her paper plate and its oil-spattered wax-paper liner. Still working on the crust, she headed for the curbside pay phone she'd been eyeing through the window during her hasty meal. From the inside pocket of her bomber jacket, she pulled the torn phone book page she'd been carrying around for weeks.

"Yeah?" the voice answered.

"Mrs. Parker?"

"No."

"Oh. Um . . . then may I please speak to Ramona?" Claudia inquired.

"She in school right now," the voice replied. "Can I *help* you with something?"

"Is . . . is this Darleen?"

"Why don't you tell me who *this* is."

Claudia exhaled, ruffling the silence that strung the phone receivers across two boroughs. "Darleen, it's Claudia Silver. You know, from the block. And from school." She pictured the black and white linoleum of the Parkers' kitchen, the open shelves of jarred tomatoes and peaches from their grandparents' place in North Carolina, the big plastic tub of Tang, and the Panasonic radio perpetually tuned to WBLS. Still no reply. "I . . . I ran into Ramona the other night, and, um, I forgot to ask her a question."

Darleen chuckled. "Oh, you *ran into* my sister, is that how we're playing it." Claudia pumped another quarter into the phone before the mechanical operator could even think about interrupting.

"Listen, Darleen," Claudia said. "I fucked up."

"That's cool," Darleen assured her, "and now I'm gonna fuck *you* up, and then we're gonna be even."

40

"Fine," Claudia consented.

"*Fine?*" Darleen echoed, incredulous. "Damn, girl. You lie down easy."

"No, I don't," said Claudia.

"What you want to ask my sister?" Darleen demanded.

"I suppose I could ask you." Claudia hesitated. "I was wondering if Ramona, or you, has seen Phoebe around. And if so, you know, how she's doing." She neither wanted to say nor think the name *Robbie*.

"How come you gotta ask *me* that? You get your phone cut off? Or your legs?"

"Not exactly," Claudia admitted. "But Phoebe and I . . . we've been out of touch."

"I see Phoebe every other damn day," Darleen countered. "*You* the one who's out of touch. Where you staying these days?"

"Park Slope," Claudia replied.

"Oooh," Darleen teased. "You a Slopie now. Too good for the ghetto."

"It's not that," Claudia said. "Please. Can you tell me how she's doing?"

"I only see her *around*," Darleen explained, with some irritation. "I ain't her *parole* officer."

Claudia's subway car was empty, except for a lone guy in a Triple FAT parka sleeping hunched over, his head resting in his own lap, and a pair of Dominican girls with white lipstick sharing a single pair of headphones. Still, Claudia rode home standing, commanding a doorway, her eyes obscured by the dark green lenses of her aviators. She looked tough and felt empty. Not particularly bereft, but hollow and disconnected from her own nerve endings.

As the F train emerged from the tunnel at Carroll Street and chugged its ascent, Claudia turned to take in the sweep-

ing view. It was a cold November day, with narrow, shredded clouds skittering high in a blue sky. Each backyard and
rooftop stood in bright relief, heightened and silent, emanating a life force that penetrated the scratched Plexiglas of the
train window, like a photo-realistic painting she'd seen at the
Whitney Museum as a child, standing at Edith's side. Claudia imagined she could see her entire life unfurling across
this landscape of brick, concrete, and metal that she knew by
heart. Her high school was over there and Edith's brownstone
was here. There was the school yard where she'd had her first
kiss. Her college was over the river and through Morningside
Park, a crosstown bus ride from where she'd been born. She
belonged to this tiny part of the world, but the feeling wasn't
mutual. Claudia's universe easily carried on without her.

At this time of day, the quiet apartment presented an ap-
pealing, shabby gentility. Claudia made her bed, and put the
kettle on. When the buzzer rang it jolted the cozy scene. It
could have been a package from UPS, filled with Bronwyn's
latest order from J.Crew, and yet, as the buzzer sounded again
a moment later, Claudia sensed danger.

Darleen was waiting at the top of the step, still with the
Jheri curl and the Air Jordans, her white breath filling the air.
Claudia opened the door and braced herself for a bitch-slap.
But Darleen merely gestured, as Ramona appeared at the bot-
tom of the stairs.

She had brought someone with her.

Standing behind Ramona was a tall sixteen-year-old girl
with broad shoulders, long arms, and knee-high Minnetonka
moccasins.

Phoebe.

She wept loudly as she ascended the stairs into Claudia's
arms. She had grown taller than her older sister, but she collapsed into the hug, hanging her body from Claudia's shoul-

ders, so that Claudia both embraced her and held her up. Ramona swiped at her own tears.

"Oh my God, oh my God," sobbed Phoebe.

"Thank you," Claudia said to Darleen. "Thank you so much." Darleen shrugged, and slung her arm around her own sister's narrow shoulders. "By the way," Darleen said, squinting at Claudia, "the ghetto is up here." She tapped her temple with authority. "You know that, right?" The Parkers turned to go.

"Ramona," said Claudia. "I'm sorry. For accusing you."

"It's cool," said Ramona.

"No it ain't," Darleen reprimanded.

"I mean, it's *okay*."

"That's right," Darleen concurred.

The Parkers headed for Seventh Avenue, and a corner table at Smiling Pizza. On the bus home, Darleen would flash the pass she'd been expertly doctoring since high school graduation, seven years ago.

Claudia gently peeled Phoebe from her body. "Are you okay?" she asked, grave. Phoebe shook her head. "Is that a stupid question?" Phoebe gave a slight laugh and nodded, wiping her nose on her sleeve. "Let's go inside," Claudia said.

They sat on the futon couch in Claudia's small living room. Phoebe looked around, taking in the brick-and-plank bookcases, the hanging plants, the rocking chair draped in a Mexican blanket, the Richard Avedon poster of a bald man covered in bees. "Your house is really nice," she said.

"What's going on?" Claudia asked. Phoebe's face crumbled as she curled into Claudia's lap. "Did you get my cards?" Claudia asked.

"Cards? No," said Phoebe. "I don't get any mail. Robbie confiscates all of it. He says I can have it when I'm eighteen unless he decides to burn it first."

Claudia clenched her jaw and stroked her sister's hair. "It's okay," she said.

"No," said Phoebe. "It's not." The only person she'd sort of told what life was like at home had been Ramona, which was why Mrs. Parker had banned her daughter from stepping foot in their house ever again. Phoebe wished she could stay right here, in her sister's lap, and not talk about anything, but felt the nagging pressure that confiding in Claudia might be her equivalent of rent.

"What I mean is, I will help you, Feebs," said Claudia.

Claudia told herself she would figure this one out. She would get another job, and her thousand bucks from Ricky Green and her credit cards would get her from here to there; she could have her own little corner of the Seventh Avenue flea market, and sell back her vintage purses. She'd call Bronwyn's dad at his law firm and ask him about guardianship and he would find her a pro bono attorney. Phoebe could have her bedroom; Claudia would sleep on the couch. Phoebe would finish high school on an accelerated schedule and get a swimming scholarship to St. John's and work part-time. She could model, people always said so.

Claudia would make a raft from a rooftop, and she would pull her sister up beside herself. Someday, when the waters receded, they would find that there was a house still standing, and that it was mostly intact.

2

Liar's Gap

C LAUDIA SILVER HAD ALWAYS STRUGGLED with Christmas Eve in New York City. She knew that happy New York Jews weren't supposed to ignore Christmas, they were supposed to *participate* in it with one of two rituals, and possibly both: the eating of the Chinese food and the going-to of the movies. Claudia wished she'd come from that kind of jolly Jewish household, taking on the gentile shopping season with an amused smile and deep pockets. Instead, her holidays were sponsored by Bronwyn's family, with Phoebe as her special guest. The sisters had been roommates for the last month.

Stepping from the shower into her apartment's crooked little bathroom, Claudia wrapped her body in one of Bronwyn Tate's monogrammed bath sheets and her hair in a coordinating bath towel. As she crossed the living room, she heard a voice coming from the answering machine, and realized

45

that Phoebe, plugged into her Walkman on the futon sofa (*Ring the alarm, I don't wanna stay calm cause I'm about to rip this psalm*), reading a *Betty and Veronica* comic she'd rescued from Edith's house and eating a bowl of raisins, was making no move to answer the phone. Claudia's brief annoyance turned to relief when she realized the nature of the call.

"... *Office of Career Services. Please give me a call to discuss an opportunity that might be a good fit. I'll be out of the office through the New—*"

Claudia dove on the nearest portable receiver, this one languishing with a largely drained battery on the coffee table. "Hello?" she cried, hurrying to the brick-and-plank étagère to fuss with the answering machine, which droned with feedback as she tried to get it to stop. "Yes, hello?" she repeated, breathless. "This is Claudia."

Phoebe didn't know that Claudia was out of a job. She didn't know that the holiday season was a shitty time to look for one, unless you wanted to slave in a remote corner of Macy's Cellar, a notion that Claudia had briefly considered and then rejected, having been taught by Edith at an early age the womanly art of gift wrapping, not yet convinced that it had come to that. Phoebe didn't know that Ricky Green's thousand-dollar severance package had evaporated considerably, and that Claudia had considered picking up some shifts at the restaurant where she'd worked through college, except hadn't, because that would feel like going backward, and Claudia was determined to press forward, gunning along an ambivalent fulcrum from dawn till dusk since she'd gotten canned from Georgica Films, her wheels growing muddier and her chassis sinking. Phoebe didn't know that groceries, takeout burritos, movie tickets, and the two six-packs of cotton bikinis that Claudia had bought her from the Modell's on Fulton Street, along with a gray hoodie to layer under her peacoat now that the weather was growing nasty, had been purchased by Uncle MasterCard. Phoebe didn't know that Claudia was stealing from herself to give her the things that she herself wanted.

Claudia didn't know that Phoebe had called Edith's house to report she wasn't dead. The first time, when Robbie answered, Phoebe had promptly hung up. The second time, Edith answered. Phoebe, paused, then hung up. The third time, Phoebe had left a message on the answering machine: *"Hey, um. It's me. Phoebe. I just want you to know that I'm okay. I'm staying with a friend for a little while. In Park Slope, actually. I'm going to school. And I'm, uh . . . yeah."*

Claudia didn't know that Phoebe missed her mother.

"Oh good," said Cheryl Polski, on the other end of the line. "Claudia. It's Cheryl, from Career Services. What are you doing at home on Christmas Eve?"

"What are you doing at work?" Claudia shot back.

"I just ran in to pick up some files to work from home over the holidays, and saw that a new posting's come in," Cheryl explained amiably. "I think it might be up your alley."

Claudia tensed, glanced over at Phoebe, and tugged at her towel. "Do tell," she said.

"Hope Valley is hiring a second assistant to the executive producer. Shelly Gerson. She's an alum."

"Hope Valley?" Claudia repeated, padding down the hall to her bedroom. She had planned her outfit in the shower, and knew it would include her one good pair of black wool trousers. "You mean the soap opera?"

"It shoots at the Avenue M studios in Brooklyn," Cheryl Polski enthused. "You live there, right? So it would be an easy commute."

Claudia allowed herself to feel marginally hopeful, trying to ignore Edith's disappointed voice in her head, accusing her of being a middlebrow. "I've got mad lunch-ordering skills," she offered.

"This is more than ordering lunch," Cheryl said. "You'd be handling script continuity. You know what that is, right?"

"You bet your bippie I do," Claudia lied, holding the phone with her shoulder and pulled her panties on under her towel. *Script continuity?* Was that where you typed *"Stay tuned for more unlikely melodrama shot on video, brought to you by Ex-Lax"* at the bottom of each script? She figured she would fake it, as women had been doing for years.

"And you know the show, right?" Cheryl continued. Claudia, who still suffered from the mortifying sixth-grade memory of Edith discovering her horde of Harlequin Romances in a Buster Brown shoe box, did not. But she glanced over at Bronwyn's television, pledging silently that the free time she currently had on her hands now served a purpose. She could become more than fluent in *Hope Valley*. She could become the freakin' *mayor*. "I think I spent my entire sophomore year in high school in a lather over the Denise/Diane evil-twin story line," Cheryl was saying. "It was Anne Heche's first TV role, you know."

"Cool!" Claudia exclaimed, having never heard the name. She flipped through her wardrobe of thrift-store blouses, selecting a drapey, merlot-red polyester number with a long, pointed collar.

"This could be your big break," Cheryl encouraged. "Who do you think hires writers on TV shows? *The executive producer.* Shelly Gerson hires you, you do a great job for her, and when it's time for a promotion, she puts you on the writing staff. If you look at the credits, a lot of the writers, actors, and directors on the show do other things, too."

"Like sell Amway?" Claudia quipped. The job sounded almost too good, like a well-lit path straight out of Dodge, with groomed terrain designed for one foot in front of the other, and as such it threatened Claudia's entrenched anxiety and despair, forcing her to retaliate.

"Like get nominated for Tonys."

"Really?" Claudia breathed, impressed and humbled, instantly picturing herself in a well-cut Calvin Klein tuxedo over a push-up bra, thrusting a cast-bronze statuette aloft. She was glad she'd stolen a ream of resumé paper from Georgica Films as one of her last hurrahs. She sternly reminded herself that under the circumstances, Edith's assured scorn was beside the point. She would update her resumé on Bronwyn's word processor when Bronwyn was at her job at the morning show, and draft a Pulitzer-worthy cover letter. She would fax it from the corner store instead of asking Bronwyn to fax it from work, which would require telling Bronwyn she was unemployed. Then: "I'm on it, Cheryl."

"Good girl," Cheryl praised.

Claudia and Phoebe hurried to the subway arm in arm. The possibility of *Hope Valley* felt good to Claudia as it began to sink in. She liked the idea that cool people worked on soap operas, and that they started there and went places. Going places, in fact, being more real to Claudia than starting. But the illuminated Citibank lobby on the corner of President Street, as it now appeared, threw a bright, threatening light across her path.

"I need cash," Claudia admitted to Phoebe, pulling her sister from the sidewalk's steady bustle. She'd earned one hundred dollars a day at Georgica Films, but had never had an idea what this sum added up to over the course of a month, or how to make her earnings last for that long, let alone how to engineer things so that there'd be leftovers when the new month began.

"I've got some," Phoebe offered, digging her rainbow Velcro wallet from her barrel-shaped knapsack fashioned from Tibetan saddle fabric.

Claudia was startled by the notion of Phoebe's solvency.

49

"And how's that exactly?"

"Babysitting." Phoebe shrugged. Claudia could see that Phoebe's wallet was neatly organized, the bills smooth and facing the same direction.

"Whose babies?"

"They're *kids*," Phoebe explained, reading Claudia's suspicion. "Friends of Edith's from temple. You don't know them. I can pay for stuff, you know. You've been paying for everything."

Claudia looked at her younger sister's expression, guileless and steady as she offered the neat, small knot of ones. "*You have no idea*," Claudia considered replying, before reminding herself that Phoebe wasn't good with sarcasm, nor was anything her fault.

"Take it," Phoebe insisted. "It's eighteen bucks."

"Uh, yeah. No way," Claudia scoffed, swiping her bank card and pushing open the lobby door.

Claudia and Phoebe took their spot at the end of the line for the ATMs. There was an air of pink-cheeked festivity among the young couples en route to ecumenical church services with full choir and the potbellied husbands who'd been sent out for last-minute eggnog, rum, and tulips.

Claudia immediately spotted Garth Kahn a few customers ahead. Garth was still clamped to the puffy vinyl headphones he'd worn as an undergrad. His curly dark head grooved in time to whatever he was listening to, the cord disappearing into his messenger bag. The same shop-teacher eyeglasses. Everything about Garth was short and thick, including his fingers, the stubble along his jaw, and what looked like a fresh pair of brown suede Wallabees. In his giant silver parka he resembled a beetle of the Volkswagen variety.

Claudia and Garth had been at Columbia together, and now they had four-odd years of adult life between them. At the miserably humid, very end of last summer, when it felt like anybody Claudia had ever met was enjoying a Campari cocktail at one of the venerable beaches of the Eastern Seaboard while she trudged a vacant city piled with hot garbage, Claudia had gone on a single, cringe-worthy date with Garth. First running into Garth at Café Roma, bristling slightly at his explanation that Roma was "his," when it had been hers all along and she couldn't remember ever having seen him there before, followed by the request for her phone number, a boldly presented invitation, Fela Kuti at the Prospect Park Bandshell, and Jamaican goat roti and sorrel drink ordered with an uncomfortable hint of swagger. Claudia had sported an unflattering vintage dress she'd bought on credit in a frenzy of eager preparations and never worn again.

But it was after smoking a joint with Garth that he'd rolled with a filter and tobacco, as he'd learned to do during his junior year in Barcelona, that Claudia had become fatally distracted by Garth's perspiration. Staring at the side of his round, beaming face, she marveled at the subjectivity of sweat. How was it that Ruben Hyacinth's was a jasmine nectar she wanted to lick, while Garth leaked bottled gravy on that hot summer night? The deal breaker, however, was when Garth rose up on the fleece blanket he'd pulled from his backpack, and, unable to convince Claudia to join him, gave his body to the music in twitchy ecstasy, just like a white-boy former Deadhead who'd taken an African dance class at the Y and was now practicing his moves as a nearby klatch of home-care aides, still in their floral scrubs and perforated white clogs from work, convulsed in laughter—all of which, Claudia had realized with horror, was in fact happening.

"I really want to kiss you right now," Garth had said to her when the concert ended.

"Thanks," Claudia mustered.

"*Thanks?*" Garth repeated. "How'm I supposed to lean in for the kill after that?"

"How about not?" Claudia countered. "Does *not* work for you?"

"Wow." Garth was hurt and impressed. "That shit's ice-cold."

"I'm sorry," Claudia said. "It's just—"

Garth raised a paw. "This is the thing," he'd interrupted. "And I don't want you to say anything, or kiss me if you don't want to. But when I look at you, I picture our son's bar mitzvah. There. I said it."

Claudia stared at Garth in disbelief. At that moment, her immediate and entire future had consisted of nothing more than the ceremonial burning of her tragic dress.

"The event itself, tasteful," Garth continued. "The after-party, bumping. I'm talking Phish. Or a Phish cover band. Or whatever the kids are listening to in . . ." He paused to silently calculate. " . . . in 2013. Because that's how this family parties." He was still talking about the bar mitzvah.

"Thank you for a lovely evening," Claudia intoned. With no idea what else to do, she reached out and squeezed Garth's shoulder, then turned and began, very slowly, to flee. She'd known it was rude.

"Don't walk away, Renee!" Garth cried, quoting pop lyrics of a bygone era, and loudly. Claudia ignored him with remarkable ease as the nighttime crowd of concertgoers buoyed her along Prospect Park West. *"You won't see me follow you back home!"* Garth hollered after her. Claudia considered turning around to offer Garth a very human shrug that would communicate her heartfelt appreciation and regret. "I always thought that was a Steely Dan song, but it's not! It's Left Banke!" Garth continued at top volume. "Banke! With an *e!*"

But Claudia *did* just walk away.

Over the next few weeks, Garth left several messages on Claudia's answering machine, but she'd never gotten to the meat, erasing them as soon as she'd heard: "Hey. It's me."

All of that had been last July.

One, two, three, four, five, six, seven, eight, nine, ten—two hundred bucks. Claudia couldn't see the bills themselves, just the relaxed movement of Garth's shoulders as he caught the money and secured it with a clip that he jammed in the front pocket of his corduroys. Claudia worried that Garth would notice her and say hello. Simultaneously, she hoped that in the five months since they'd last seen each other he might have forgotten they'd ever met. Garth's eyes immediately lit on Claudia and brightened. He wasn't angry, just hopeful. He ambled over, bowlegged.

"Will you look who the cat drug in!" Garth bellowed, his headphones still on.

"Boy, that's loud," said Phoebe.

Garth pushed his headphones up. They leaked music, making a halo of hip-hop around his head. "Wow. You are so gorgeous right now with your pink cheeks." Claudia noticed Garth's eyes, Siberian husky bright and pale, and his chapped lips, shiny with goo. "You're like Sabrina from *Charlie's Angels* meets Rhoda," he praised.

"No, I'm not," said Claudia.

Garth gave Phoebe a polite, disinterested smile. "And who are *you?*"

"Phoebe," said Phoebe.

"My sister," Claudia explained, adding pointedly, "she's sixteen."

"Cool." But Garth clearly wasn't interested in Phoebe. Penetratingly, he admired Claudia. "So how are two sophisticated Jewesses celebrating Christmas Eve?"

"We're headed uptown to my roommate's parents' house," Claudia told Garth.

"East or west?"

"Side?"

"What else?"

"West. Eighty-First and the Park."

"Picturing that," said Garth. "Me and my pop, we do the movies–Chinese food thing. In a strange twist, on Christmas Day we do movies and Vietnamese. You guys wanna come?" Garth scanned the sisters' faces hopefully. "The pork chops on Bayard Street are crazy good, and as we all know, Jews love swine."

"I don't think so," said Claudia.

"Don't think, *feel*," Garth urged. "That's what went wrong last time."

"Maybe next time."

"But next time is a year from now."

"By then we'll have so much to catch up on," said Claudia.

Garth smiled and slid his earphones back onto his ears. "It was a misstep," he remarked loudly, as other customers turned to look. "If I'd just taken you to *The Umbrellas of Cherbourg* at Film Forum and tomato soup at Fanelli's, we'd be making out right now." Garth saluted Phoebe and ambled from the bank.

"Oh my God," Claudia remarked as the line moved forward. "Freak show."

"But you guys sound like you're from the same planet," Phoebe observed. She waved to Garth, who was now gesturing from the sidewalk.

Claudia glowered. "Don't encourage him."

"I wasn't," Phoebe said as the bustle of Seventh Avenue carried Garth away. "He seems pretty encouraged in general."

By now it was Claudia's turn at the ATM. She turned to face her foe.

Claudia punched in her PIN number and angled her body while the money machine churned, not wanting Phoebe to see her balance. When the numbers appeared on the screen, Claudia's chest constricted.

"You sure you don't want a few bucks?" Phoebe asked.

"I'm good," Claudia said lightly, withdrawing her last forty dollars.

Claudia and Phoebe hurried down the stairs of the Grand Army Plaza subway stop into a holiday block party. It was hard to believe that Christmas held the possibility of disappointment or loneliness, what with the chatter and laughter hanging low over the crowded subway platform like cigarette smoke at a zinc bar. A young guy from across the park, his knit cap housing his dreadlocks in a striped mound, serenaded the guests with reggae-infused carols on a battered acoustic guitar as his open case gathered an impressive pile of bills on a bed of coins.

Claudia observed the Park Slope families: Wall Street dads in good wool overcoats and leather gloves, mothers in fleece earmuffs and Wellies, children in ripped jeans and new sneakers. They resembled one another effortlessly and took their natural, mutual devotion completely for granted. Claudia wished that she and Phoebe could fasten themselves to one of these solid pods, like the segment on *Live at Five* where a plump Riverdale house cat had taken in an orphaned gorilla. They could even share a wallpapered bedroom under the eaves and do their own laundry and light housework.

Will work for family.

Claudia and Phoebe emerged from the subway into Bronwyn's neighborhood, where progressive Brooks Brothers Jews, deeply empathetic WASPs, tenacious LaGuardia High School Puerto Ricans and wide-hipped Eileen Fisher divorcées were minted, to be turned out to the rest of the city. Snow was sketching paisley patterns on the shop awnings along Eighty-Sixth Street. "We need to bring them something," Claudia said. They were about to duck into a Korean grocery when a lanky, lacquer-haired man with a leather trench coat appeared in their path.

"Excuse me." His accent was fruity and Claudia immediately pegged it as a sham. "Hello." He ducked his head slightly, as though doffing an invisible cap. "I'm Paolo Crespi."

Claudia gripped Phoebe's arm, tightly. "Of course you are," she said.

Paolo swung his droopy eyes between the two girls as snowflakes melted on his leather shoulders. "You are sisters?"

"No," Claudia shot back. "I'm her trigger-happy bodyguard."

"I wonder," he continued, pointing his smile and his gaze at Phoebe, "if you model?"

"Wow, great line," said Claudia. "You get that from the *Date Rapist's Handbook*?"

Paolo hesitated. "Because you have a great look."

"Move along, Father Sarducci," said Claudia, firmly steering Phoebe into the market and gearing herself up to get loud if he followed them in, which he did. Paolo brandished a business card in each of his long, outstretched hands, ineffectually insulated with perforated leather driving gloves. "Please. My card. Give me a call and we chat." Claudia made direct eye contact with Paolo, memorizing his sallow face with its thickly lashed, deeply set eyes so she could select it from the inevitable lineup. She plucked a card from his hand—IMAGE MODEL MANAGEMENT—as did Phoebe, but Claudia pointedly tore hers in half and deposited the scraps in Paolo's gloved hand before he'd had time to retract it.

"Maybe not you," Paolo said to Claudia. Phoebe, who was familiar with Claudia's occasional grocery-aisle smackdowns, slid Paolo's card into the pocket of her peacoat and hungrily eyed the cigarettes.

"What was that?" she asked Claudia rhetorically when Paolo had moved on.

"The shit that happens to you on a regular basis," Claudia replied, piling a bunch of berried branches, a pot of lemon marmalade, and a box of Bahlsen Afrika cookies onto the checkout counter. She pulled the string shopping bag from her green vinyl purse as the storekeeper rung up her purchases. Claudia selected one of the two twenties from her wallet. Releasing the soft bill, she felt a pang, but was heartened by the crispness of the four singles returned to her as change.

The Tates lived in the Anselmo. The grand building had its broad shoulder to Central Park West and kept its face to the side street, in this way exemplifying a balance of prestige and humility.

"Oh no," laughed Mr. Pettijohn when Claudia and Phoebe entered the lobby, "look who Santa brought me now." The petite doorman came around from his desk and made his way across the marble checkerboard of the lobby in little dancing steps. Mr. Pettijohn's singsongy lilt of the islands seemed utterly sincere, not like he was hiding his Bushwick for the sake and comfort of his clientele. "I want to say you got bigger since the last time I seen you, but I know how the ladies are. You gonna get mad, right?"

Claudia handed Phoebe her bulging string bag and entered Mr. Pettijohn's familiar embrace.

Mr. Pettijohn was just Claudia's height, with a short, impeccably kept salt-and-pepper afro. With his bay rum cologne, corduroy trousers, and drugstore reading glasses on a chain, if Mr. Pettijohn wasn't hailing a taxi in the rain under a striped umbrella, or signing for another delivery from Gristedes, or monitoring the messy midnight comings and goings of the Anselmo's teenagers as they obliterated another winter break, he could have passed for a visiting humanities professor. He now held Claudia at arm's length. "You all grown now?" he asked with a rhetorical twinkle. "You got a job? You workin' hard? Or hardly workin'?" His friendly questions caused Claudia's skin to chill and prickle uncontrollably. She managed to nod and smile.

The elevator opened with a clatter, depositing Claudia and Phoebe in a wood-paneled corridor. Swathed in fresh pine garlands and festooned with plaid taffeta rosettes, the Tates' front door announced itself from the far end of the hall. The L.L. Bean boots and running shoes lined up neatly under long rows of enameled hooks from which all manner of foul-weather gear and faded Harvard sweatshirts hung suggested long walks over the heath, inclement weather be damned, decent sailing skills, and high SAT scores.

"I know," Claudia remarked, as Phoebe absorbed the intimate sprawl. "It looks like Vermont exploded, right?"

Phoebe nodded at two decades' worth of law-firm-boondoggle golf umbrellas stuffed into a majolica stand. "At least we'll stay dry," she noted.

Claudia rang the bell.

Paul and Annie Tate had bought their place in 1966, when the Upper West Side was still considered overly ethnic and dangerous. One of the first things they did was replace the shrieking buzzer with a proper bell. Its confident, brassy herald of the sisters' arrival now reverberated through the apartment, the sound snaking around many highly polished surfaces.

"Merry goddamned Christmas!" Bronwyn cried as the door flew open. Flushed with champagne, she stooped slightly in her towering heels to snatch Claudia into a skinny, fierce hug. "To say that the two of you are a sight for sore eyes would be the understatement of the millennium."

"Exaggerate much?" Claudia grinned. Bronwyn grabbed Phoebe's wrist. In her stiletto sling backs she was just shy of the younger girl's considerable height.

"Why can't you be my sisters instead of mere *roommates?*"

Bronwyn complained, pulling Phoebe into the circular foyer, already infused with the lively energy of the party.

"It's better this way," Claudia countered. "If we were your sisters, you'd be complaining about us to somebody else." As swingy Christmas carols played from hidden speakers, an eager young man approached Phoebe, his arms outstretched in a gesture she mistook for an invitation to dance.

"Maybe later," Phoebe offered apologetically.

"He's asking for your coat," Bronwyn explained, grabbing a pair of champagne flutes for her guests as Phoebe hesitated.

"*Give* it to him," Claudia instructed firmly, holding on to her string bag full of offerings for the Tates and downing her champers like a shot. In the time it took Phoebe to struggle with the fan of cocktail napkins presented by another party helper, Claudia tossed back a second. The third glass Claudia was willing to nurse for the moment as, from her corner perch at the top of a wide set of steps, she surveyed the familiar sunken living room, dotted with clumps of chatting adults. Throughout the year, the Tates' home could always be counted on for whimsical seasonal decor, fresh flowers, thoughtfully selected ambient music, and a selection of stinky cheeses, but Annie Tate outdid herself at Christmas.

The towering tree, strung with cranberry ropes, emerged from a sea of wrapped gifts to scrape the ceiling. Bulging needlepoint stockings hung from the fireplace mantel, its hearth crackling. Claudia nodded to a miniature table, set near the tree with holly-printed linen and china, around which a pair of worn Steiff bears in matching Stewart-plaid vests and a Madame Alexander doll dressed in a form-fitting, fur-trimmed red ensemble enjoyed a tea party.

"So who all is here besides High-Priced Call Girl Claus and her gay best friends?" Claudia asked, enamored of the scene.

"Oh, Carter Kemp and the rest of Dad's boring-as-dirt associates from work that we might go to Odeon with later," Bronwyn replied, indicating a group of ruddy young men in sports coats, clutching pilsners, as Annie's unruly older sister, Throaty Aunt Toni, held them prisoner. Aunt Toni's fuzzy curls, seasonal caftan, Frye boots, and childlessness bore a notable contrast to Annie's tidy presentation. "And Martha and her boyfriend, the couple most likely to be eaten by bears on the Inca trail." Bronwyn gave a nod to her oldest sister, Martha Tate, a lean, deeply tanned young blond in a simple shift and bare legs, just back from her most recent Guatemalan research junket. Martha stood closely to an older man with a shaggy gray mane and matching crumb-catcher beard.

"Those two are *dating?*" Claudia marveled. "I thought he was her graduate thesis adviser or something."

"He *was*," Bronwyn replied. "And now he's her boyfriend. He's five years older than Daddy."

Phoebe was incredulous. "Wait. Your *father?*"

"*Ding ding ding*," Bronwyn confirmed. "We call him Married Michael."

"Do you think they'll ever get married?" Phoebe asked, unable to take her eyes off the unlikely couple. It was fascinating to see another woman of substance, besides her own mother, dating against type.

"No time soon," Bronwyn guessed.

"Because he's too old?"

"Because he's too *married*," Bronwyn explained. "Hence the name, hello. He and his wife have no kids, but they hyphenated their last names. *Curry-Baum.* How queer is that? They're like the John and Yoko of the orthopedic-sandal-and-safari-vest set. Except John never cheated on Yoko." Here, Bronwyn paused, and frowned. "At least, I don't think he did." She looked over to Claudia for confirmation. "Yoko wouldn't let him, right?"

"Whoa," said Claudia. "That's cool with Annie and Paul? Their daughter *shtupping* Charles Darwin?"

"She's almost thirty years old," Bronwyn observed. "What are they going to do?"

"Dock her allowance?" Claudia suggested, assuming correctly that Martha still received one.

"So where's his wife?" asked Phoebe.

"In remission."

"*Jesus!*" Claudia cried.

"In *what?*" Phoebe asked.

"Hey," Bronwyn shrugged, effectively ending the debate.

Agnes Tate, the dark-haired, sharply drawn middle daughter, who'd been living at home, stormily, since bailing on her master's degree in European history last spring, was draped over the back of a wing chair. Tucked inside the chair, a slight young man curled up with a worn Chomsky anthology, his slim legs folded coltishly.

"I see Aggie's cut bangs," Claudia observed. "They're very French."

"She looks like an escapee from *Sweeney Todd*," Bronwyn remarked.

"Who's the guy?" Claudia asked.

"That's Joel," Bronwyn explained, settling into her role of docent. "I heard Aggie introduce him as her 'partner,' which is hilarious, considering they're both living at home in separate states."

"Claudia? Claudia Silver!" The trilling voice made a cheerful accusation of the girl's name. Bronwyn and Phoebe joined the crowd as Annie Tate, a spotless Christmas apron tied over her crisp Anne Fontaine blouse, emerged from the swinging, quilted double doors that led to the kitchen suite. By the fireplace, at the sound of her name, one of the associates turned expectantly, and Claudia caught his eye, realizing immediately that this was in fact her host, Paul Tate.

Boyish in his Levi's and loafers, with his monogrammed cuffs rolled above the elbow, Paul had been temporarily camouflaged by his younger guests. But now his retreating hairline, the laugh lines that crinkled his temples as he tucked his smile into the mouth of his beer bottle, and the heavy, five-figure wristwatch that glinted from his wrist as he raised his ropy hand in casual greeting gave him away.

Claudia had, of course, seen Paul Tate plenty over the years. With Bronwyn as her date, and feeling vaguely conspiratorial—as though they'd been playing hooky with their former T.A.—she'd enjoyed several more rounds of burgers and beers at the Corner Bistro since the miserable week of her college graduation. With the entire Tate household, including boyfriends and hangers-on, she'd attended elaborate meals at cavernous restaurants co-owned by Robert DeNiro, where Paul held court and did all the ordering. Claudia had watched Paul call for the check, tip the coat girl, and hail a taxi with a crisp arsenal of masculine gestures. She'd sat in the front passenger seats of various uptown-bound taxis while Bronwyn and her two parents occupied the backseat, and, drowsy and comfortable, had caught snippets of their familiar banter. She'd slept over and seen Paul and Annie head out to the park for a power walk in the morning, Annie in a coordinated tracksuit and visor, Paul in a faded and frayed sweatshirt from his varsity crew days.

But tonight, through Claudia's mud-splattered windshield, Paul looked different. Despite the twinkling lights, the sea of gifts, the houseful of guests, the swingy carols, the stinky cheese, and the undulating waves of chatter and laughter, he seemed to be maintaining an aura of cool, cordial remove. As though, quite like Claudia, he was *in* this living room, and yet, somehow, not quite *of* it. Had he always been this way? Simultaneously occupying the spotlight and the periphery, and she was just noticing it now? Or was this something new?

"Claudia," Annie was saying. "How happy *happy* we all are to see you." She pulled the girl in for a hug. "Merry, merry, *merry* Christmas, darling." Claudia smelled Annie's Chanel No. 5 and felt the cool smoothness of her pearl earring against her cheek. Annie held Claudia at arm's length and scanned the girl's face intently. "Know that when I say 'how are you,'" Annie continued, "you can say 'just fine,' with no further questions asked. At least not on Christmas Eve." It sounded to Claudia like a request to keep things light and breezy: she wondered how much Annie knew about her new role as Phoebe's illegal guardian. Annie lowered her voice. "So how are you, darling?" she asked.

"Just fine," Claudia dutifully replied, noticing that the older woman's eyeliner and mascara were an earnest navy blue.

"Wonderful," Annie replied briskly, giving Claudia's hand what seemed like a grateful squeeze for having delivered a manageable answer. Claudia's heart quickened as she presented her hostess with the string bag. "What's this?" Annie asked.

"Thanks so much for having us, Annie."

"Don't be ridiculous," the hostess scoffed. "We love filling the house with strays during the holidays." She opened the string handles of the bag and peeked inside. "Is that *Silver* Shred marmalade from Claudia *Silver?*" The hopeful girl nodded. "Have you seen *Six Degrees of Separation?*" Claudia shook her head. "There's just the most marvelous speech where the black—I mean the *African American*—boy talks about giving pots of jam to rich people." She circled her long, slim arm around Claudia's shoulder. "Not that we're either," she added. "Come. I want to show you the most beautiful thing in the whole world."

The tiled bones of the Tate's long, narrow kitchen had gone untouched since the 1930s. The entire suite of rooms, including a small laundry, pantry, and maid's quarters, were Annie's sentimental territory. She had refused Paul's many offers over the years to gut the space and install a kitchen island and a wine fridge. Instead, she'd decorated every available surface with paper ephemera. Snapshot collages of Martha's Vineyard holidays had been assembled on a row of bulletin boards, with felt banners from the various schools and summer camps the girls had attended draped above them like bunting. There were holiday cards and finger-painted masterpieces from Martha and Bronwyn's Brick Church School days—Agnes, swiftly expelled for painting a swastika on the shell of a live turtle, having been exiled to a pilot nursery-school program at Teachers College. There were yoga schedules and a recipe card for cornbread from a Cape Cod grist mill. Marching around the upper seam of the rooms, where the tile met plaster, was a large collection of watercolors painted by Annie in a former life and preserved in Lucite box frames. Swans beneath willow, gourds in a bowl, still life with Ball jar and ball of twine: domestic snippets and cooperative wildlife in the vein of a particularly innocuous *New Yorker* cover.

Annie beckoned Claudia to the perfectly good, very old refrigerator. Pressing her finger to her lips as though a newborn might be napping inside, she tugged on its wide metal handle.

"Have you ever seen anything so gorgeous?" she asked Claudia, revealing an artful trompe-l'oeil log fashioned from sponge cake and butter cream. Chocolate twigs jutted from the cake at realistic angles, and meringue mushrooms, dusted with cocoa-powder dirt, sprung up in clumps from loamy chocolate curls. "Bûche de Noël," Annie said reverently. "Payard Pâtisserie. I ordered it before Thanksgiving."

Because all of this, Annie wanted to add, *is what I do now.*

Claudia had seen cakes like this before in the bright windows of pastry shops. Glancing upward at the framed gallery, she recognized there was even a watercolor of a cake just like it tilted above the laundry-room doorway. But Claudia hadn't known what you *called* a cake like this, or what it had to do with Christmas. Unsettled, she glimpsed her string bag, now collapsed forlornly around her meager offerings in the forgotten corner where Annie had dropped it. The berries needed water. "It's so pretty," she said. "It's a shame to eat it."

"But you see," Annie marveled, "that's the whole *point*. That's why it's my favorite Christmas tradition. It reminds me that before Santa there was Jesus, and before Jesus there were trees. It's both pagan and exquisite." Annie had majored in classics at Radcliffe, and Claudia had assumed, until this very moment, that she'd replaced her intellect with motherhood. Annie slid her vodka rocks in its collectible Scooby-Doo Welch's grape-jelly glass from where she'd tucked it, and swallowed a cold mouthful. "Bûche de Noël is just like life, Claudia," she said. "Too heartbreaking to be eaten but it *must* be eaten. That's what it's there for."

The assembled found their place cards, surrounded by the vast population of books lining the dining room in built-in cases. Annie had sent the party helpers on their way, having learned after twenty years of hosting that she needed extra hands for prep and cocktails, but preferred autonomy for serving the meal itself. In this way, Annie was able to approximate the feeling of actually attending her own party. She'd engineered the seating to encourage everybody's best qualities, suppress their worst, and develop dormant potential where possible, counting on the steady flow of cold Veuve to help things along. Paul, who now emerged from the kitchen to great applause, bore the largest turkey they'd had at Ottomanelli's. He took his place at the head of the table and began to carve.

Paul had made partner years ago. He'd nearly won countless charitable 5K races, been a capable steward of major purchases and projects, and took on pro bono cases both at work and at home. At many a midnight Annie had discovered him deep in counsel at the kitchen table, his chin propped on his clasped hands, listening with utter focus and sympathy to an anguished daughter, a daughter's pregnant friend, a Lebanese law student desperate to stay in New York to live as a gay man, all the while churning capably with answers and solutions. Pretty images could stir the actual soul, of *course*, they could—that's how Rockwell sold all those magazines. Somehow, it was from twelve feet away, watching Paul announce that they'd say grace, that Annie felt closest to her husband.

"God," Paul was now saying, clasping Claudia's and Joel's hands respectively and bowing his head, "or, if you prefer, the Creative Source of the Universe that's also the engine of your life, otherwise known as your instinct . . ."

At this, Claudia opened her eyes to consider her host. Throaty Aunt Toni's eyes, also open, caught hers across the table. Aunt Toni winked, and Claudia quickly fled to the darkness behind her eyelids. "We acknowledge this moment, this table, this company," Paul continued. "Christmas dinner is a symbol of the abundance and richness of our lives and of our choices. And it's also an actual feast we're fortunate to enjoy, so we give thanks for it. There's a prayer my grandfather used to say—"

"Back when we were Jewish," Agnes interjected darkly.

"Aggie," Annie warned.

In three generations the Tarnows had become the Tates, traveling from steerage to first class, from the Meseritz Shul to Ethical Culture, from City College to Harvard. Paul dusted off this notable fact a few times a year, in intimate settings like this one, where his family's successful assimilation could be couched as a well-executed PBS documentary. But Agnes, who pitted herself against whatever she could, and who, as a young teenager, had received novel offers of bat mitzvah tutoring and Israel teen tours with nothing short of disgust, could be counted on to rail against Paul's slightly proud, slightly guilty sentiment. Agnes was her father's emotional Dorian Gray. Her reliable distress allowed him to remain serene. *"Baruch a'tah adonai, elohanu melech ha'olam . . ."* Paul began plainly, even as eyes along the table blinked wildly, loose shutters anticipating a growing squall.

Claudia waited until the coast was clear and slowly opened her eyes again. Scanning the table and confirming that everyone else had settled into darkness, she let herself consider the side of Paul's handsome face, his trim jaw and throbbing temple vein, the movement of his mouth, as he continued to say grace. *"She-hecheyanu, v'key he'manu, v'hig-heyanu l'azman ha'zeh."* In all the time she'd spent with the Tates, this was the first glimpse she'd ever had of Paul's distant Mosaic past. That Paul Tate would know a Hebrew prayer by heart, that he would trot it out on Christmas Eve, that this household had something deeply in common with her own, boggled Claudia's perceptions. Yet Paul's secular confidence transformed the familiar prayer. Edith's *she-hecheyanu* was anxious and lisped; Paul's was "Amazing Grace" as sung by James Taylor at a private party. "We thank the universe for bringing us to this moment. Let us all be here now. Amen," he concluded.

Claudia suddenly noticed her hand in Paul's, and stared at their entwined fingers. She considered the smooth hollow beneath Paul's ear, the freshly laundered and pressed turn of his collar.

Paul gave Claudia's and Joel's hands brief, businesslike squeezes as the rest of the table stirred.

"Praise the Lord and pass the gravy," Aunt Toni declared as she tucked her cloth napkin into the neckline of her caftan.

"Wait," said Paul. "Now that the God stuff is out of the way, let's raise a glass to the goddess." He smiled down the table at his wife. "Annie, we are all thankful to you for making a beautiful Christmas Eve with all the trimmings and then some."

"It's my great pleasure to have all of you here. Merry Christmas!" Annie said graciously, beaming around the table as she remembered both the dinner rolls and the jelly glass of vodka she'd left behind in the kitchen.

After dinner, the Tates and their guests gathered at the baby grand for the customary sing-along with Throaty Aunt Toni. Annie bustled between the kitchen and the dining room, setting up the dessert buffet.

"Can I help you with anything?" Claudia offered, as the bûche de Noël emerged on its porcelain platter to take its place of honor.

"Would you like to lead the group in a Hanukah song of some sort?" Annie suggested distractedly.

"That would be a resounding *no*."

"In which case," Annie said, emptying the last of the Veuve into Claudia's glass, "you just have a marvelous time and enjoy." She tucked the empty under her arm. "I'm sending you girls home with plenty of leftovers." Annie retreated, leaving Claudia with the unpleasant reminder that there was less of the evening ahead of her than behind. Claudia took a deep breath, considered her options, and soon found herself venturing into the deep, unchartered territory of the apartment.

She wandered the length of the long central hall, lined in framed family photos, and found herself in the doorway of Paul and Annie's master bedroom. Quietly, she turned the cut-glass knob and entered her hosts' private quarters.

A stretch of windows along the far wall of the enormous bedroom overlooked Central Park. The windows continued around the corner of the room, offering an unbroken north-bound view of Central Park West.

Her body drifting slightly from the champagne, Claudia placed her palm against the glass. She thought her breath would fog the cold window and leave a wet print, but the substantial double pane ignored her touch. Outside, the gentle, persistent snow sugared the trees and muffled the midnight traffic, making the taxis into darting yellow fish going about their business under the softly frozen skin of a wintry stream.

Claudia moved to the large bed and sank down at its edge. She ran her hand over the block-printed coverlet folded at its foot. Chagrined and determined, she vowed that if she ever had a master bedroom and a husband to put in it, she would have a bed like this one, high off the floor, and a rug like this one, faded and extravagant, and a dresser like this one, tall, glossy, inherited from someone, topped with a lacquered tray and bottles of scent, and Paul's wallet, an old Gucci with an elastic band striped red and green, its rich, burnished leather evoking Paul's own skin, his forearms vaguely tanned even months after summer due to his weekly doubles at the Ninety-Fourth Street courts with his law-school roommates.

Claudia rose from the bed.

Paul's wallet pulled her close, then closer.

Her racing heart yammered in her ears, startling her from her champagne trance. She told herself she just wanted to see what was *in* there. What pictures, if any, he carried with him. She quickly devised a simple game to explain the motion of her hands, which were moving faster than her conscience. She hoped to find outdated school photos of the girls, a decade or more older, that would prove Paul was as detached as the next corporate father. Then Paul would be pushed safely back into the fog of parenthood.

Claudia slid the elastic from its grip and opened the wallet.

She could hear Aunt Toni's voice, belting out over the jolly chorus of dinner guests: *"I have no gifts for you pa-RUM-pah-pah PUM . . ."*

Inside the wallet, credit cards peeked from their slots. Five one-hundred-dollar bills, crisp and facing the same direction, were tucked neatly into its main compartment. In between the two halves of the wallet, Claudia discovered a thick strip of folded paper. It was a photo booth triptych of Paul and Bronwyn, laughing and tan, probably taken on the Vineyard, not long ago. She stared at the lively image and heard footsteps in the hall. The looming threat of being caught in Paul's wallet might have caused her to desist, but instead it urged her forward, past the point of choice.

She plucked a hundred dollar bill from Paul's wallet and shoved it deep into the pocket of her one good pair of black wool trousers.

She secured the elastic band.

She glided over the rug and found herself gazing contemplatively at the snow as Paul entered his room.

"There you are," he said. Claudia heard only mild surprise in his voice, tempered by pleasure. "Annie's about to serve dessert and she requests your presence for the cutting of the ever-loving bûche."

"Okay," said Claudia, not moving as Paul crossed to the dresser. In her mind, nothing had happened, so much so, that nothing had happened.

Paul disregarded his wallet as he opened the top drawer and removed a slim silver case. He cracked the window that was right behind Claudia, letting in a puff of soft, snowy air as he folded his frame into the deep sill and rested one foot, still in its loafer, on the upholstered bench that ran the length of the windows. Paul snapped the silver lid open, offering Claudia a smoke as he selected one for himself. She shook her head.

"Good for you," Paul said, as the Rothman bobbed in his mouth. The flare from his old Zippo lighter illuminated his face. "Healthy lifestyle." He cupped the flame and the scene was briefly reflected in the window.

Claudia had never been alone with Bronwyn's father before, let alone after a night of drinking, let alone in a darkened bedroom, let alone with cigarettes. But it was the dirty loafer now resting on the expensive striped fabric that gave Claudia a pang of something, and suggested that either Paul had some degree of disregard for the house rules, or that perhaps he had begun to chafe under them. Claudia pictured him as a patrician prep-school senior, sick to death of the same place that held him firmly in its bosom. Paul pulled his knees up, tucking himself deeper into his perch. He rested his wrists on his knees as he considered Claudia, his cigarette burning. "Mind if I ask you a personal question?"

"I wish you would," Claudia replied. If Paul was a senior, and Claudia was an underclassman, she could talk to him like this.

"What's really going on?"

"With what?"

"You and your sister. Bronwyn says she's been living with you for more than a month." In fact, Bronwyn had illuminated the situation to her father in far greater detail. Worried, and amazed that Ivy Leaguers could have problems that she'd typically associated with Appalachia, Bronwyn had reported to Paul a variety of troubling anecdotes regarding Claudia's family of origin and sworn him to absolute secrecy. "Are you okay?" he asked Claudia, lightly.

" . . . Sure."

"You're on your own, working full-time, and now you've got a teenager to keep an eye on. That's got to be stressful for you."

"*You've* done it." Claudia countered. "Three times."

"I have a wife."

"Me, too," said Claudia. "In another county."

"Enough with the jokes," said Paul, not unkindly. Claudia looked away, temporarily humiliated, but the warmth of Paul's large hand as it briefly touched her shoulder brought her back. "Where's the money coming from?" he asked.

71

You, Claudia considered replying. She didn't want to tell Paul that there was no money and now no job, because that would make it true. "From the engines of capitalism, I guess." She shrugged.

"And you can't ask your dad for help," Paul reflected. Bronwyn had long ago reported Claudia's quasi-bastard status.

"Who?" It was hard to stop the jokes.

Paul took a long, squinting pull on his Rothman. "And what about *Phoebe's* dad?"

"He makes mine look like Dick Van Patten."

"Maybe you and your sister should explore the idea of Phoebe becoming an emancipated minor."

"Um . . . a *what?*"

"An emancipated minor," Paul repeated. "Legally declaring herself independent from your mother."

"I . . . I guess I'm not familiar."

"If you're going to keep up this arrangement," Paul advised, "I recommend you look into it. The State of New York will grant Phoebe all sorts of rights and protections if she becomes emancipated. But if she doesn't, your mother can make things difficult for you. She can have Phoebe declared a runaway, or worse, she can accuse you of kidnapping her. It sounds intimidating, but the process is manageable. It's something I can help you with, Claudia." Paul let his cigarette droop in his mouth as he looked out at the snow. Claudia easily pictured them standing outside a bar on upper Broadway during Christmas break after two pitchers of Rolling Rock, Paul having just said to her, "Let's get out of here."

"Okay," said Claudia.

"Here." Paul propped his Rothman on a small, lidded silver ashtray and returned to the dresser.

Claudia watched him reach for his wallet. The hundred-dollar bill pulsed in her pocket. She picked up Paul's cigarette. "Cigarettes are cool," she said.

He glanced at her in the dresser mirror. "You can have your own, you know. You're a grown woman." Paul was now standing before her, his arm outstretched, a thick ivory business card in his fingers. "I want you to call me," he said.

Claudia hesitated, then took the card as Bronwyn appeared in the doorway.

"What are you guys doing?" There was mild accusation in Bronwyn's voice. She carried a pair of dessert plates, each one bearing a slice of bûche de Noël.

"Just watching the snow," Paul replied easily.

"Do you know what I had to do to defend your meringue mushrooms?" she asked. In a fluid motion, she handed Claudia a cake plate, kissed her father's forehead, and extinguished his cigarette.

Paul popped a meringue mushroom into his mouth and sighed as it dissolved on his tongue. "You want to get out of here?" he asked his daughter in between rapid forkfuls of cake. "Take a walk in the snow?"

"I thought you'd never ask," Bronwyn replied.

Paul rose from his perch. "You, too, Claudia." He and Bronwyn were the same shape, tall and lean, more leg than torso.

Claudia sensed unenthusiastic vibrations emanating from Bronwyn. "Actually," she volunteered, lifting her cake plate for emphasis, "Meringue mushrooms are about as outdoorsy as I get. And I've got my eye on seconds." With that, she excused herself discreetly from the farthest corner of the Tates' apartment with the priceless view, and left the man and his daughter to make their preparations for a midnight stroll.

Three days later, at 11:50 in the morning, in the week between Christmas and New Year's, on a bright, cold corner of West Twenty-Seventh Street, Phoebe Goldberg drained the dregs of the hot chocolate with whipped cream that the guy at the Cuban diner had insisted on giving her for free. The flower district was a red and white sea of poinsettias, which Edith had always vociferously loathed. Phoebe, stopped in a stand of shivering ficus, pulled a folded-up business card from the back pocket of her jeans for the millionth time: PAOLO CRESPI — IMAGE MODEL MANAGEMENT. She lobbed the blue and white takeout cup and sunk it neatly into the trash as the light turned.

Ambling across the street, oblivious to the heads that turned to follow her appreciatively, Phoebe calculated with mild pleasure that she was keeping up her truancy skills even during Christmas break. It had been easy to drop Claudia and Bronwyn at the F-train stop and head off to the fictional Trivial Pursuit tournament that she'd convinced her distracted sister was being conducted on a classmate's sun porch in Ditmas Park.

Image Model Management was located on the fifth floor, past the inconsistent guardianship of the lobby security guard, a hulking, uniformed woman with lacquered hair and nails, both shot through with plastic pearls and streaks of hot pink. Her beard was faint, her transistor radio tuned fuzzily to WLIB. Her security policy included the chatting up of all UPS men, the harassment of most non-English-speaking food delivery boys, and the random interrogation of the young Miss Things with portfolios under their scrawny-ass arms.

"Ex-*cuse* me, lovely ladies," she warned. Phoebe kept going, since the security guard was confronting a ramrod suburban blond who looked like a Pan Am stewardess and her matching daughter, with duct-tape-wrapped Weejuns, most definitely not *her*. "You think this is a puzzle book in front of me? 'Cause it ain't. It's a *sign-in book* and it's waiting for your autograph and I don't *care* how many times you been here before . . ."

The lilting tirade continued as the elevator doors bumped closed.

Phoebe followed a narrow hallway around so many bends she thought she might end up where she began, and eventually arrived at the unassuming offices of Image Model Management. The reception area was lined in molded plastic chairs occupied by ambitious mothers in fresh lipstick. Snaking through the center of the small room, an anxious queue of slender, permed, and processed girls from the perimeters of the city bristled with pride. The dusty silk orchid on the coffee table gave the place the neutral but benevolent air of a Planned Parenthood, dulled the impact of the framed magazine covers lining the walls, and put Phoebe at ease as she took her place at the back of the line. A moment later, the statuesque mother-daughter duo from downstairs sailed in.

"We have an appointment." The mother was firm as she threaded through the crowd, gripping her daughter's hand. "Terrific new glasses, Dennis. They really suit you."

Dennis the receptionist, a pear-shaped young man with bleached hair, red-framed glasses, acne scars, and a bolo tie, framed Phoebe in his crosshairs as he leaned sideways from his perch. "Can I help you?" he asked.

"Only if you have a cure for jet lag," the mother replied with a knowing chuckle. "Tokyo always takes the stuffing out of us."

But Dennis was pointing at Phoebe. "No," he said. *"You."*

"Me?" Phoebe looked around.

"Come here."

Phoebe shifted in her moccasins, feeling the eyes of the wary hopefuls upon her. "Hey," she grinned at Dennis, giving an easy wave as the knobs of her wrist jutted from her sleeve. It was the cockeyed grin of beautiful tomboys everywhere who don't give a shit in the nicest possible way, girls shot through with a rusty vein of testosterone, and so up for whatever. She approached the front desk in her loping glide. A chubby girl in a chair followed Phoebe with her eyes and opened a sugarless candy; the taut silence was instantly filled with crinkle.

"Jesus, Mary, Joseph, the donkey, and a bucketful of myrrh," Dennis exclaimed quietly as she arrived before him. He was fixated, with a strictly entrepreneurial arousal, on the space between Phoebe's teeth—otherwise known on the block as her *liar's gap.* "Lauren Hutton."

"Phoebe?" she corrected uncertainly.

"Your *teeth.*"

" . . . Excuse me?" Phoebe poked her tongue into the space that she never thought about.

"How tall are you?"

"Yeah, um . . . so Paolo told me to stop by."

"That's how tall you are?"

"Five-ten," Phoebe replied. "My mother says I'd be five-eleven if I did the whole stomach-in, chest-out thing." Posture was an area in which Edith had remained vigilant. "Stomach?" Dennis bored a hole through Phoebe's peacoat. Beginning to understand, the girl stared back at him, slowly opening her jacket and pushing up the hem of her sweater to display a sliver of sunken belly.

"Nope."

"Bitch don't got no ass, neither," one of the waiting girls muttered, to the delight of her friends. Like Claudia, Phoebe had long ago developed eyes in the back of her head. She now reached behind herself in silent retort, subtly cupping a butt cheek with one hand and flipping the bird with the other without shifting her eyes from Dennis. The girls doubled over in ragged peals.

"Or manners," Pan Am murmured.

"Or shut the fuck up," a round-the-way girl with a sleek

wrap growled, having just decided she liked Phoebe. Pan Am inhaled sharply.

Dennis hit the intercom button. "Drop-in," he announced flatly.

Paolo Crespi emerged from the back of the office. He still had the slicked hair, fingerless driving gloves, and gangly carriage that Phoebe remembered from their first meeting outside a Korean market on Christmas Eve. Dennis hid his half-eaten package of Donettes with a pink message pad.

"Darling, what a surprise," Paolo said, extending his hands to Phoebe, then pulling her in to kiss her cheeks. He looked around, feigning anxiety. "Where is your bodyguard?"

"My sister?"

"She did not appreciate my sophisticated recruitment methods."

"She's cool," Phoebe offered uncomfortably, unwilling to conspire against Claudia. Gently pivoting her chin with the tip of his index finger, Paolo examined her jaw and throat.

"And you," Paolo marveled, "are maybe perfect."

"Are you thinking *Moxy* outdoor?" Dennis asked, right there with him.

"Among other things." Paolo took Phoebe's broad hand. "Come back and meet everybody, darling."

Paolo fancied himself a Milanese cowboy leading a fresh filly along the inner corridor of Image Model Management. He was perfectly aware that booking agents were emerging from their cubicles to form a murmuring crowd, but kept his breathing steady and his eyes on the warm, dry stall of his glass-walled office before Phoebe reared and bolted. As she was removed from her peacoat, fed a Diet Coke, and spun gently around, as her arms were checked, as she was led onto a digital scale that Paolo produced from under his desk, he marveled at the way the girl seemed to relax *into* the strange ministrations of his staff. Finally, Phoebe was deposited onto a puffy black leather loveseat, a relic from Paolo's first apartment. She stretched her arms along its back and folded her legs, hooking the foot behind the ankle. In this iconic pose struck only by the very slim, Phoebe commanded the office, and from there, Paolo quickly plotted, the entire Western world. And Japan.

"So," he said, leaning forward, "you have always wanted to model, yes?"

"Actually," she replied, "no. Definitely not." Paolo paused, allowing himself a deep inhalation. Her not caring was *brilliant*.

"Absolutely wonderful," he marveled. "So I assume that the pictures, you don't have."

"Of myself?"

"That's right."

"Not really." Phoebe frowned. "I could get somebody to take some—"

"No. We will make the arrangements. And give your hair a health trim. It is only two inches, no big deal. You don't even need highlights, because God, he already gave them."

"Okay."

"And there is something I must tell you right now," Paolo continued gravely, "before we start down this road together. It is one of the most important things you will ever know." He coughed wetly, clearing the contained excitement from his throat, closed the door, and assumed a gargoyle perch. "It is a life lesson, but please God you don't have to learn it, because you trust me now. You must always trust me, Phoebe. Because when you give something away that is so precious, you can never get it back. So you must protect it. And I must protect you. No matter what they say, no matter how powerful they seem or how fabulous the evening is or what covers he promise us. Do you understand me, Phoebe?"

" . . . I guess."

"You must never, never, *never* get your teeth fixed."

"Okay."

That was easy, they both thought.

"And you are how old?"

"Sixteen."

"And you will be seventeen when?"

Through the glass walls of Paolo's office, Phoebe glanced at the framed *Seventeen* magazine covers lining the corridor, and wondered if you had to be that age to get that job, and whether it was a mistake that she hadn't already lied. "Next August," she answered, truthfully.

"Eight months," Paolo calculated, with some concern. He knew from experience that much could happen to a young girl in eight months, and did not want to delay for a moment. "So do you have working papers?"

"Not really."

"In this business, Phoebe, there are not so many yes or no questions, but this is one of them."

"Then . . . no."

"Ah. Well, you must get them right away. That is the law, so that is the *first* first thing." In a swift movement, Paolo produced a bureaucratic form from a desk drawer. "You are with Mother and Dad?"

"No."

"I don't mean right now, Phoebe. I mean this is where you live, yes?"

"Um . . ."

"Dad, he is not in the picture?"

As Phoebe pulled the long strands of her legs into a tight knot and wondered how Paolo could tell, he silently praised himself for the insight that had gotten him out of the *quartieri dormitorio*, and eventually the down payment on his Spring Street loft. "And so you live with mom."

Phoebe paused. Then: "Pretty much."

"So you must have Mother sign," Paolo declared. Phoebe quickly pictured herself forging Edith's signature in the elevator and returning to Paolo's office first thing tomorrow morning. "Well, not just sign. She must come into the office in person and then we will also discuss how you get paid, the range of assignments, where to send the checks and such. And we will sign your contract. This will not be a problem, yes?" Phoebe dropped her chin into her hands. Once again, she resolved that a thing was only a problem if you called it that.

"It shouldn't be," she said.

On that very same Tuesday in late December, a gleaming midtown atrium thrummed with workaday traffic. Those who had not fled to Nevis or Aspen were working a short week. While the cavernous lobby was the portal to a major record label and the world headquarters of the conglomerate that owned several pet care brands, the interior lobby of Golden Fenwick Tate Stein and Lowe, with its curved mahogany staircase lined in Audubon prints and symmetrical flower arrangements tucked into ginger jars, had the thickly carpeted hush of a patrician funeral chapel. Claudia removed her lumpy fur cube of a hat and lowered her voice respectfully as she announced herself to the receptionist. She'd barely settled herself in a club chair when a young woman approached on a bright wave of pert energy, her coppery bob swinging and her arm extended.

"You must be Claudia," she declared. "We met on the phone." Claudia rose to meet the hale handshake, picturing the girl pirouetting through the foyer of her efficiency apartment at the Barbizon Hotel, circa 1963, without spilling a drop of her sherry. "I'm Kelly Welch, one of Paul's paralegals." The Cartier bangle spun on one freckled wrist. High on her forearm, in the working girl's version of a serpentine garter that cinched her sleeve at the shoulder, Kelly wore a stretchy plastic spiral from which a lone key dangled. "Paul's stuck in a staff meeting, so what else is new, but he knows you're here. He'll come get you as soon as they spring him."

Claudia followed Kelly to her office. She had never before been mesmerized by another woman's backside, and yet with Kelly, packed into her straight wool skirt and emanating a soap-and-water sex appeal that deserved a bossa nova soundtrack, she couldn't help it.

"Please, make yourself comfortable," Kelly urged Claudia, plucking her coat from the chair of the unoccupied second desk. "Can I get you anything? Coffee? Does your dog need some water?" Kelly nodded at Claudia's fur hat with an acceptable giggle. "So you're Paul's daughter's roommate, is that right?"

"*C'est moi*," Claudia replied. Kelly swept aside the small pile of bills she'd been paying at her desk. Claudia noted the personalized labels printed with a horsey motif and the Scarsdale return address.

"Career advice?" Kelly guessed.

"Okay." Claudia was certainly willing.

"I mean is that what Paul's going to give you?"

"Oh," Claudia realized. "Um . . . I don't think so. He's helping me with some legal research, I guess. A thing with my family."

"Sounds private," Kelly observed, slipping into her coat. There was an urgency behind the girl's chitchat that Claudia sensed but couldn't pinpoint. "I thought maybe he was going to have you apply for the paralegal job." She indicated the empty second desk. "I lost my roommate. Big promotion."

Claudia didn't know a single person who'd gone to work for a big company like this one, or even attended a recruitment fair. Had there even *been* a recruitment fair at the college? Of course, there must have been, for the football players, but her friends had all been slated for entry-level jobs in glamour fields, ski-bum stints in Telluride, or Fulbrights. "Promoted to what?"

"Married," Kelly sighed enviously. "At the Pierre. All the trimmings." Kelly's rump positively switched as she crossed the room to close the door, then pivoted neatly. "Senior Partner, Litigation," she continued admiringly. "Bad news? Now she's the twenty-five-year-old stepmother and the kids hate her guts. Good news? The last one leaves for Groton in the fall, and then she's going to *completely* redecorate in the city *and* get a place in Bucks County." Kelly gave Claudia a pragmatic once-over. "This is the best job in New York City for girls like us and you should totally apply for it. Get transferred to Intellectual Property or Entertainment as soon as you can and give it two years, tops." She arrived at Claudia's pointy black toes. "You won't be able to wear those, though, without getting the stink-eye from some biddy in H.R."

Girls like us? Kelly didn't seem to be kidding. "I'm not really the legal type," Claudia admitted.

There was a brief knock on the door. "Who is?" Kelly laughed. "Half the attorneys in this place aren't legal types. They're *making a good living* types. They're *little blue box* types." She opened the door to a young man in a cashmere coat and a Lawrenceville baseball hat whom Claudia immediately recognized from Christmas Eve at the Tates'.

"Let's go, m'lady. Time to feed the beast," said Carter Kemp, his gaze landing on Claudia indifferently. He made no move to press the flesh.

"Mr. Carter James Kemp," Kelly announced.

"Yes, we've met," Claudia pointed out.

Carter frowned. "We have?" His doubt at having crossed paths with Claudia rendered him instantly dead to her. Still, she hoped dearly that he'd spontaneously combust.

"She's thinking about applying for the paralegal job." Kelly winked at Claudia as she pulled on slim, green leather gloves.

Carter drifted from the doorway. "We'll have a blast. And don't let silly Carter Kemp give you the wrong impression," Kelly added brightly. "I promise you. There are much, *much* bigger fish at Golden Fenwick."

Moments later, Claudia was standing unseeingly in front of Kelly's large framed Seurat poster. She wondered vaguely whether it had come from the firm's decorating coffers or Kelly's former dorm room at Colgate, when she turned at the sound of Paul Tate's voice.

"Hi. Sorry." Bronwyn's father had been a rakish young man on Christmas Eve, but he had clearly aged since that night. In his velvet-collared charcoal wool greatcoat he dominated the doorway of Kelly's office, exuding barely contained impatience. "Look. I hope you don't have a problem with going out," Paul said, curtly. "There's turkey meatloaf and filet of sole in the partner's dining room. The former is hell to digest and the latter makes me feel like my grandmother."

"Sure," Claudia replied.

"Good. I made a reservation at Pippi." Claudia looked at Paul blankly. "The new Marcus Samuelsson over on Washington? I suppose you haven't heard if it's any good?"

Indeed, Claudia most certainly had not.

A town car waited outside, and Paul held the door as Claudia slid in. The interior was a soundproofed leather parlor, immaculately kept, with fresh magazines and the Modern Jazz Quartet playing quietly. No conversation was required with the driver. "I know we have important things to talk about," Paul said as they settled, "but they have to wait."

Soon the car was traveling south along the wintry Hudson River. Claudia was troubled by the silence and expected herself to fill it. She busied herself with sucking in her belly. She didn't know how long Paul expected her to wait, or whether she was waiting for him to speak next, and in the meantime, who she was to him now, a mentee, an acquaintance, a curiosity, or an obligation. It helped to fix her gaze on the Circle Line as she caught it keeping pace among tumbling white-caps. Claudia could make out the miniature tourists gathered on deck despite the cold.

"I have to confess to you, Claudia," Paul eventually said. She caught Paul in profile and felt a rush of tenderness for the lines around his eyes that made her hand want to reach out and touch his cheek. "My chief personality flaw. It's gotten me in more trouble over the years than I care to recount."

"I'm all ears," she ventured.

"I forget to eat, and then I become pretty much an ass-hole." Paul turned to face her in a rush of familiarity. Claudia suddenly knew who she could be between here and the restaurant. A wry, Hepburn-esque sidekick with empathetic womanly intuition beyond her years, intellectual bravado, and a smoldering core.

"And is that where we find ourselves?" she asked, congratulating herself on making him smile.

"Sadly, it is where we find ourselves."

"And yet it must be a relief to unburden yourself to me." Paul chuckled and shook his head. "Shall I amuse you with tales of my day," Claudia asked, "until the waitress brings us warm rolls and butter?"

"I wish you would," he said.

Phoebe strolled from the offices of Image Model Management into the cold, bright afternoon. Paolo had given her a plastic sleeve, into which he'd slipped two blank copies of the working papers, a brochure, his business card, and the business cards of the hairstylist and the photographer he planned to employ on Phoebe's behalf, "so that Mother, she can get comfortable before we all sit down." Phoebe had slipped the sleeve into her Tibetan knapsack and walked west to Seventh

Avenue. At the first working pay phone she found, she dug out a quarter and dialed Claudia at work.

"Georgica Films," Gwen answered, with her gentle lisp.

"Can I speak to Claudia Silver, please?" Phoebe asked. "This is her sister." Obviously, Claudia would have to be her fake mother for the meeting with Paolo. There was a long pause. "Hello?" Phoebe repeated.

"Yes," said Gwen. "Could you hang on a second?" Gwen placed the call on hold. Phoebe watched the F.I.T. students swarm about the entrance to campus in their different costumes. Gwen, who did not like to be caught walking, rose from her creaky chair and lumbered across the office to Faye's desk. Faye's eyes instantly filled with tears at Gwen's report: it was Claudia Silver's sister on the phone, the sister Claudia hadn't heard from, the unfathomable mother, Claudia Silver who seemed long gone. Faye shushed the rest of the office and picked up the line.

"Hello, dear," Faye greeted Phoebe, unnaturally. "You're calling for Claudia?"

"Um, yeah," Phoebe replied, instantly aware of the worried strain in the strange woman's voice.

"Is this . . . Claudia's sister?"

Phoebe considered hanging up. In the street, truck drivers lay on their horns, yet Phoebe could hear the woman's breathing. "Yeah," she finally answered. There was a long exhale on the other line.

Faye stumbled forward. "Darling, I'm sorry. But Claudia doesn't work here anymore. We had to let her go almost a month ago."

"You mean, like, *fired?*" Phoebe asked.

Faye screwed her eyes shut. "Yes," she confirmed. "But is there anything I can—"

Gently, Phoebe returned the receiver to its cradle. Why

wouldn't Claudia turn out to be both more and less than Phoebe had expected and trusted her to be? No job. No job for *a while* now. Fired! Lying! *Of course.* Of course, Claudia had something fucked-up going on and, *of course*, it was hidden in plain sight and, *of course*, Phoebe had a sign on her back that said SUCKAH and whether it was Claudia who'd taped it there, or Edith, the fact was *this family was totally fucked.* She would forget it, Phoebe decided. Forget it and move on. That was just what you did. It was just a matter of figuring everything out. Phoebe stood on the sidewalk in a funnel of thick dust, and decided it would be best to wait for a minute, until she could see.

Pippi, the Scandinavian restaurant earning raves for its Ethiopian-inflected tapas, occupied a former photo studio on a secluded West Village corner. The coveted dining room murmured with an offhand, in-the-know afternoon crowd. "I'm uncomfortable with the idea of herring and yams," Paul admitted, dropping into the limed-wood booth upholstered in kente cloth and dressed with white tulips. He'd checked his coat and loosened his tie. "But don't let that get out." He pulled a pair of reading glasses from his jacket pocket. "I don't want to get dumped by the cool crowd." The menus were heavy white cards printed in blue, and Claudia scanned hers rapidly for the cheapest combination, as Edith had instructed her always to do, arriving at a cup of peanut soup and a side of collard greens with lingonberries. Paul, nibbling an anise cracker, plucked the menu from Claudia's fingers and pushed it away, print-side down. "You relax, let me order a bunch of everything, and we can decide what's good."

"Love it," said Claudia, meaning it. "At this rate, I may never have to think again."

Paul frowned at the cracker in his hand. "This thing is like a licorice crouton," he said. "Absurd." He dropped it with disdain. "Let's get down to business. First of all, remind me of your sister's name."

"Phoebe."

"That's right. Phoebe Silver."

"Goldberg. We have different fathers."

Paul glanced up sharply. The different-father thing seemed to be least of it, but always got a reaction. "Silver and Goldberg," he mused.

"Yup." Claudia wanted to try an anise cracker as a warm-up to eating in front of Paul, but struggled to make a move.

"And she's how old?"

"Sixteen. She'll be seventeen in August."

Paul instructed his signature concern to overtake his utter starvation, dug for his Montblanc, and flipped his menu to its blank side. At the top he wrote *Emancipation*, and underlined it. "So," he began. "Emancipation applies to kids between the ages of sixteen and eighteen who are not living with their folks; who don't receive financial support from their folks except by court order or benefits that they're entitled to, like Social Security; who live beyond their parents' custody control, and who aren't in foster care." There was an expected thrust to the shape of Paul's letters as he jotted bullet points on the menu:

- *16–18*
- *no live mom*
- *no money mom*
- *no custody control mom*
- *no foster care*

The waiter arrived, and Paul placed the order with similar pith. "We'll do the herring fritters, the mixed greens, the lingonberry meatballs, the lamb special, and the compote," he rattled off from memory. "Bottle of bubbly water, no ice." Paul turned to Claudia. "Unless you want to start with the peanut soup? Ruth Reichl says you'll see Jesus."

God no, Claudia thought. The peanut soup had become the enemy. "It's a lot of food," she said, instantly regretting her queasy observation.

"She sees right through me," Paul said to the waiter, handing him the menu. "I'm an over-orderer." He leaned across the table. "It's a socially acceptable panic attack," he confided amusedly as the waiter strode off. Claudia was trying hard not to be distracted by Paul's mouth and hands. He clicked his pen and returned to the task at hand. "Do you know what emancipation means?"

"Freedom."

Paul hesitated. "With a price," he warned. "A big one. It means mom renounces her legal obligations as a parent. She surrenders her parental rights to your sister. She is unwilling or unable to meet her obligations to Phoebe, or Phoebe officially refuses to comply with the terms of her household and officially leaves home." He continued to draft his list:

- *parental obligations renounced*
- *parental rights surrendered*
- *can't fulfill obligations*
- *Ph. no comply, leave*

"And what are parental obligations, exactly?" Claudia asked, heartened, as ever, to learn the rules.

"Very good question. Are you sure you don't want to go to law school?"

"Maybe after lunch."

Paul smiled. "The primary parental obligation is to protect the health and welfare of the child."

"That's how the court defines it?" Claudia asked.

"And that," said Paul, impressed, "is a perfect segue. And

88

here's where I owe you an apology." He paused to scan the dining room. "For Christmas Eve. I blame my ego, which requires me to fix everything, and the fact that I practice real estate law and haven't thought a lot about this stuff since I was studying for the bar. Plus I was drunk as a skunk."

"Okay," Claudia replied, wondering if he remembered being alone with her in his bedroom.

"I made it seem that emancipation is something you simply *apply* for and Bob's your uncle. But I totally forgot a key point. In New York State, while the courts recognize the status of emancipation and the rights of emancipated minors, there's no emancipation statute *per se*. In other words, there's no court proceeding in which you actually *obtain* emancipation. It all depends on the facts on a case-by-case basis."

"So that's good news if you're me," Claudia decided, "which I am." She had been unable to imagine the scene in the courtroom, *Silver and Goldberg v. Mendelssohn*, without forcing Edith into a rolled hairstyle and restrictive tweed skirt suit in the vein of Mildred Pierce, which, of course, would never happen, as most of Edith's waistbands were elastic. "What are the facts?"

"These puppies here." Paul indicated the first set of bullets with the tip of his pen. "Over the age of sixteen, not living with mom, not in foster care, beyond custody control, and one more."

SELF-SUPPORTING, Paul now wrote in caps. "But d'you want to hear the rub?"

"With a dream scenario like this one," Claudia replied, "there's got to be a catch."

"The State of New York still requires emancipated minors to obtain parental consent to get working papers," Paul explained.

Claudia scowled. "You mean have to get permission from the same person you're trying to get free from to acquire the key credential you need to get free of them?" Paul nodded. "That's some fucked-up Joseph Heller bullshit," she concluded.

"But it's within the realm of possibility, and kids do it all the time, or, at least, when circumstances demand it," Paul continued. "So once Phoebe handles things with Mom, and I'm not saying it's easy, she has the legal right to retain all her own wages and establish her own independent legal residence. Of course, since minors in the State of New York can disavow a lease, most landlords won't rent to them."

"So is emancipation going to help my sister," Claudia asked, "or hurt her?"

Paul shrugged. "She could tough it out until she turns seventeen, at which point it will be a whole other ball game. And I assume that the two of you are experts in toughing it out."

A movement across the dining room caught Claudia's eye. She glanced its way and froze, recognized the gleeful wave, the bobbing mop of dark curls.

Garth Kahn, grinning in his cardigan.

Raising his lingonberry spritzer high, to toast the happy couple.

"Dang," said Claudia.

"Who the hell *is* that?" Fretting, Paul propped his reading glasses high on his forehead. "Is he one of my summer associates we didn't hire?" Paul squinted, taking in Garth's big head of hair. "Is he, you know, *light skinned?*" Garth consulted with his gray-haired luncheon companion, who glanced over his shoulder at Paul and Claudia and quickly returned to his *mitmita pastejköket*. Now Garth was bouncing toward them on his Wallabees. "You *know* this guy?" Paul asked.

"Sort of."

"Is he your boyfriend?"

"I just said I only sort of *know* him," said Claudia.

"The last time one of my daughters said *sort of,* she was calling from the Edgartown jail."

"He's not my boyfriend."

"Hey, sweetie," Garth said as he arrived. "Small world." He bent to peck Claudia's cheek with a light, ritual affection, instantly clocked her palpable anxiety, then aimed a meaty hand at Paul's chest. "Garth Kahn at your service." With easy authority, Paul half rose from his seat to shake it.

"Paul Tate."

Garth wedged himself next to Paul with a quick nudge. "I won't be long," he said, folding his hands in preparation for an extended interview. Quizzical and dogged, Garth sniffed back and forth between the older man and the younger woman. "You're Bronwyn's dad?"

"You know my daughter?" Paul raised an eyebrow at Claudia, who shrugged.

"Choate summer school," Garth explained, shoving an anise cracker into his mouth and crunching messily. "I bought my first string bracelet because of her. Plus Live Aid in Philly. And who could forget college." He turned to address Claudia, the crumb flurry continuing. "Which makes you and me practically related." With a sweep of his forearm, he transferred the crumbs to the floor. "So what do you guys make of this place? Stockholm and Addis Ababa—two great tastes that taste great together, or dangerous miscegenation we must put a stop to? Personally, I'm agnostic. Although my pop's having a religious experience." He attempted to bore his eyes into Claudia's, then nodded to the busy gray head across the dining room.

"Paul thought he might know you from work," Claudia offered, smiling weakly as she looked between the two men.

"Oh, so we're not unpacking the restaurant? That's cool. And where does Paul work?" Claudia noticed the clench of Paul's jaw.

"I'm an attorney," said Paul, considering heavier weaponry as he drained his champagne.

"At Golden Fenwick," Claudia added.

"I'm sorry to hear that," said Garth. "I was selling pot for about three minutes after graduation. Is it possible we know each other from hemp circles?"

"I don't think so," said Paul.

"Because you get all of your hooch on the Vineyard and bring it home in a coffee can, then promise yourself you'll make it last till Memorial Day?"

"Excuse me," Claudia announced, lurching from the teacup ride that her perfect lunch had become. Somehow, Garth's smitten antics left her miserably exposed. Her cheeks burning with shame, she fled for the ladies' room.

A postcard rack was mounted to the wall between the restaurant's bathroom doors. Furiously, Claudia scanned the images for a card she could send to Phoebe, despite the fact that Phoebe lived with her now. As recently as last month, Claudia spent her evenings writing and pasting collages in a notebook, swinging into her sister's life on an imaginary chandelier to whisk her out of the circus. But that was then.

Or maybe it was their circumstances that had been imaginary.

These days there were burritos to order. There was angel hair pasta to overcook into a mash. There was homework to talk about double-checking, and then blow off. There were Monie Love lyrics to memorize and recite while dancing around the living room, and there was the futon sofa bed to make up with Bronwyn's extra linens.

"Hey." Garth had padded up behind her, wearing his smile sideways.

"Jesus fuck," Claudia snapped, quickly swiping at her eyes. "What is your *deal?*"

"I was about to ask you the same question."

"Except that it's none of your fucking business."

"He's thirty years older than you and he's your best friend's *father*."

"What are you *thinking?*"

"Hey, baby. I'm picking up exactly what you're laying down." Garth paused. "You should be dating a loose cannon with youthful joie de vivre and everything to live for, like myself."

"Paul is my *attorney*," Claudia declared, suddenly overcome with wanting out. She pointlessly rattled the doorknob of the locked ladies' room.

"There is somebody in here," somebody's nasal grandmother proclaimed determinedly from inside. Claudia stepped to the men's-room door.

Garth gaped. "You're not actually going to—"

"What? Like pee has a gender?" Claudia pushed open the door and scanned the empty row of urinals for pederasts. "It's how they do it in Paris." She didn't actually need to pee.

"When's the last time you were in Paris?" Garth asked.

"Never," Claudia snapped. Garth wedged his foot into the doorjamb, blocking her escape.

"Claudia."

"*What?!*" She was caught and frantic.

"Somebody else's husband is no way for you to have your first orgas—"

—CRACK!

Claudia's palm shot from her shoulder on a taut fulcrum to strike Garth's face, hard.

The slap rang in Garth's ears.

Having learned long ago to put her weight behind a punch, and sporting a giant flea-market ring in the shape of an eagle, Claudia deposited a notable splotch across Garth's cheek. He made no move to touch his burning cheek, which deepened in color as the seconds froze.

"Really?" was all he said.

But he was alone in the hallway, addressing the bathroom door, as by now Claudia was gone.

In the time it had taken Phoebe Goldberg to recalibrate everything she thought she knew about Claudia Silver, wander southeast from the Flower District, and eventually emerge from the F train at Bergen Street to face her old neighborhood, the afternoon had begun to fade and the pothole puddles of Smith Street were growing dark and glassy. At the top of the subway stairs Phoebe stopped to survey the busy corner and review the facts. Her sister, whom she'd been living with for the last month, who'd been buying her stuff and telling her not just *what* to do in the day to day, but *how* to do life in general, was a liar. A weird one. It was one thing to fake going to school—that was a *classic*. It was what you were *supposed* to do when you were sixteen and clearly not cut out for a life of letters. But to pretend to go to *work?* When you were out of a *job?* While declaring yourself the boss of the situation? That made Claudia Silver a pretty fucked-up choice for a fake mother. Unpredictable Edith Mendelssohn, on the other hand, was a fucked-up choice for a *real* mother, along with the motherfucker who'd come up with the idea that somehow you choose your parents. At least Claudia had never let anything bad actually *happen* to Phoebe, whereas Edith had Robbie Burns. And while the things that Robbie had done to Phoebe maybe weren't as bad as they *could* have been, as bad as the shit you read about in the papers, walking out of Edith's house hadn't been the solution to getting rid of Robbie. At night, Phoebe churned on the futon sofa in Claudia's living room. The scent of Robbie's filterless cigarettes and English Leather tirelessly pursued her dreams, with an impish torment scurrying after: Did Edith sort of know and turn her back? Or could she not see even the most fucked-up shit on earth when it was happening in her own house? Was she a laser beam or a blind bat?

Phoebe swept the corner for Robbie. Satisfied that he was nowhere in sight, staying focused on the working papers in her Tibetan knapsack, and taking a deep breath, she gathered herself together and headed down Smith Street. The very least Edith owed her was a motherfucking signature. Phoebe would get it, and she'd be gone. Tomorrow, or soon, she'd have a job. And eventually, a place.

Phoebe knew the strip by heart: the Chinese variety store with its cotton Mary Janes and plastic bucket of baby turtles, this morning's *platanos* long congealed under the heat lamps at Castillo de Jagua, the acrylic fumes gushing from Elvira's Beauty Box, and the tubby Bensonhurst cops scarfing slices at the counter of Pino's, anticipating signs of criminal activity with a relaxed disgust. The nameless candy store, however, where once she and Ramona Parker had pooled their pennies for Fun Dip and Pixy Stix, was a surprise. Long shuttered behind a scrolled metal gate tagged thickly by every Basquiat in the Gowanus Houses, it had apparently since blinked open to reveal a dark socket. A small crew of young white guys in painter's pants did demo in the dimness. As Phoebe loped past, one dropped his sledgehammer heavily at his hip to watch her.

Phoebe could remember when she'd been pretty much the only white girl around. That's what had taught her to clock other white people. Still, Phoebe didn't seek white people out for comfort like she was pretty sure other white people did, especially in neighborhoods like this one. In fact, Phoebe *preferred* to be the only white girl, and quite truthfully felt she was a better representative of white people everywhere than most of the white people she'd known.

A crooked figure twitched into Phoebe's sight line. "Hey, girl," he croaked, ashier than ever. Benny Crackers, the block's most vivacious crackhead.

"What's up, Benny," Phoebe offered in reply. This neighborhood had taught her that a simple "What's up" would do in response to just about anything. That offering an easy "How's it goin'" to your neighbors before being spoken to, over time, forged loose alliances.

Still, as Phoebe neared Hector's Hardware, her worry began to mess with her cool. Hector's was Robbie's joint. Robbie liked to load his suede fanny pack with chump change, shrug on the fur-collared parka that Edith had chosen for him from the Eddie Bauer catalog, and light a Pall Mall for the trek to the corner, where he'd regularly spend his allowance from Edith on an addition to his hand ax collection before returning home to fry a triumphant baloney sandwich and rest up for his noonday NA meeting.

Phoebe really, really, *really* did not want to see Robbie. So, before turning the corner onto her former block, she pulled the favorite move of frightened white people everywhere.

She crossed the street.

This deceptively simple adjustment to her usual route angled Phoebe differently to the past. Walking along the tall chain-link fence that Darleen Parker had long ago taught her to vault, Phoebe was curious whether she could see her mother's house and not feel anything.

Turns out, she couldn't.

Too anxious, Phoebe cruised straight past the tilted little building, then jaywalked to the corner of Hoyt. She pushed open the glass door collaged with stickers for Coco Lopez and Utz chips, and with the clatter of bells sewn to a leather thong, ducked into Mickey's. The dry wooden floorboards creaked as her racing heart slowed to a jog. Tina, one of Mickey's myriad nieces, perched, as always, on her cashier's stool behind an elaborate candy and notions counter displaying the competing cassette tapes of local emcees. Engrossed in the 4:30 movie on the tiny black and white TV, with a bulky cordless phone tucked into her shoulder, she bickered vehemently with her married boyfriend in Spanglish, while cracking her gum spectacularly and acknowledging Phoebe with a tough-love chuck of her dainty chin.

Phoebe arrived at the back wall of humming, leaking fridges, wherein every flavor of Yoo-Hoo chilled, even banana, and reached for a grape Fanta.

"Where the school bus at?"

Darleen Parker, in her tracksuit, Triple FAT, and wrap-around plastic shades, leaned against a stretch of paneled wall. Due to persistent winter hat head, she'd traded her Jheri curl for tight cornrows that tugged her eyebrows scalp-ward. Presidente posters hung behind her, featuring glistening girls in hot pants and knotted soccer jerseys. Tucked among the high rumps, a small square had been punched in the wall and fitted with a sliding window.

"What's up, Darleen." Despite the utterly chill delivery that Darleen had taught her by example long ago, Phoebe had never been happier to see anybody.

"You *got* to be on some kind of class trip. Come over from Park Slope for the *anthropology*, right?" The window slid open. La Mega played quietly from whatever lay inside. "Come on, gal," Darleen chuckled. "You know I'm just messin'." She cocked her voice in the direction of the little window. "Not you," she clarified edgily to the unseen clerk. "Lemme get a dime of Violet Crumble." The window slid closed, taking La India and the timbales with it. Darleen cocked an already-taut eyebrow at Phoebe. "You back home now?" she asked.

"Nah."

"You wanna smoke?"

"I gotta see my moms," Phoebe demurred.

As the little window opened, Darleen exchanged a faded ten-dollar bill for a small ziplock Baggie. The window closed.

It used to be that Phoebe let herself into her mother's house with a key hung on a tooled-leather key chain shaped like a strawberry. But on the recent November afternoon when Darleen and Ramona had escorted her back into Claudia's life, she had left her key behind, smack in the middle of Edith's dining room table. The gesture was a fuck-you parting gift that also guaranteed she would be unable, even in a moment of punk-assed weakness, to return. Darleen now slipped the dime bag into the coin pocket of her track pants and retied the drawstring. "Shit," she mused, sympathetically. "If I was gonna hang with your moms, I need to bake me an entire dime *pie*."

"Yeah," Phoebe agreed, picturing Darleen sitting next to her in Paolo Crespi's office at Image Model Management, telling Paolo she was Phoebe's mother, even though she was only eight years older, the wrong color, and possibly didn't like boys.

The clang of Mickey's homemade doorbell ushered Phoebe and Darleen back to the sidewalk. Phoebe pocketed the Fanta cap she'd popped on the door frame, took a brief purple gulp, then belched neatly.

"Nice," Darleen praised.

"Thank you, Obi-Wan." Scanning the corner, Phoebe observed the pulse of the Gowanus Houses at their main artery. Up the wide front steps at the entrance to 211 Hoyt, young mothers bumped granny carts of damp laundry as the men, in Gazelle glasses and bulky leather jackets, ignored them en route to the night shift. Thanks to Darleen's various lectures over the years, Phoebe could tell the difference between this, the *real* business of life, and the jumpy, manufactured daily grind of the crack trade. As she always had, Phoebe felt safe next to Darleen, who came to her shoulder. Darleen was both the gatekeeper and the gate itself.

"You ever have working papers, Darleen?"

"*Working papers?* Shit. I was born with 'em. My moms ain't never *forgave* me for the paper cuts."

Staring straight at Edith's house, Phoebe took a longer pull on her Fanta, then let rip a stunning belch, wet this time, during which she recited the first few letters of the alphabet, getting all the way through *g*.

"Damn," Darleen marveled. "We *got* to get you on *Star Search*."

"All right," Phoebe declared. "I'm going in."

"What was that all about?" Paul asked. He held open Claudia Silver's bomber jacket, with her big black scarf draped over his arm. Had a man ever held a jacket for Claudia? No, he had not. Not to mention that in Claudia's former life, one she'd occupied until this very second, Claudia would have found the gesture skin-crawlingly twee. Paul watched Claudia wind her scarf around her neck, then deftly helped her on with her jacket.

"What was *what*?" she feigned, awkwardly thrusting her arm about.

"If that reaction was for a fellow you only 'sort of' know," Paul explained, referring to Garth's turn through their lunch, "what happens when there's history?"

Suddenly, Paul was touching her, from behind. Well, not *her*, exactly, but her hair. Slowly, gently, lifting her hair out from where her scarf had bound it. The ends of her hair dragged along her shoulders like Paul's fingertips. He then placed his hands on her shoulders and turned her to face him. She was limp now, a doll.

"Is it chestnut?" Paul's voice sounded like it had grown

thick. And maybe other aspects of himself had grown thick as well. But Claudia wasn't sure of anything, including the placement of the floor in regards to the ceiling. She felt herself swimming, her ears clogged, no idea what he was saying, rededicating herself with every passing millisecond to her posture, erect, and her hands, to herself. "Your hair," Paul explained. "The color."

"I don't know. Yeah. Maybe." Somehow, she was speaking.

"Postprandial perambulation?" Paul asked. Claudia stared at him woozily. "An after-meal stroll, for digestion," he translated.

"Let's call it 'an after-meal stroll for digestion,'" Claudia replied, finding her footing. "That other thing sounds like a Whiffenpoofs medley."

"Fuck it," Phoebe said to herself as she rang Edith's bell. Hearing the metallic shriek reverberating through Edith's lower duplex, she grabbed her knapsack straps. The police lock scraped and the front door opened, answering Phoebe's prayers, sort of. It was Edith at the door, not Robbie. Phoebe always forgot how much taller she was than her mother.

"Phoebe," Edith said, matter-of-factly, after a brief pause.

"Mother."

Edith cocked her head, piled precipitously with its dark, wavy mane shot with gray. Loose silver strands clung to her pilled navy turtleneck, on which her reading glasses, hung from a tortoiseshell chain, rested at chest level. "What winter wind has blown you this way?"

"I . . . I'm not sure which one," Phoebe answered. She hadn't exactly been expecting a bear hug and freshly baked snickerdoodles . . . but *damn*.

"I was just making tea," Edith relayed, opening the door wider as she stepped aside. "Would you care to join?" Teatime was *the* civilized ritual of Edith Mendelssohn's household.

Unlike supper, when Edith usually seemed to be faking it at gunpoint, teatime was assured. Her little trays of crackers and dates were charming, whereas crackers and dates for supper were sad.

Edith closed the brownstone's front door behind her, revealing Robbie's collection of axes and baseball bats arranged in a white plastic bucket. She crossed the building's foyer and padded into her parlor in her old boiled-wool clogs, embroidered with springs of dingy edelweiss, and Phoebe, more nervous than she wanted to be, followed. The absence of cigarette smoke, jangling, and throat clearing confirmed Robbie's absence. Only the teakettle whistled.

"Are you alone?" Phoebe asked anyway. She had never told Edith what Robbie had put her through, because she suspected that telling her mother would make things worse, not better.

"We are *all* alone, darling," Edith replied, donning her glasses to pour boiling water into a heated brown teapot, "especially at birth and death." She peered over the top of her glasses at Phoebe, who hovered by the apartment door. "But at the moment, you and I have privacy. Robert's at a job fair."

In your dreams, Phoebe considered replying, as she closed the apartment door with a clank of the police lock.

Phoebe decided she'd ask Edith to sign her working papers as soon as the quilted tea cozy had been removed from the teapot and the PG tips poured. Maybe she could slip the paperwork from Image Model Management in front of her mother without even an explanation, and Edith would sign her autograph blindly, with a dreamy smile. Or maybe Ziggy Marley would ask her to prom.

"Take off your coat and stay awhile," Edith demanded, mashing tinned sardines into a paste with Dijon mustard.

"I'm cool," Phoebe replied.

"No, you must be overheated," Edith countered.

The doorbell rang, and Phoebe jumped slightly, glancing quickly at the parlor windows. Through the lace curtains she made out a familiar figure jittering at the top step. Of course, Robbie wouldn't ring the bell. "It's Benny Crackers," she announced, assuming that seeing her up on Smith Street had put the idea in his head to stop by.

Edith wiped her hands on a linen towel. "Another country heard from," she commented, retracing her steps to the front door as Phoebe shrugged off her knapsack, sank into the shredded Victorian wing chair flanked by a magazine rack stuffed with scholarly rags, and splayed her long legs in front.

The parlor windows were cracked an inch or two, and Edith's voice floated in from the stoop. "Yes, Benjamin," Edith said, benevolently.

"You got any handyman-type stuff you need done?"

"Not today, I'm afraid."

Street angel, house devil. Claudia had once described Edith thusly, and Phoebe thought that shit was true enough. There was a way in which Edith loved and respected all humanity, while remaining unlikely to pee on you in a firestorm.

"How about the stoop?" Benny Crackers was insisting. "It need sweeping? I see you got some leaves down there, and whatnot. Them kids, throwing they bottle caps all over th'place. You let me get all that mess picked up for you."

Briefly alone in her mother's apartment, Phoebe could help herself to anything she wanted. She surveyed the faded cotton bedspread over the futon sofa that became Edith and Robbie's bed at night, the tilted standing ashtray mounded with Pall Mall butts, the red lightbulbs that Robbie had screwed into the parlor's ceiling fixture, the busy formation of fruit flies hanging low over the mottled bananas. But there was no object in sight for which Phoebe *felt* anything, not even the wooden animal napkin rings of her youth, still on their bed of dust in their pewter bowl set in the middle of the old dining room table.

"All right, Benjamin," Edith agreed. "Help yourself to the broom."

"Yes ma'am," Benny Crackers replied, excitedly. Phoebe could picture his little scarecrow dance, and his unsteady descent to the steep lower stairwell.

"This is all I have today, I'm afraid," Edith was saying.

"Three bucks lookin' real good to a workin' man."

It was then that Phoebe found herself inexplicably rocketing from her seat to snatch an ancient bag of Chinese ginger candies from a chipped ceramic jar on Edith's kitchen counter. In a flash, she wrapped the bag into a tight cylinder and shoved the entire thing down the sleeve of her peacoat.

"I've got my younger daughter over for tea," Edith was saying to Benny, "so I'll see you next time."

"Yes, ma'am." The rhythmic scrape of Benny's sweeping had begun.

Phoebe dropped into a dining room chair and wondered why the fuck she hadn't a) asked for the bag of prehistoric candies if she wanted them that much or b) shoved them in her knapsack, where they would be far less likely to make noise and cause a scene.

"From each according to his ability and et cetera," Edith remarked as she returned.

"Word," said Phoebe, trying not to move.

"So," Edith began, placing a little delft pitcher filled with skim milk on the table, "do you have a toothbrush?"

"Excuse me?"

"A molded implement, fashioned from nylon and plastic. With which you clean your teeth. At your current address." It was always impossible for Phoebe to tell what Edith really meant. Was everything Edith said always sort of joking? Edith knew exactly where Phoebe was staying, because Phoebe had told her. Unless Edith hadn't gotten the message, because Robbie hadn't relayed it, in which case wouldn't Edith have been happier to see her? *Relieved?* Was Claudia dead to her?

"Oh," Phoebe replied. "Yeah. It's pink."

Making several more trips between the table and the kitchenette, Edith set out Jacob's Cream Crackers, farmer cheese, dates, sesame cookies, radish roses, and cold ratatouille in an old blue Pyrex mixing bowl, stuck with a scalloped silver spoon, a survivor from her own mother's trousseau.

"And do you continue to grace school with your presence?" Edith asked, placing a lone radish and two crackers on a flowered saucer and settling in her chair.

"Affirmative."

"And having arrived at school, are you staying there?" Edith placed the whole radish rose between the two crackers, and steered the unwieldy, rolling sandwich toward her mouth.

"Yeah."

A shower of broken cracker plunged to the saucer, the radish bouncing down after it. Edith frowned in surprise and brushed the crumbs into her hand. "And are you doing drugs, including malt liquor and cigarettes?"

Phoebe sighed.

The fact was, Phoebe had neither confirmed nor denied whether she drank malt liquor and smoked blunts like every other red-blooded American girl in the 718. Instead, she'd always responded to her mother's occasional inquiries with a studied, long-suffering patience that was partially true. Yes, Phoebe had done everything, just about, nothing with needles but whatever you could smoke or drink and plenty of what you could swallow, and also no, she wasn't really *motivated* by that shit at all. Phoebe was Wile E. Motherfucking Coyote, zooming along a desert road with a repeating backdrop of stone monuments. She was gaining speed, churning. She'd always known she couldn't live in Claudia and Bronwyn's living room forever, and now it was clear that Claudia couldn't afford to keep her for probably one more minute. Soon she would find herself in midair, a disintegrating, wedge-shaped dead end behind her. To land, she'd have to launch herself. Really put her back into it. That's what Phoebe cared about. At some point, coming down, not too hard.

"I need to ask you something," Phoebe began, buying herself another minute as she sugared her tea.

"Spit it out, child."

"I need you to sign my working papers."

Edith, whose shoulders were perpetually braced for an accusation, relaxed imperceptibly. "Working papers?" she repeated.

"So I can get a job."

"What kind of job requires papers? Will you be a guard at the Canadian border?" Edith scooped ratatouille.

"Nah."

"I am asking you for reasonable details, Phoebe," Edith said messily, her mouth full.

"I . . . I met this guy. Uptown."

Edith lifted her faded Kliban Cats mug. Phoebe heard the rattle of ice cubes, and marveled once again that her mother was some kind of Jesus, turning tea into whiskey right under your nose. "How I wish this tale had a more propitious beginning," Edith lamented.

"No, he's cool," Phoebe hedged. "He's an agent. He represents models." As Edith sipped, Phoebe grew quickly aware of her mother's creeping unhappiness. "No, seriously," she insisted. "He's, like, totally legit."

Edith set down her mug and removed her glasses. They dropped on their tortoiseshell chain. "This phrase you use," she said, pressing her fingertips to her closed eyelids and holding them there. "This 'totally legit.' As in legitimate, yes?"

She dropped her hands from her eyes and glared at Phoebe. "So this would suggest you've done a complete and thorough check on this individual's profile with the Better Business Bureau."

"It . . . it would?"

"You are able to confirm, without a shadow of a doubt, that this individual is a licensed representative of a *legitimate business enterprise*. That he holds no criminal record. That he faces no outstanding litigation for charges of statutory rape." Two spots of high color had appeared on Edith's cheeks.

"His company's called Image Model Management. They're in the Flower District, near F.I.T.—"

"Ah, the Flower District. How appropriate a milieu for fresh blooms, swept into the gutter when no longer a prized commodity to be replaced by a fresh crop."

" . . . *What?*" It was perfectly obvious to Phoebe that this shit was going south. It was perfectly *wack* that Edith cared so much about virginal bullshit while having a skank boyfriend like Robbie Burns. Phoebe pressed her back against the chair, steadying herself.

"It's prostitution," Edith declared flatly, taking a deep swallow.

"No," Phoebe said. "It's like *Seventeen* magazine."

"It's *prostitution*," Edith repeated, her voice growing louder, "and while I assure you I've learned over the years to adjust my expectations according to your apparent devotion to the lowest common denominator, I certainly held out hope that at some point you'd consider a trade, a vocation."

"You mean like air-conditioning and refrigeration?"

"I mean *not* the oldest goddamn profession, is what I mean!" Edith cried. And then suddenly—SMASH!—Edith's fist hammered the table. The silverware jumped, the pale blue milk quivered. "Goddamnit!" Edith cried again, at the edge of a raw scream. A delicate garland of saliva hung between her bicuspids. SMASH! SMASH! The fist came down. "Shame! *Shameful!*"

Edith plunged her head into her hands.

The room thrummed with a ringing silence.

There was nothing for Phoebe to do, she knew from experience, except hold very still. Only suckers got jacked by their mother's rages, especially since there'd been warning in the slow boil of Edith's curlicue questioning punctuated by the spots of color on her cheeks. But somehow, Phoebe was, once again, a sucker. The trick was to sit still now and *act* not surprised. To sip tea. To leave the building in your mind, to pretend Edith was a stranger, just a crazy lady on the F train, to switch cars, to get adopted, or maybe married. To concentrate on the tea, on the steam, settling upward on her face as it rose, maybe cleaning out her pores. You couldn't know, Phoebe knew, what was going to happen next. Maybe Edith was done, or maybe this was the pregame warm-up. If Edith kept going, Phoebe decided, she would get up and walk out. She would go next door and ask Mrs. Parker to come with her to Image Model Management in the morning and be her mother for half an hour. She could have a black mother for thirty fucking minutes. She had the mouth and no father, right? Phoebe thought Mrs. Parker would do it, too. There was love lost all up and down Hoyt Street, but none of it was between Edith and Mrs. Parker.

Edith sighed loudly and pressed the heels of her hands into her closed eyes, digging at her hairline with her fingertips.

Slowly, Phoebe began to rise in her seat.

She was backing away and getting gone.

That's when the police lock scraped and her mother's front door shuddered open.

Suddenly, Phoebe found herself flash frozen.

With a stamp, and a rattling cough, with the jangle of keys and change, on a cloud of cold city air, and without a friendly whistle or a *honey I'm home*, Robbie Burns had returned.

For several blocks they'd walked along the charming streets of the far-west Village in a parallel silence—comfortable for Paul Tate, uncertain for Claudia Silver—and now stopped in front of a proud but tired apartment building. A scalloped green awning declared its name, *The Powell*, in faded gold cursive. "This stuff with your mom," said Paul. "It's a lot of information to digest. Do you have any questions?"

Claudia looked up at Paul, cocked her head, and tucked a strand of her chestnut hair behind her ear, wishing she'd reapplied her matte lipstick somewhere between Garth's bitch-slap and here. She followed Paul's pale breath, visible in the cold air, and willed it toward her mouth so that she could draw it in, shotgun-style. *Let's see. Any questions. What if Phoebe stays, and what if Phoebe goes? What if Edith reappears, and what if she disappears? What if* Hope Valley *requests an interview, and what if I end up homeless?*

What if I kiss you?

Right now?

Claudia shook herself into the matter at hand. "I guess I'm slightly hung up on the self-supporting thing," was what she came up with.

"You don't think your mom will sign working papers?"

"It's the conversation that happens right *before* that one," Claudia explained. "Eating glass comes to mind as a pleasant alternative."

"How about I talk to her?"

Paul began to speak, then paused. And in this brief moment, something came over Jane Street. Everything suspended and shimmered around the edges as Paul deposited a dry cough into his glove.

The cough was so *fake*. Which confirmed the essential thing.

Paul was nervous.

He shape-shifted before Claudia's eyes into the gangly youth pounding beers by the Christmas tree.

"D'you want to come up to my studio?" Paul indicated the Powell with a glance.

So there it was.

There was Claudia's former life, B.P., Before Paul, when Bronwyn had been merely her best friend, the buffer between the guest bed and the curb, and Paul Tate had been the father of them all. There was what would happen next. And this moment was the portal between the two. The only way through it was to push, hard and determined, to shut the toy chest of the college years without looking at its sentimental contents too closely, refusing to succumb to Bronwyn's imagined stare as the lid closed. Starting now, things would be different. They would be dangerous and delicious. *Adult.* She considered the building, strung with a lone fire escape and studded with ancient air-conditioner units. She made her voice amused and controlled. "Are you actually asking me to see your etchings?"

"Not exactly," Paul confessed shyly. "I . . . paint."

"As in *Dogs Playing Poker*?"

"Something like that."

Claudia grinned.

Moments later, in a creaking elevator the size of a powder room, a reverent silence descended upon Claudia and Paul. Dutifully, they faced forward, as in a lineup facing a one-way mirror. Their heels clicked down a linoleum hallway, yellowed like an old tooth. "Place smells like rent control, unfortunately," Paul apologized, pulling the keys from his pocket without fumbling. "I've held on to it since my second year at law school."

The inside of the little one-bedroom, however, was bright

and blond, from the renovated floorboards to the tweed sofa bed, with the distinct stillness left by a recently departed cleaning lady. Near a triptych of windows, in an ideal spot for a wintry landscape to emerge against a backdrop of New Jersey, an easel stood. But the pencil sketch in progress, waiting to join stacks of finished canvasses propped against the walls, suggested a hunched human form. The paintings were pale washes of gouache highlighted with telling details. The despairing drape of a loose hand had been rendered with only a slash or two of black oil pastel. Claudia assessed the pictures and found them to be actually pretty good.

"So," she asked, "being a fancy-pants lawyer. That's like your day job, while you wait for the call from Mary Boone?"

Paul stood before the windows, staring out at the steely river. "I don't think Mary Boone's going to track me down any time soon," he replied. "Not that my work is any good." Here, he paused. Before Claudia could sort out how on earth to compliment this man's artwork, he continued. "The painting is my little secret."

"Only the one?" Claudia asked. Paul turned to face her, but said nothing. "Do you come here every day?"

"I wish," Paul replied. "More often I use this place when I'm pulling an all-nighter on a closing. It's a place to catnap and shower. And, you know. Express myself." Paul could have nodded at his oeuvre for emphasis, but instead he kept his eyes on Claudia. She felt a tremor as she glanced into the bedroom doorway. The room was spare, anchored by a platform bed. She drew closer for a better look, Paul's eyes pulling taut the space between them. "Once you make partner," he said, "You get to stop sleeping on the floor under your desk."

Claudia wandered slowly into the bedroom, pretending to be drawn in by the paintings stacked around its walls. Paul followed her in. "This place needs a chair, I'm afraid," he said, lowering himself down.

"That's cool," said Claudia, joining Paul at the edge of the bed as he lay back and folded his arms behind his head.

"I guess I paint because, somehow, I *have* to," Paul explained, a warm drift of Grey Flannel, mixed with Right Guard and laundry starch, rising from his collar. Claudia propped herself so that she was looking down on him, realizing they were already on to plan B, that Paul wasn't going to push her up against the wall with a hand cupping her breast and his mouth lunging toward hers in a muscular crush, like Ruben Hyacinth would. Neither of them glanced to the radiator when it moaned, jarringly. The dizzying yellow circles on Paul's tie, it turned out, were owls. The strand of hair that Claudia had tucked earlier now fell loose.

"Bronwyn reports that you won a writing prize. At school." Paul reached up and touched the strand. His thumb grazed Claudia's cheek, but his fingers were too thick to tuck it, and it bobbed back into frame. Their breathing had become synchronized. Claudia was gratified that he touched her first.

"I won three, actually," she whispered.

"You see that?" His voice was husky.

"But I don't write the way you paint," Claudia said. "I mean, not because I *have* to."

"No?"

"I do everything else because I have to." She laid her hand against his jaw. Finally, he pulled her to him. The kiss was so tender, dry at first, but sure. They were in a dorm room.

They were away for the weekend.

They were at the edge of a private meadow, sheltered by blossoming boughs.

Right now everything Claudia had in this world was her mouth against Paul's.

The room tumbled as Paul rolled her onto her back.

Testing the waters, she lifted her hips to press herself against his thigh.

When Paul groaned, the roof blew off the building.

Claudia saw a jaunty little plane hurrying to Teterboro, and an escape balloon.

Then she closed her eyes.

Robbie never said hello. His silence, along with his sunglasses, his silver rings, his tattoos, and his shit-kickers were costume elements. Narrowing his eyes, Robbie surveyed the scene.

"Jesus," he complained, tossing his parka on the futon. "You two at it again?"

"Only moments ago it seemed I was minding my own business," Edith said, her head still in her hands.

Robbie opened the fridge and stared inside. "You got to show up and upset your mother?" he accused Phoebe.

"She shows up when she wants something," Edith remarked. "This has been established."

"You got coffee?" Robbie asked.

"Tea," said Edith, surveying Robbie with blatant desire.

Phoebe was pretty sure Robbie wouldn't know what to actually *do* with one of his hand axes if an intruder lay at his feet, bared his throat, and *begged* for it. Edith smoothed her hair and rearranged a hairpin. Robbie found a can of Coke.

"I can make coffee," Edith offered.

"Congratulations," said Robbie. He filled a cranberry-glass goblet with soda, selected a Hostess lemon pie from his drawer, and took his seat at a carved Victorian throne.

"Tell him what you told me," Edith instructed Phoebe.

"I didn't tell you anything," Phoebe said. "I *asked* you."

Robbie opened his lemon pie. "Can I get you a plate for that?" Edith asked.

"This suspense is fucking killing me," said Robbie.

Edith pushed her own empty plate before Robbie. "She asked me to register her for prostitution."

"And here you was," he said, pushing the plate back, "worried she wasn't going to make nothing of herself."

"*Say* something to her," Edith insisted.

Robbie took a swallow of Coke. Finally, he stared at Phoebe. She stared back. "The fuck you bustin' your mother's balls for?"

"I have a chance to sign with a modeling agency," Phoebe explained plainly, "but I need my mom to sign working papers."

Robbie considered Phoebe, clearly weighing his response. "You get what you give," he said. "You familiar with that one?" He crumbled up his pie wrapper, lobbed it at the sink, and missed. "You got my prescription?" he asked Edith.

"It's downstairs."

"Hey, *Sanford and Son*. I can never find shit down there. You know this." Phoebe watched Robbie and her mother exchange a knowing look. It was almost entertaining, how they thought they were slick like that.

"I'll get it," Edith declared, leaving Robbie and Phoebe alone. Phoebe had promised herself she would never be alone with Robbie again. She'd learned that Edith being nearby didn't make a difference.

Robbie pulled his Pall Mall box from the snap front pocket of his corduroy shirt. He held a cigarette in his teeth and produced his Confederate flag Zippo. "I got an idea," he said, touching the flame to the tobacco. He took a deep inhale, crossed his legs, and exhaled a plume at the yellowed ceiling. "You want something from your mother? You want your papers signed or what have you?" He pushed his sunglasses up on his forehead. The small, pale eyes were always a surprise. "I'm asking you a question."

"I guess."

"You guess, huh." Robbie picked a fleck of tobacco from his

tongue with a long pinkie nail. "There is one way we can play this," he said, focused on Phoebe as he tapped a plug of ash onto the glazed rind of his lemon pie.

"Okay."

"You move back home. Where you should be, anyhow, by the way. You come back here where we can keep an eye on you." Robbie exhaled another plume and moved his hand to rest high on his thigh. "And in return for that, you get to try your little cockamamie modeling crap." Phoebe wondered if he was going to start playing with his thing outside of his jeans as she'd seen him do before.

"Would you like your sweatpants?" Edith called up from the basement.

"You think about it," Robbie said to Phoebe. But Phoebe already had. By the time Robbie had descended the basement stairs and deposited a loud slap across Edith's ass, Phoebe yanked open the stiff apartment door. Its ancient, floor-mounted police lock, comprised of a steel bar wedged between the door and the floor, provided dual service as an acoustic alarm. It clattered loudly as Phoebe bolted.

Out on the stoop, Mrs. Parker was arriving home from a temp job, trudging up to her own front door with her Met Foods shopping bag and her headphones. She gave Phoebe a tired, distant smile. Phoebe pictured the bear hug that Darleen would offer. She could see Mrs. Parker at the Crock-Pot, ladling out stew studded with soft carrots and sprinkling the steaming bowls with oyster crackers. Phoebe opened her mouth to speak when she heard movement inside her mother's apartment. She leapt Edith's stoop in a single bound as Mrs. Parker disappeared into her own home. At the curb, Phoebe fought the urge to sprint. She reminded herself that she'd just escaped—again. The point now was what to do with it. With the utter determination required to slow the fuck down, Phoebe unfolded one long leg after another and, with her signature lope, made her way to Smith Street.

At suppertime, Claudia returned to the apartment she shared with Bronwyn to find that the door had once again been left unlocked. In their two-year stint as roommates they'd debated this habit numerous times. Bronwyn held the optimistic view that an unlocked door promised "I'm home, all is well." Claudia considered it an open invitation for homicide.

Tonight, stunned by her afternoon with Paul, Claudia found the door resting on its latch and quietly entered, as a criminal might.

Adrenaline thrummed her veins, burning body fat and lengthening her throat so that its ring of pudge, noticeable in photos, melted away with the passing seconds. Simultaneously, Claudia was no longer occupying her body. She would be bobbing against the ceiling, looking down on her life with a giddy remove, were it not for the new, droning weight that held her to the surface of the earth.

Bronwyn was blasting *Hey Ladeez*, the mixed tape featuring romantic chanteuses that Claudia had made for her twenty-first birthday. Doris Day, bubbly and knowing, floated down the airless entrance hallway from the brightly lit living room to greet her, along with a waft of something hot and delicious. Claudia considered tiptoeing the length of the hall, but under the unwieldy circumstances it would be cruel to surprise Bronwyn. In Manhattan, Paul Tate was merely somebody else's husband. But here, he was something both rare and permanent. He was Bronwyn's *father*.

"I'm home!" Claudia called.

"Hooray!" Bronwyn called back, from far down the hall. Bronwyn's puttering had a distinct physical rhythm, and Claudia could picture her shuffling about the kitchen in her rag-wool slipper socks, an apron from Balducci's triple tied around her lean waist, taking an occasional gulp from a Mexican-glass tumbler of decent pinot noir. Claudia paused at her darkened bedroom, tossing her bomber jacket and fur hat to the futon bed and turning on the desk lamp. She scanned her wall of flea-market purses and the curtain made from a vintage lace tablecloth that prettied the dire view of the air shaft.

Claudia agreed that money creates taste, and briefly wondered how hers might differ if she had any.

A messy stack of Phoebe's school notebooks and papers had spread across Claudia's sawhorse desk. "Feebs?" Claudia hollered.

"Not here!" Bronwyn called from the kitchen. A particular sheet of Phoebe's crumpled schoolwork, scrawled in red ballpoint, now caught Claudia's eye. *Phoebe*, the note from the concerned teacher said, *let's talk. Please make an appointment to see me during lunch.* And the grade, D-plus. And the title of the paper: *Water Imagery in Huckleberry Finn, by Phoebe Goldberg.* Claudia seemed to have remembered writing one of these, before she got sprung from gen pop and placed on the AP track, but she'd always favored cheeky essay titles, and would have gone for something more like *H2 Oh No, Twain's Watery Ambivalence.* Her first sentence would not have been: "There is quite a bit of water imagery in *Huckleberry Finn.*" She would not have written her essay in faded magenta Magic Marker. But a D-plus? It was strangely shocking. More so, even, than the sight of Paul's snowy boxers peeling from his muscular thighs.

She had no job. She had no business. She had Paul Tate's fingerprints on her. *The roof, the roof, the roof was on fire —*

"I have a lasagna béchamel from Cucina and those cookies you like, the pink leaves with the chocolate filling," Bronwyn announced happily, appearing in the doorway. She grabbed Claudia's wrist and pulled her down the hallway. "And I made a wilted-spinach salad," Bronwyn was saying, "and I have all sorts of cheese—"

Strung liberally with winking Christmas lights shaped like hot peppers, the living room had recently been tidied. Bronwyn had contained most of Phoebe's sprawl in the cubbies Claudia had fashioned from a pair of wooden wine crates. On the coffee table, a stunning florist's bouquet of white and pale blue hydrangea, the gift card emerging from the blooms, towered over bowls of glossy purple olives and toffee cashews.

"Nobody told me we're hosting the varsity crew dinner tonight," Claudia quipped. She was grateful for her ability to act normal, and poised to put air quotes around her entire life.

"I have *news!*" Bronwyn cried, doing a quick bouncy dance of anticipation. She handed Claudia a Parmesan straw and skated into the kitchen on her slipper socks. Claudia kept her eyes on the flowers. Their tailored freshness exuded respectable festivity, rather than romance.

Claudia waited until Bronwyn was out of sight, then plucked the gift card from the bouquet. "You're pregnant?" she called out, nonchalantly.

"No! Jesus!" There was an unseen clatter of ceramic and stainless. "It's *good* news!"

"Bruce Springsteen invited you onstage to dance in his music video?" Claudia called, reading quickly. *Congratulations, Darling! We're so proud of you! With love from Mother and Dad.*

Claudia heard a celebratory pop as she swiftly returned the gift card to its envelope, her heart pounding as a bolt of anguished jealousy thrummed her veins. "Stop guessing, I beg of you!" Bronwyn begged, emerging from the kitchen with a monogrammed Lucite bucket she'd nicked from Annie's pantry and a pair of champagne flutes. A bottle of Veuve was plunged into the ice.

"Daddy sent champagne, *already.* Isn't his bionic timing

ridiculous?" Bronwyn rhapsodized. Claudia, whose long-absent father had still not sent an IOU, had to agree. "He is why I don't have a boyfriend, by the way," said Bronwyn. Claudia smiled thinly, feeling gypped. Bronwyn raised her glass. "To the newest addition to the *Moxy* team, Associate Photo Editor, Bronwyn Margaret Montgomery Tate, aka yours truly." She clinked her glass to Claudia's, tilted her chin, and sipped with refined zeal, as Claudia dispensed with her bubbly like a Hoover. "I got it!" Bronwyn squealed. "I got the job!" Claudia set down her glass and the friends embraced. "I start on Monday."

"Mazel tov," Claudia said, elevating slightly to rest her chin on Bronwyn's sharp shoulder. Bronwyn wore old-lady fragrances, thick with gardenia, and a plain leather choker that Claudia coveted, knowing it would make her own throat resemble a bratwurst. The pudge, apparently, was back.

"I'm finally going to *have* something, Claudia," Bronwyn said. "For the first time in my life, I really know that. I mean . . . Martha and her old, married boyfriend. Agnes and her terminal . . . personality. Sometimes I look at my sisters and I think there has *got* to be more to life than the quest for *attention*. D'you know what I mean?"

"I feel you," said Claudia, pressing her palms against Bronwyn's shoulder blades. Her throat had grown tight. She knew it must be a good sign, Bronwyn growing up and becoming a Successful Young Media Professional. Bronwyn's budding career would help her handle everything that was coming, because she might be too busy doing whatever it was that Associate Photo Editors did to care what her father and her best friend were up to in *their* off-hours. Claudia hugged Bronwyn tighter. She couldn't imagine leaving this clinch, nor the permanent deep freeze that must be rolling in. Unless, of course, Paul called.

"Are you okay?" Bronwyn asked.

"Don't let me rain on your parade," Claudia said quietly.

Bronwyn held Claudia at arm's length, her expression furrowed with concern. "You won't. You *can*. What is it?"

"I . . . ," Claudia began. *I just slept with your father, and I'm quite certain it's not the last time, so just bear with me here, because if we put our heads together on this I think we'll both realize* — "I got fired."

Bronwyn's large violet eyes immediately filled with tears. "Oh no!"

"Yup. Shit-canned." Keeping the *almost a month ago* part to herself, Claudia slapped back the tears that threatened to scuttle up. The relief she felt to finally tell a truth threatened to loosen every secret she'd ever stuffed. She scrambled to outrace disaster.

"Oh, Claudia," Bronwyn commiserated. "How could those idiots fire you? You're so much smarter than they are!"

"They say blonds have more fun," Claudia said, letting her eyes, and only her eyes, spill. "But I'm pretty sure it's idiots who do."

Bronwyn pulled Claudia onto the futon sofa. "Tell me everything."

Claudia took a moment. Then: "I was born a poor black child."

"Come on, Claude. Don't do that."

Claudia swiped at the two fat tears racing toward her jawline. "The first thing I want you to know is that I am one hundred percent thrilled for you." That part was true. "I have no idea what an Associate Photo Editor does all day, but I look forward to finding out."

"Thank you." Bronwyn pressed her hand over Claudia's. "You'll be among the first to know."

"And thank you for making this lovely dinner." *Manners before morals*, Claudia remarked to herself, ruefully quoting her mother.

"You're very welcome. Now tell me what happened."

"I don't know," Claudia began. "I'm supposed to organize family-style lunch every day, but I just couldn't *take* that shit anymore . . ."

"You just outgrew it, that's all. It was time."

"I guess."

"Trust me on this," said Bronwyn, topping off Claudia's champagne with a twinkle in her eye. "You have perfect timing. Because we are in this thing together, Claude. What did your horoscope in the *Post* say?"

"'Your mother wears army boots,'" Claudia replied.

Bronwyn shook her head. "You're going to have something, too."

"Yes," Claudia sniffled, allowing the idea of Paul Tate as her something to rise, wonderfully, in her mind. She would savor it much later. "I look forward to fetching your cocaine and slippers," she said.

"No!" Bronwyn bounced and clapped her hands. "*You* got a call, too." Beaming, she crossed to the answering machine that occupied a shelf on their brick-and-plank étagère. Claudia made quick work of several more olives as Bronwyn hit PLAY.

"*This is a message for Claudia Silver,*" the voice said, nasal and slightly bored. "*Claudia, this is Shelly Gerson's office over at* Hope Valley. *We got your resumé, and we'd love you to come in and meet with Shelly at your earliest convenience. Please give us a call—* "

Here, Bronwyn stopped the message. "Did you hear that?"

"Yes."

"Do you get what it *is?* Ricky had to fire you so you could be available! It's absolutely *incredible*." Claudia deposited her olive pits into the little majolica saucer that Bronwyn had provided just for that purpose. "Um, *hello*," Bronwyn admonished. "Why aren't you smiling?"

Claudia sank back against one of Bronwyn's bargello throw pillows and closed her eyes, overcome by a wave of familiar exhaustion. A call from Shelly Gerson's office was "good news," and given all that Bronwyn had done to make a festive evening, to stand unshakably in her corner, the least she could do was smile pretty. But for Claudia, successful turns were necessary and largely joyless. Did *Australopithecus* man feel joy when he bagged a saber tooth? Did the Artful Dodger bounce around in his slipper socks when he nabbed yet another Covent Garden pocket watch? Successes were how Claudia *survived*. They were peat, potatoes, kerosene. Each one merely begat her bleak strategy for the next. Claudia opened her eyes. Bronwyn had returned to the sofa.

"Is it the interview?" Bronwyn asked, baffled by Claudia's nonreaction. "Do you want to borrow something to wear?"

"Maybe," Claudia allowed. She wondered how she would emerge victorious from the first firing of her so-called career, get Phoebe through junior year, and wreck her roommate's childhood home between now and the immediate future, plus put together a smart ensemble for her *Hope Valley* interview with Shelly Gerson. *Nose to the grindstone and all that*, she reminded herself, grimly.

Bronwyn sighed, determined to coax her friend into enthusiasm without losing her patience. "I think we're going to be very rich old women," she predicted, crossing to the answering machine and hitting REWIND. "I think I'm going to have a place near Cap d'Antibes, like Tina Turner." The tape wheezed backward. "And we'll sit on striped chaises and read and chat and have fabulous streaks of white in our hair, like .Mrs. Robinson, and look back on all this . . ."

"And then we'll die," said Claudia.

"This is no time to be thinking about mortality, Claude," Bronwyn admonished. "We're twenty-four. Now's when we think about *immortality*, okay?" She hit PLAY.

"This is a message for Claudia Silver," the voice repeated, sounding even more bored the second time.

"Oh shit, my brownies!" Bronwyn remembered, dashing back into the kitchen.

"Claudia, this is Shelly Gerson's office over at Hope Valley . . ."

"They're the good kind of brownies," Bronwyn called.

"Hash brownies on a Thursday night?" Claudia dug deep for a second wind. "I thought tomorrow was the first day of the rest of my life."

"We got your resumé, and we'd love you to come in and meet with Shelly at your earliest convenience."

"So eat half!"

Just then, the phone rang. *"Please give us a call,"* Shelly Gerson's *Hope Valley* staff member droned on, *"and we'll set something up for you . . ."*

Claudia sprang up, panicked by the relief she would feel to hear Phoebe's voice. "I got it!" she cried, finding the cordless phone among Bronwyn's Murano glass paperweights. "Hello?" she answered.

In the next room, the old stove door creaked open. "Tell Phoebe to get her butt over here," Bronwyn called. "This lasagna is a thing of beauty."

"Claudia?" the voice asked. "I need to talk to you." It was Paul Tate. "Are you alone?"

Bronwyn appeared in the kitchen doorway with a lasagna in her mitted hands and a glad expression. "Is it Feebs?" she asked.

Claudia shook her head. She knew it was too soon for Paul to call here, too dangerous. Bronwyn frowned.

"No, I'm not," Claudia said to Paul.

"Well, we are eating in ten minutes," Bronwyn warned, as she disappeared into the kitchen. "Lasagna béchamel, unlike revenge, is a dish best served hot."

Claudia took a pause, wondering what Bronwyn would come to mean, exactly, by "revenge."

"Claudia," Paul said. "We need to talk." With her eye on the kitchen, Claudia backed down the hall toward her bedroom. She braced herself for Paul's apology, for his lament. Furiously, she tried to sort out whether she should ask for his help with the job thing before or after he pleaded with her to burn his number. She stood in the middle of her little bedroom and closed her eyes. "I need to know if you feel like I do," he said.

"I . . . I don't know," Claudia hesitated. It all depended on how he felt.

"What happened with us this afternoon. It was . . . ," Paul trailed off, his voice husky.

Us. If there was an "us," then all of this was really happening. Claudia glanced at her desk, then down at her feet in her striped kneesocks. One day, fairly soon, this sad little room would belong to somebody else.

Us.

"Claudia . . . are you there?"

" . . . Yes."

"Can I . . . keep going?"

"Yes."

"I've never . . ."

Claudia lay back on her futon and touched her fingertips to her mouth. It was tender and swollen from her hours entwined with Paul. Claudia breathed in and out a few times, not deeply. She could hear Paul breathing, too. "Are you there?" she finally asked.

"Yup," Paul replied. Somehow, that was enough. "Claudia . . . I want to see you again." He hesitated. "And again." Claudia closed her eyes in the holy silence. "And can I tell you something else?" he asked.

"You can tell me anything, Paul." *Paul.* It was funny how saying his name out loud was borderline unbearable.

"What you need to know," Paul continued, lowering his voice to a murmur, "is you've got the sweetest ass I have ever seen in my life."

"Whoa," said Claudia, suddenly flushed with heat and about to dissolve. "You have got to get out more."

Paul laughed. "Trust me on that one."

Bronwyn appeared in the bedroom doorway in a mild huff, brandishing her bottle of pinot. "Um, hi, hate to interrupt. But hosting a celebratory meal, here. Guests of honor, us."

Claudia raised her head from the bed. "I'm getting off."

"I want to watch," Paul said on the phone. Bronwyn stood there, tucking a blond tendril behind her ear. Claudia raised her index finger in the international sign for *one sec*. Hand on hip, Bronwyn cemented her stance.

"Do you like when I talk like that?" Paul asked. "Is it too much?"

"Yes," Claudia said, her index finger still raised.

"Should I stop?"

"Probably. For now." Bronwyn stepped into Claudia's room and reached for the phone. Just as Claudia thrust out her hand in a halt, there was a beep. "Call waiting," Claudia announced to Paul and Bronwyn simultaneously. Bronwyn paused. Paul breathed. Claudia pressed the button. "Hello?"

"Hi, Claudia, this is Annie." Annie Tate sounded brisk. "May I speak with Bronwyn, please?"

"Actually, I'm on the other line," Claudia said. "Would it be okay if she calls you ba—"

"I'm returning her call, darling," Annie trilled, brightly trumping Claudia's business with her own. Claudia hesitated. It was enviable, Annie Tate's sort of mother love, and its unfamiliarity stirred Claudia's shame. There was the temptation to just go ahead and tell this lovely lady—her rival, apparently—just exactly who was panting evenly on the other line.

Claudia clicked over to Paul. "I have to get off right now."

"Call me back on my direct line at the office."

"In a few minutes."

"I'll wait."

Claudia clicked the call waiting again and handed Bronwyn the receiver. "It's your mom," she said, wishing she'd confirmed that Paul was no longer on the line.

"Hi, Mommy," Bronwyn said, cradling the phone as she wandered back to the kitchen.

At the corner of Seventh Avenue and Seventh Street, Claudia waited for the light to change. Across the street, glowing yellow, with its front door shut snugly from the cold, the phone booth, because it held the promise of Paul, looked more like a cozy little home than any place she'd ever lived.

Once inside, Claudia closed the door firmly, and wished there was a velvet curtain to pull, and a roaring fire, and a wing chair and ottoman upholstered in witty Brunschweig & Fils fabric, and a side table with a glass of champagne and a few slices of buttered baguette and chicken-liver pâté and cornichons, and a pedicure, and a pair of Moroccan leather slippers with funny curled toes, and a plaid mohair dressing gown in muted grays and creams with a thick silk cord, and a place by the beach, and her college loans paid off, and a job. She dialed Paul on his direct line.

"Hey," he answered with a warm chuckle, knowing that it would be her.

"When last we left our heroine," Claudia began, then paused. She hoped Paul was smiling.

"You're brilliant," he said.

"Aw, shucks."

"You are," he insisted. "Brilliant and beautiful." Then: "You're not used to being told that, are you."

As it wasn't a question, Claudia was unsure of the correct response. "Actually, I'm sick to death of it," she said. "Enough already."

"We should discuss logistics," said Paul, with a slight tinge of apology. "I know it's not very sexy, but we're both busy people, with plenty of, uh, moving pieces."

"I think our moving pieces are actually quite sexy," Claudia teased, emboldened. It was then that she spotted a familiar silhouette, very tall and very lean, gloveless hands jammed in peacoat pockets, long mane twisted into a knot and held with a chewed pencil, approaching her well-appointed side-walk cottage from the direction of Flatbush Avenue. Despite the long stretch of city sidewalk between them, the sisters' eyes met magnetically, at which point Claudia's typical relief at the sight of Phoebe plowed headlong into a fierce, new covetousness. Wanting nothing to interrupt the delicious naughtiness of her fireside chat with Paul, she turned her back.

Phoebe saw her do it.

So it's like that, Phoebe thought.

"In general," Paul was saying, "we should probably talk and confirm our plans before meeting."

A firm knocking on the side of the phone booth startled Claudia. She turned to see Phoebe staring at her through the glass. No irritated *what the fuck* gesture, just a long, even glare. Claudia held up an index finger. In response, Phoebe flipped her the bird, not rudely. "Can you hold on for a sec?" Claudia asked Paul. Praying that he would hold, Claudia let the receiver hang, then opened her front door, letting the winter air rush in. "Hey!" she greeted Phoebe, holding out her arms, sick with her own irritation. "We were about to call the hounds."

Phoebe made no move toward Claudia's offered embrace, and glanced at the phone. "Who's 'we'?" she asked, edgily.

"It's an expression, Feebs," Claudia replied. She took a step closer and absorbed Phoebe's entire existence in a single sweep, picking up on something that was off, and dropping it just as quickly.

"So who are you talking to?" Phoebe demanded.

Claudia hesitated. "Miss Krinsky," she lied. In a swift, clean motion, born on the block, Phoebe now lunged for the phone. Matching her speed, Claudia grabbed the receiver and abruptly hung it up. Anguished, Claudia prayed that Paul would forgive her, that he would speak to her again, and all the rest of it. She prayed that he'd understand the road before them would require the deft handling of hairpin turns like this one. "Actually," Claudia continued easily, "we were just wrapping up. I mean . . . *wrapped.*"

Phoebe frowned, indicating the bustling nighttime avenue. "You were talking to Krinsky out *here? Now?*"

"Bronwyn is on the phone and, well, to be honest . . . ," Claudia trailed off. Then: "I didn't think it should wait." She swore to herself that tomorrow morning she'd wake early, no matter how much hash Bronwyn had baked into the brownies, and would return to this very pay phone, and call Ms. Krinsky, at which point what she was saying to Phoebe now would be, retroactively, the truth.

Phoebe folded her long arms. "Because of the D-plus on my book report?" Claudia nodded, wondering if Paul was staring at the phone on his desk and wondering what the fuck was taking her so long.

"Personally," Phoebe said, "I think that shit could have most definitely waited. Like until you talked to me about it."

Claudia hesitated. She had never heard this tone from Phoebe. Was it possible that Phoebe sensed her infraction? But Phoebe wouldn't care if she had a new boyfriend, would she? A new boyfriend with some moving pieces? She tried to picture a day when she, Phoebe, and Paul might do something together. A long weekend somewhere warm, with Phoebe in the main hotel building and the two of them in one of the casitas, surrounded by an adobe wall, the breakfast tray ignored for now at the trellised front door. "I was going to talk to you about it first," Claudia insisted, "but then *she* called *me*."

"Krinsky called *you?*" Phoebe asked, doubtful. "But she doesn't know I'm staying with you. At least, I never said anything to her about it."

Claudia shrugged. *Fuck me*, she thought. "I wanted to get back to her before she called Mom."

Phoebe squinted at her sister. It would be easy to call her on her bullshit, but she wasn't sure where it began. "So when are we going in?" she finally asked, having already planned to return to Paolo Crespi's office during school hours.

"She's going to get back to me with some options," Claudia replied. "I'll run them past you." Then: "I promise."

Phoebe couldn't help herself. "Your work is going to let you go all the way to Bedford in the middle of the day?" she asked.

Claudia hesitated, then nodded. "Sure," she said.

Phoebe shook her head. *Unfuckingbelievable*, she thought, as Claudia drifted further away on her phone-booth ice floe. She would no more ask Claudia to help her solve the business with the working papers than she would join ROTC. "It's cool that you have a—what d'you call it?" she said, just to see what would happen. "A flexible schedule. At your job."

"True dat," said Claudia.

"But you know that I don't care about grades, right?"

"You need a Regents diploma," Claudia declared.

"For *what?*" Phoebe questioned, stepping to the curb as the light turned green.

"For *college*," said Claudia. "You won't get in anywhere half decent without your Regents."

Phoebe shrugged and began to cross the street. "I'm not going to college," she said. "I'm getting a job."

"As what?" Claudia asked.

Phoebe stopped in the middle of the street. Soon, the light would change and she'd be potential road pizza. "You think that bad grades are wrong," she said, as loud as she ever got, which wasn't terribly.

"I think they're a red flag," Claudia called, "and so do a lot of other people." She remained watchful as Phoebe continued on to the other side of Seventh Avenue with no incident. She hoped that she hadn't made Paul angry by making him wait.

"Are you coming?" Phoebe yelled. Traffic surged between them.

"I have to make another call!" Claudia yelled back as Phoebe trudged away. *"We're all good!"* she cried after her.

Bronwyn set a Mexican blue-glass pitcher of chilled cucumber water on the kitchen table and heard movement in the hall. "You're lucky my béchamel hasn't cracked!" she called.

At the front door, Phoebe hesitated, having no idea what the older girl was talking about. She pulled off her peacoat and calmly observed the bag of ginger candies she'd removed from Edith's house as they rustled from her sleeve to the floor. She scooped them up.

Bronwyn, puttering to and fro at the stove, looked up to see Phoebe in the kitchen doorway. "Feebs! Fantastic!" she yelped, spotting the bag of old ginger candies in Phoebe's hand. "I thought you were your sister!" Bronwyn snatched the bag. "Can I have those?" she inquired, rhetorically. In addition to the Veuve and the pinot, Bronwyn had licked some of her hash-brownie batter earlier and then pinched a sizable crumb from the pan. She wanted a whimsy to finish her table setting. Shaking out a handful of candies, she artfully placed a pair on each of the Pierre Deux napkins she'd arranged in the center of her purposefully mismatched plates.

"Do you have cigarettes?" Phoebe asked.

"Yes, ma'am." Bronwyn nodded to the shelf over the stove as she lit a pair of tapers jammed in champagne bottles that were drizzled with the wax of many parties. Phoebe helped herself to a Rothman and a Bic. "Ashtray, please," said Bronwyn, removing her apron. "And out the window." She stepped up into the skinny, yellowed bathroom.

Phoebe cracked the kitchen window and tucked herself into the sill, letting one leg drape to the floor and bracing her other foot against the frame. She was ducking her head toward the cupped flame when the bathroom door opened and Bronwyn, patting her face dry, suddenly considered the younger girl from an entirely new vantage, as though noticing her for the first time. "Oh my God," Bronwyn announced, inebriated. She gripped the edge of the bathroom sink and glared at Phoebe. "I just had the most incredible idea."

Phoebe raised an eyebrow and French inhaled with extreme skill. "You want me to take off my shoes?" she guessed.

"Fuck that." Bronwyn had folded her arms tightly. She squinted at Phoebe, assessing the girl with intent. "I have a new job," she declared.

"Cool," said Phoebe.

"I'm the new associate photo editor at *Moxy*." Bronwyn slouched into a kitchen chair. "Have you heard of us?"

Phoebe waved ineffectually at the cloud of smoke hanging before her, as she'd seen Claudia and Bronwyn do.

"It's a very important new title," Bronwyn continued, reaching for a cigarette and the lighter. "We're *alternative*. Just launching. And we're looking for our first *Moxy* girl. The *face*. Is that something you'd be interested in?"

Phoebe hesitated, letting the wind devour her cigarette. "Do I need working papers for that?"

Bronwyn sighed, unfamiliar with daunting bureaucratic obstacles. "Did Penelope Tree have working papers?" she asked. Phoebe didn't know who that was. "*Moxy* is *authentic*," she declared. "We're the voice of real teen girls. We have a brain in our heads, and brass ones. We want a real girl for our launch campaign. We just fired our ad agency because *they didn't get it*. We're going to stick with our media buy but handle our own creative. Outdoor rolls out ridiculously soon."

"So, it's like off the books?"

"Phoebe, I'm telling you I think you could be the new face of *Moxy* and you're utterly stuck in this dreary, practical minutiae!"

"I don't have working papers."

"This is *fashion*. And lifestyle. It's *culture*, Feebs. Not management training at Bain & Company. We're going to feature every alternative band you need to know. We have a *sex columnist*. She's going to tell you how to give the perfect *hand job*."

"Damn," said Phoebe.

"So will you come to the open call?" Bronwyn implored. "It's the Monday after next."

Phoebe pulled on her cigarette and peered out the window into the air shaft's permanent dimness. "I should ask Claude," she said. Despite Phoebe's frightening new doubts about Claudia, the notion of her sister's permission seemed comfortingly necessary. She reached for Bronwyn's wine and took a gulp.

"Treat yourself to a glass," Bronwyn said, nodding to the cheerful rack of blue glass goblets she'd installed over the counter.

"This is glass," said Phoebe, pouring a few inches of wine into an empty tahini jar. It was hard to imagine what a conversation with Ms. Krinksy was going to do for anybody. It was easier to imagine wandering into Covenant House with all her worldly possessions stuffed in a pillowcase, begging for a bunk after getting the boot. "Claude's not going to want me to do something like that."

Bronwyn was disbelieving. "What do you *mean?* You're a beautiful girl, Phoebe. A lot of successful women in a lot of different fields started out as models. Take a look at whatsher-name, you know, the blond. Mike Nichols's wife."

"Claude wants me to go to college and become, I don't know. Respectable."

"You already *are* respectable."

"Yeah, right."

Claudia's boots clomped in the hallway. "Honey, I'm home!" she called. In a fluid motion, Phoebe stubbed out her cigarette, flicked the butt out the window, set the ashtray in front of Bronwyn, gargled a swig of pinot, grabbed a Granny Smith from the hanging basket, took a bite, and returned to her perch in the windowsill.

As for Claudia, she had sworn to herself that once she re-turned to the little party she'd behave appropriately. "Hey, DJ, we've got no tune-age," she complained from her bed-room. "How can the two of you live like that?"

"Do you want me to talk to her?" Bronwyn asked Phoebe. Despite her stocking feet, the vibrations of Claudia's heavy footfall shook the framed posters as she approached.

"You're full-on tripping," Phoebe replied through her mouthful of apple.

Bronwyn lowered her voice. "But do you want to come to the casting call in a couple of weeks?"

"Maybe."

"Neneh Cherry?" Claudia asked loudly, unseen in the liv-ing room.

"Sounds good," Bronwyn replied over her shoulder. She

leaned closer to Phoebe. "You can tell Claudia after you get the gig."

"I guess," Phoebe said, doubtfully.

Claudia strode into the kitchen. "Hey, *ladeeez!*" She grinned. "Let's get this party started! Somebody give me a cigarette. Not you," she said to Phoebe, grabbing a chunk of hash brownie from the pan on the stove and shoving it into her mouth.

Bronwyn swatted Claudia good-naturedly. "Those are for dessert!"

Claudia wedged herself into the windowsill and put her arms around Phoebe. Despite everything, Phoebe decided to lean her body into Claudia's. "Hey," said Claudia, kissing Phoebe loudly on the cheek, "it's dessert somewhere."

3

Dial 9 to Get Out

JANUARY 1994

LOVE, CLAUDIA HAD BEEN LEARNING, was not without its awkwardness. Sometimes she experienced mild distress about possibly looking like Paul's daughter, even though nobody could see them in the miniscule Jane Street elevator. There was the big emptiness afterward, when Paul's town car, arriving mysteriously and purring patiently, swallowed him as his frank lust dwindled to appreciation, his gloved hand waving farewell as he glided away. There was only one way to survive the departures, and that was to turn every cell in her body toward *next time.*

Claudia now had access to the glittering best midwinter Manhattan had to offer between the hours of noon and three on Tuesdays and Thursdays, and Thursday nights starting at eight, and Friday mornings until 7:40. In just over a fortnight, she'd sipped the best of the new Beaujolais at several bistros tucked below street level on the farthest eastern edge of midtown. She'd had beers and shots in the back of Corner Bistro, Paul's favorites on the jukebox once again, but now the formerly senseless lyrics to "Box of Rain" promised that love would see them through.

There had been a too-brief gallery trawl along Fifty-Seventh Street, during which, with wit, wisdom, and semiotic insight, Claudia had analyzed the outrageously priced French advertising posters from the 1930s that Paul could well afford to buy. Paul apparently loved Claudia's wit and wisdom. The smarter and funnier she was for him, the more he stood behind her, cupping her ass under her jacket and breathing outrageous suggestions in her ear. That is, until Paul thought he recognized a member of his co-op board, and was forced, briefly, to pretend that he and Claudia had never met. Back out on the street, they made a quick recovery, and soon, Claudia had beautiful new black leather gloves.

Their afternoons all led to Jane Street, where new gloves and wit and wisdom were shed with urgency. There wasn't *time* to think between the hours of noon and three on Tuesdays and Thursdays. There wasn't *room* for guilt in the bright little studio, not when Paul's considerable power, channeled directly into their union, banished all reason.

Picturing Bronwyn, or Annie, while Paul was in the midst of showing Claudia things she hadn't known would have been, somehow, sacrilege.

In the last two and a half weeks of Claudia and Paul's . . . arrangement . . . she had been told that she was beautiful more times than in the two decades prior.

But right now, at 12:46 on a Friday morning, Paul seemed impossibly far away, to the point of full disappearance. The digital clock on Claudia's nightstand mocked her, and the portable phone, resting regally in the center of a nearby pillow like a black plastic glass slipper, was decidedly not ringing.

She reached for the phone and pressed REDIAL. *"You have reached the offices of Golden Fenwick Tate Stein and Lowe,"* the dulcet recording repeated for the fuckteenth time. *"If you know the person's extension, please press it now."* She did. *"You have reached the offices of Paul Tate, Senior Partner, Real Estate —"* Frustrated by this conspiracy of robots, by Paul's relentless work schedule, by the closing he had tonight when he should have been with her, Claudia hung up and smothered the phone violently with her pillow. She threw back her duvet and stood in the middle of her bedroom.

I use this place when I'm pulling an all-nighter on a closing, Paul had said. *It's a place to catnap and shower.*

Claudia found her bra among the pile of clothes on her desk chair and slipped halfway out of her tie-dyed long johns to put it on. She pulled her jean skirt on over the long johns and added an argyle vest, and over that, a long cardigan, and over that, a belt. She liked the idea of Paul unwrapping her. Claudia padded into the living room, where Phoebe was sleeping. Phoebe's feet stuck out at the end of the futon; one of her mismatched sweat socks had sagged down, leaving her heel exposed. Even asleep, her features slack and her lips parted, Phoebe's expression was watchful. Claudia arranged the patchwork quilt over Phoebe's long body and tucked Barkella, her stuffed dog with the rubbed-out plastic eyes, inside. Phoebe sighed in her sleep and snatched at her worn friend.

What demanded guts, Claudia realized as she stared down at her sleeping sister, was futile devotion. Futile devotion was the human force that engineered prison breaks and chastity vows, and nothing threatened it like daily contact. Watching Phoebe clutch Barkella, Claudia feared that in order to preserve her relationship with Paul she must never see him again.

Back in her room, Claudia perched at the side of her bed with a yellow legal pad in her lap. It was 1:11 A.M.—time to make a wish. Claudia closed her eyes and pictured an old rowboat arranged in the Chilmark sand, filled with ice and stocked with cold beers and novelty sodas in vintage glass bottles for the kids, at her Martha's Vineyard wedding to Paul. Before she could conjure other positive steps toward an entirely new life, it was 1:13. She reached for her desk lamp and blinked as it threw her little room into light and shadow.

There on her crowded sawhorse desk, Phoebe's crumpled D-minus paper on *Huckleberry Finn* had been smoothed out and stacked more neatly. As she'd promised herself she'd do, Claudia had arranged an appointment for the two of them to sit down with Phoebe's teacher, Ms. Krinsky, and discuss it. The more time she spent with Paul, the better she felt she was able to perform her duties as guardian. And the better her employment outlook, too. It had been rescheduled twice, but tomorrow's interview at *Hope Valley* had been set, or so the production office had claimed, in stone.

Claudia reached for the hardcover journal that had once, in the ancient past, been her stalwart café companion. The first third of the book bulged with bulky collage work and impassioned verse; the rest lay tight, white, and dormant in its binding. A gust of wind found its way down the air shaft and rattled the old window behind her—it sounded cold outside. She tore out a blank page.

Peeps, she wrote, *can't sleep. Meeting the muse at Purity Diner.*

The diner down the avenue would be awake at this hour, and glad to serve as her alibi.

Be back when the sun comes up, sort of like a vampire with a concentration in creative writing.

Claudia signed with *x*'s and *o*'s. She affixed the note to the refrigerator with an Adam Ant magnet she'd been carrying through her life since the seventh grade.

The dark end of the hallway was even darker at this hour. At the front door, Claudia slipped into the thrift-store army parka that made her look like a freezer chest. She strung her messenger bag across her shoulders and dug for her change purse. Inside it were two subway tokens, a package of rolling papers, a single, disheveled stick of blue Trident gum, and a folded slip of paper torn from a little pocket notebook. She unfolded it. "*Garth*," the note said in ballpoint, with Garth Kahn's phone number jotted underneath. Disgusted, Claudia crushed the paper in her fist and hurled it into her wastepaper basket. She remembered her journal and shoved it into her bag. She opened her wallet and counted and recounted the three bucks a few times. Was she really going to take the F train at this hour? If she was robbed and raped on the platform, the cops would call Edith. She'd bring Robbie with her to the emergency room while half pretending not to know him.

Claudia wished she had Paul's driver's pager number.

It seemed the least Paul could do was to send his driver out to Brooklyn on freezing nights like this one to deliver Claudia in safety and comfort.

She would ask him about that.

Claudia headed for Bronwyn's bedroom.

She knew where Bronwyn kept her wallet. It was an Il Bisonti number, eggplant in color, buffed by time to a rich patina. Carefully, she opened Bronwyn's bedroom door. Bronwyn seemed to be fast asleep on her loft bed, tucked under the ceiling strewn with postcards, with barely enough room to sit up. A long drafting table ran the length of the loft, bearing a large lacquered tray on which the wallet sat, along with Bronwyn's rings, a few books of bistro matches, a leather barrette, Beacon Theatre ticket stubs, and Bronwyn's collection of silver shells. Claudia lifted the wallet. It was heavy and chubby, and she half expected it to animate in her palm and protest, so she gripped the leather flap to muffle the snap as she entered. Sixty-two dollars. She slipped a twenty from the pile and quietly returned the wallet to its tray. Silently, she made her way to the front door and the desperate pleasures that lay beyond it—

"Claudia?"

Bronwyn, inexplicably, had appeared at the mouth of the living room, knotting her old flannel robe. Claudia froze. Bronwyn whispered hoarsely, so as not to wake Phoebe. "Did you just take money out of my wallet?" she asked.

"What?" Claudia whispered back.

"Did you just take money from me?"

If the living room was a space station, pumped with fresh oxygen, the hallway was an air lock. Beyond the front door lay the icy soup of deep space, into which Claudia's corpse, frozen in spread-eagle, would plunge forever. "What?" she repeated, stalling.

Bronwyn took a few steps closer, her head cocked to the side. She was groggy and alert. Sure, and not sure she wanted to be. "I heard you in there," she said. "You woke me up."

"Oh," said Claudia. Moving slowly, she backed away a few steps, ever closer to the front door, brushing against the sleeves of their coatrack, a peewee version of the sprawling display in the Tates' Anselmo hallway. She'd always loved the moment in *The Lion, the Witch and the Wardrobe* when Lucy first discovers the cold, fresh night air of Narnia where a wall is supposed to be. Suddenly, she landed on her epitaph. *Here lies Fast & Sloppy*, it would read. *Get me out of here.*

"What's the deal?" Bronwyn pressed.

"I . . . I couldn't sleep."

"And where does my wallet come in, exactly?"

"No. I . . . I was going to the Purity to write," Claudia replied uncertainly, "and I didn't have any cash, so—"

How else could Claudia explain what came over her again and again? To confess that something beyond her control had placed a brick on the accelerator, that it was operating the gears from behind her eyes with grim determination, that she was still *in* there, Claudia would have had to separate herself from the impulse. From Paul.

"So there's something called an ATM," said Bronwyn.

"I know. But my card has been acting weird, so just in case, I thought I'd borrow a few bucks and then see if I could get the cash on the way back to pay you ba—"

"In that case," Bronwyn pressed, "when I ask you if you just took money from me, the answer is *yes*."

"I . . . I know. It's just . . . 'take,' you know? That's like . . . wow. Because, you know. I was borrowing," Claudia faltered. "*Jesus*, Bronwyn."

Bronwyn folded her arms tightly and took a few more steps. "Claudia," she said, "I want to help you. But you have to ask me. If you ask me for help, it's one thing. If you go in my wallet, it's something else that's really fucked up."

Really fucked up. That sounded about right. "You're right."

"Are you okay?"

"Yeah," said Claudia. Could she ask Bronwyn for help? Right now, if she told Bronwyn where she was headed with Bronwyn's own money, would there be a chance, unlikely but still in the realm of possibility, that eventually things would all work out? "Jesus," Claudia said. "Of course." She dug in her messenger bag for her own wallet. "Here." She would hand the twenty back, even though she had just earned it in pure mortification.

"No," Bronwyn said. "You keep it. Pay me back when you can. Just, please, don't ever go in my stuff like that again, okay?"

"Yes," Claudia said. "Okay."

"I love you, Claudia."

"Thanks," she muttered, disappearing into the building's chilly foyer.

"Right here," Claudia said to the Black Pearl Car Service driver, as they pulled up in front of the Powell. It was odd to consider the lives behind the other lit windows at this hour of the night.

Claudia rode up in the tiny elevator. She breathed deeply, anticipating Paul's greeting. Because he had told her long ago, when all this began, that they should always speak first before meeting, there would be a brief pause of surprise, but then a release as he pulled her inside, a surrender to something inexorable that was working to realign the entire world and place the two beloveds at its center. Even the apartment door was breathing, in and out with her own breath. She could feel new life, hopeful, pushing up from a crack in the sidewalk. It was behind that gentle door.

Claudia knocked. She felt a presence approach as the lock's cylinder slid from its case. Claudia let her lips play into a smile. She pulled in her belly and fastened it to the invisible hook she'd installed at the base of her spine, willing it to stay latched.

The door opened.

Inside Paul's pied-à-terre, the lights were on, and WBGO played softly. The easel had been arranged in the center of the room on a splattered drop cloth. Painting supplies were placed about, and on the canvas a haunting, tender image had begun to appear.

But the painter, who stood in the doorway in Harvard

sweatpants, old leather sandals, and a frayed oxford shirt of Paul's, who had a streak of burnt sienna along the temple, but had not had the heart, for some time, to work with paint, was not Paul.

Confusion now raced over the threshold in an unruly swell.

Claudia's balance toppled. She reached for the door frame to steady herself. Her mind sped ahead, but could not outpace the roar of the wave.

"Claudia?" Annie Tate asked. "What are you doing here?"

Claudia held herself very still on the threshold, noticing her own hand, in its beautiful new glove, braced against the door frame. Annie Tate's old duffle coat, tossed across Paul's tweed sofa bed with a paisley shawl peeking out, her pony-hair boots, askew on the rug, her picked-at takeout, coagulating on the little café table by the windows—and, of course, Annie herself, staring back, frozen—were all abominations. How had this woman dared help herself to Claudia's honeymoon suite? Her mind continued to race itself. Annie was clearly to blame, but for what exactly Claudia wasn't yet sure.

As for Annie, she wondered exactly *how* Claudia Silver even knew about her West Village retreat, when Bronwyn had sworn to help her keep the place a *secret*. Neither of the older sisters knew it existed, nor that Annie spent nights here sometimes, with the simple, low bed to herself and the tender promise she'd made not to fix herself a drink. Annie glanced at her father's old Rolex. It was two-twenty-something.

Twenty-something, she thought, looking at the girl. *Ha*.

Claudia removed her gloved hand from the door frame and found that she remained standing.

"Claudia," Annie asked her gently, tucking her paintbrush into her hair and putting all that aside, "what's going on? Is everything all right?" Because, after all, she was a *mother*.

"I'm going to go with apparently not," Claudia said, stepping, somehow, into the apartment.

Annie, who usually realized what she'd wished she'd said long after the incident had passed, envied her surprise guest's quick response time. She stepped past Claudia to close the apartment door. The bedroom radiator moaned.

"Is it Bronwyn?"

"*Bronwyn?*" Claudia repeated. What, at this point, would Bronwyn have to do with *anything?* It pained Claudia to picture her, so she refused the image. "No," she answered emphatically. "Bronwyn's fine."

A brief rush of relief carried Annie to the galley kitchen as Claudia remained rooted to her spot. "She told you about this place?" Annie asked lightly, rustling in the cabinets among the many teas. How many, many, *many* tea trays she'd made in her life. Far more trays than paintings. She switched on the electric kettle, then turned, uncrossing her arms, not wanting to appear defensive. "How do you know about this place, Claudia?"

"I've been here before."

"With Bronwyn?"

Now Claudia hesitated. She had no idea what anybody in her position would be expected to say at a time like this. Briefly, she wondered if she was the only person who had ever been in this position. If this was a funeral or an inauguration. An emergency or a strangely lucky break. If there was a hidden camera. She wished Paul were here. She thanked God he wasn't. She didn't want to get Bronwyn in trouble. She realized that worrying about getting in trouble was for babies. She knew she should dissemble, make something up, quickly, about how Bronwyn had asked her to come here in order to *who the fuck knows.* "No," she said, "not with Bronwyn."

Annie cocked her head, baffled. Bronwyn had simply *told* Claudia about this place? Given her the *address?* To come here in the middle of the night? To . . . to *what?* "I'm afraid I don't understand," Annie confessed.

"With Paul."

With Paul. Slowly, Annie considered both these words, so strange, and the girl, just standing there, bristling in her getup like she owned the place. Or was about to bolt. She should paint her soon, Annie thought, before Claudia hardened. She could call it *Stunned Jewish Girl in Mannish Coat.* Painting Claudia would be a lively departure. It would be pure ease, compared to what had just been said. Why on earth would Claudia Silver have been here with her *husband?* Unless Paul was thinking of subletting the place out from under her. He'd never liked her subject matter. Paul had wanted her to paint flowers. Or seascapes. Every painting in his mother's goddamned apartment had been glorified hotel art, come to think of it.

"With Paul?" Annie asked Claudia, steadily. "Whatever for?"

Claudia drew in a breath. She felt a vague urge to simply let go, to drop the unwieldy burden of her lie, to spew, then beg Annie to help clean her up. She pressed forward, blindly. "Look, Annie," she began, somewhat sternly. She halted. There was another sharp intake of breath. "We—"

The "we," of course, was the tell. Annie was already freefalling as the rest of Claudia's announcement unfurled.

"We didn't mean for this to happen. But it's—" Here, Claudia paused, surprised to have run out of breath again so quickly. The words had taken over, a marauding band of invaders. "It's gotten serious."

Annie shook her head. "Serious? What are you talking about?" she somehow asked.

"We're in love, Annie," Claudia blurted. So this was where she had arrived. Seized territory. Somehow there was nothing else to do but plant her flag. She told herself it was the simple truth.

"In love," Annie repeated.

Claudia tried to make direct eye contact, as Edith had always instructed her to do when speaking to an adult. "Yes."

"He brought you *here?*"

"To show me his art."

"My God." Annie rolled her eyes in pity and in mirth, having been rendered instantly grotesque and agonized, ungainly, a *Guernica* horse. Her hand managed to cover whatever was happening with her mouth—Annie couldn't tell what. A strange sound crawled up, and was blessedly muffled by the electric kettle as it burst forth with a plume of steam and clicked off. Her face contorted. She knew she looked hideous when she cried, which is why she never did, but now she had no choice. "This is my studio, Claudia," she was somehow able to say through her twisted mouth. Her voice belonged to the person she used to be. "This . . . work," she said, immediately ashamed to call it *work*. Work was something you did that was *useful*, that other people *saw*, and that they *paid for*. "It's mine." Annie's legs were wilted stems beneath her. Wobbling forward as best as she could, she reached into a cabinet for a box of cookies and set about the familiar ritual of assembling a tea tray.

Claudia glanced around the room, doubtful and unmoored, scanning for evidence. She never considered that Annie had talent beyond graciousness, menus, and the exact placement of a brooch on a lapel, nor intelligence beyond guiding her daughters to make the most of their own. But alarming details quickly stacked up in Annie's favor. The mini Mason Pearson hairbrush in the medicine cabinet, the British *Vogue* that Paul convincingly explained when it had appeared on the doormat, the chocolate kefir yogurt drink in the little fridge, the fat Korean-market peonies in a cut-glass pitcher that Claudia, charmed, had pictured Paul selecting—

And now, Annie tore the box top clean off, unceremoniously dumping its contents directly onto a tray. Afrika cookies, in fact.

The very chocolate cookies Claudia had chosen for Annie with such care, a lifetime ago, on Christmas Eve. That she had broken her second-to-last twenty to purchase.

"I was at the Rhode Island School of Design for two semesters," Annie announced, reminding herself once again. "Before I got pregnant with Martha." She had gotten halfway across the room with the tray before realizing there was no place to set it down.

"*RISD?* I thought you went to Radcliffe."

"I started over." Annie considered dropping the tray. She could hurl it, spoiling her wool Berber. Claudia, meanwhile, was aware she could help her hostess by clearing some space, but that would mean moving, and as long as she held still, nothing else would change.

"Paul is a liar, isn't he," Annie remarked after a moment, breaking the spell. "A spectacular one." She wondered briefly what she would do with all these paintings. "Make some room, won't you?"

Claudia removed the Thai food cluttering the table to a counter. Annie wasn't bothering with the wetness flooding her face. "I should go," Claudia said.

"Go where, exactly?" Annie asked.

Annie had a point. From this heightened vantage point, Claudia could survey that every home she had ever known was now rubble, while the solid ground on which she and Paul would establish their homestead had not yet been broken. If she looked down, she might find herself standing in a pool of her own shame. So she didn't look down.

"You can't go anywhere at this hour," Annie declared. "This is when most of the crime happens in this city." She dunked an Afrika into her tea and, uncharacteristically, popped the whole, melting wafer into her mouth. "Are you ever going to sit *down?*"

Moving slowly, Claudia approached the sofa and lowered herself onto an armrest. She removed her fur hat and messenger bag, placing them on the sofa, and eyed the telltale cookies.

"I'm curious," Annie said. "What did he say about my art?"

"That it was his." The passing off of Annie's art as Paul's own *was* a curious choice, Claudia had to admit to herself. But maybe Paul felt that he'd *had* to lie, for some reason. Or didn't realize that he *was* lying. Maybe he considered himself the owner of the things he paid for. That made some sense. "I . . . I should probably go," Claudia eventually said.

"Surely you're collecting belt notches," Annie explained to herself out loud. "Or one of you is, at least. That's obviously what this is all about." The sky seemed to be growing lighter, differentiating itself from the dark movement of the river. Over the years Annie had found tacky hairpins in Paul's coat pockets, decorated with chipped enamel flowers. She'd scooped several unfamiliar lip glosses from the bottom of the dryer. And once, the law firm had hosted a weekend retreat at a hotel with a nonworking phone number. Paul had blamed an unexpected rash of summer thunderstorms, but his running shoes and jeans cuffs had returned home entirely devoid of mud. "How long has this been going on?" she asked.

Claudia wondered if there was any way to respond to Annie. As Paul's beloved, she felt a responsibility to protect the details. "Awhile," she replied, with some pride.

"Awhile," Annie repeated, considering the sturdy, glossy-haired, pink-cheeked girl. Size ten, size twelve maybe. What could a few weeks matter to a couple of rotting decades, with fine lines around the eyes? "It's hard to imagine that you would do such a thing to us," Annie said. "But there you have it." Claudia shifted uncomfortably on the sofa.

"Does Bronwyn know?"

"Of course not," Claudia replied.

"So here's what we'll do," said Annie.

There is no "we," Claudia thought, standing up.

"I will make up the sofa and you will sleep on it," Annie continued. "And tomorrow, you will tell Bronwyn."

"You're fully tripping," Claudia found herself saying out loud as she pointed herself toward the door.

"Fully tripping," Annie mused. "I may well be. But either you tell her yourself, tomorrow, or I will."

Yes, Claudia acknowledged to herself, Bronwyn would have to be informed, but surely not by Claudia *telling* her. By some other means. Osmosis. The wedding pages in the Sunday *Times*, which she and Bronwyn used to jokingly call the business section. The sight of Annie Tate pulling neatly folded pillowcases from a wardrobe in which Claudia hadn't bothered snooping when she'd had the chance was mind-boggling. *That's the real headline,* Claudia told herself. *How batshit crazy Annie is.* Claudia would wander. She would ride the F train all the way to Coney. She would no more stay here on Annie Tate's dowry linens than fly to the moon. It was obvious she'd made some kind of mess of things, but Claudia couldn't tell where tonight's disaster began and all the other ones ended.

What if Paul was angry?

She could not tell Bronwyn.

"I'm not staying here," Claudia announced. Was Annie her boyfriend's daughter's mother? Or her best friend's father's wife? Swaying with sudden nausea, Claudia sank back on the armrest. "But I'm just going to sit here for a second, if that's okay with you."

"By all means," Annie said. "Make yourself at home."

When Claudia awoke some time later, toppled over on the sofa, her head leaning against the armrest, the apartment was filled with dove-gray morning light. Annie Tate stood outside on the frigid balcony, wrapped in a duvet and staring out at the river as the sun rose on Friday morning. Claudia sat up, plucking her fur hat from the carpet and setting it firmly on her head. Taking care, she crept to the bathroom, silently closed the door, peed, and looked at herself. Her cheeks were creased from sleep, her mouth stale, her dark brows in need of the little brush she kept in her makeup bag. Her reflection split as she opened the medicine cabinet. Only recently she'd seen this charming assortment—the Mason Pearson, the tooth twine, the *vih*-tah-min tablets, the mysterious unguent, the Kneipp pine bath—and understood them as Paul Tate's refined toilette. But it was Annie Tate's dental floss she'd been borrowing. Plus her *husband*. Claudia squeezed a plug of anise toothpaste onto her index finger and scrubbed it across her gums, then slipped from the bathroom, grateful that Annie was doing her best pillar of salt on the balcony. Last night's scattered cookies called to her: Claudia grabbed a handful on tiptoe, refusing the notion that Annie could turn at any moment, then backed her way out of the apartment.

Last night this passageway had been breathing, warmly beckoning to her. This morning it was just another airless New York corridor, smelling, as Paul had once apologized, like rent control. She piled the cookies into a solid block and stuffed them into her mouth, where they molded to her palate.

The elevator was a tomb.

She needed to get Paul on the phone so they could go somewhere. A shingled refuge strung with glass buoys at the far end of Montauk, with no phone and a roaring fire. If Claudia could just catch Paul at work before he returned to Jane Street to freshen up after his closing, only to find his wife on the balcony, all cried out—

Outside, the West Village on an early Friday morning

hummed with promise. Claudia let the prosperous flock of commuters carry her along to the familiar corner of Sixth Avenue and Eighth Street.

Work and money.

Somehow Claudia was made of them, but had neither.

Bedford High School was big, old, brick, and pulsing. It sat across the street from Brooklyn College, capped with a cheery white cupola. It had tall sash windows and a wholesome history of Jews and Italians in bobby socks, but that was then. Thanks to various global diasporas, Bedford's classrooms and hallways had become hectic with the competing college ambitions of sixteen hundred rainbow-hued, motormouthed, science-fair attending, viola-schlepping, gumsnapping, grandmother-fearing overachievers. Their maniacal focus on fully funded Ivy League admission did away with any potential ethnic combat, and their currency was grades. Tribes at Bedford included State School Future MDs, Zeitgeisty Literary Magazine Snobs, and Elite Armed Forces Pragmatists.

Phoebe Goldberg belonged to none of these.

Her nature, fluid and chill, had led her to smoke blunts with Cambodian physics prodigies under the bleachers, paint a few backdrops for the eunuchs of musical theater, toss a Frisbee on the Brooklyn College quad with fellow City University faculty-and-admin brats, split a Blimpie with the cocaptain of the Math Team, and drop some choice words with the menacing riffraff in the back row of homeroom. She *was* the riffraff, was how she saw it. Phoebe knew she was supposed to be grateful for Bedford High School, grateful to Edith for pulling strings to get her in. For *having* strings.

Because her beauty incited a following, despite her cloak of mellow and her deliberate pace, Phoebe couldn't quite melt into the pot. The offerings she'd received to date at Bedford included: knishes, with and without onions and mustard, black and white cookies, notes, lots of them, shoved into her locker, live goldfish in plastic bags she'd felt too worried about to bring home to Edith's and released instead into Prospect Park Lake, feathered roach clips, chapbooks, and the smooth company of various cocoa-butter-scented varsity soccer players on the walk to the Flatbush Junction subway.

Pretty much every morning, Phoebe was the last one to walk in when the bell rang for first period. Not *late*, necessarily, but *last*. Her hanging back was what did it. Phoebe didn't like crowds, particularly the Bedford bazaar, all those operators hawking their personalities. Her stamina waned the instant her name was called for attendance, at which point her thoughts would turn to getting the fuck out of there.

When she'd lived at Edith's, Phoebe was often the first awake. She'd sleep in most of her clothes, finish dressing in the harsh glare of the clamp-on lights affixed to the overhead pipes, splash her face and brush her teeth at the utility sink next to the old washing machine, and emerge, squinting, from the basement doorway. She'd already be turning the corner past Hector's Hardware, headed for a hot chocolate at Castillo de Jagua, while Robbie greeted the day upstairs, coughing his brains out like a tubercular rooster.

This morning, Phoebe awoke on Claudia's futon sofa, having slept on the diagonal to maximize the cramped space. She could tell that Bronwyn had left for work and Claudia had left for wherever the hell she had been going for the last couple of weeks. Having never had a bed built for lounging, Phoebe swung herself quickly to a seated position. She scrubbed at her face, wondering if any cigarettes were lying around, and discovered, one after the other, the notes left by her roommates.

Bronwyn's note, cleverly safety-pinned to her pillow, had

simply presented the address and time of today's open casting call for the new face of *Moxy*.

Noon.

That would give her twenty unrealistic minutes to get from Flatbush to SoHo, if she cut out of school directly after her meeting with Claudia and Ms. Krinsky at 11:10, as Claudia had annoyingly arranged. Truthfully, Phoebe had been *psyched* for that D-plus on her *Huckleberry Finn* paper. She felt like Ms. Krinsky had done her a *solid*. She didn't see why she needed to show up for a bullshit parade in the first place. But the idea that Claudia could save her had once meant so much, and Phoebe was letting go of it slowly, saying a quiet and lengthy good-bye instead of hurling it on the fire, Edith-style.

The note from Claudia had been written hours earlier, and stuck to the fridge by a magnet featuring a photo of some gay guy in war paint and a pirate blouse. Phoebe glanced at the clock on Bronwyn's microwave oven. She peed, didn't flush, and wandered into Claudia's bedroom to paw through her pile of clothes and see if there was anything she could borrow from her sister's carefully staged closet. Claudia had always told Phoebe to help herself, but her jeans were too big and too short, and a lot of her clothes that *could* work—Claudia's brightly colored vintage polyester shirts and acrylic sweaters, her shiny jackets and junk jewelry—looked like they'd been jacked from somebody's old Jewish grandmother or a backup dancer.

Now, the collar of her peacoat turned up, her hands jammed in the pockets, the chain-link fence of the faculty parking lot bouncing her stance as she leaned against it, and her headphones secure (*Who's the black sheep, what's the black sheep? Don't know who I am, or when I'm coming so you sleep*), Phoebe waited for the surge up the wide front steps that indicated the bell had rung, and scanned the crowd intently for her target.

Afros, ponchos, Mohawks, cornrows . . . *BAM!*

Raising the volume on her Walkman, she loped across Bedford Avenue, her sights set on Ramona Parker.

Ramona and her soft-spoken gaggle were arriving in an affable pod, JanSport backpacks pulling heavily on their shoulders. Ramona didn't do the whole relaxer thing, but the angle of her skinny braids suggested the blunt, slightly asymmetrical bobs that the white girls in her group wore, dipped lower on one side. They were nice girls, Ramona's Bedford friends, and with their dogged scholarship, orderly creativity, and unassuming flair, just a tad interchangeable.

"Hey." Phoebe appeared at Ramona's side, towering over her.

Ramona smiled, a little sadly. Back when Ramona and Phoebe commuted endlessly between each other's houses, it would have been a grin. But when Ramona told Mrs. Parker how creeped out Robbie Burns made her, and how bad she felt that Phoebe had to live with him, Mrs. Parker's reaction wasn't what she'd expected. Ramona had wanted her mother to have a solution for Phoebe's problems. She'd wanted her mother to get *involved*. Instead, Mrs. Parker had flatly declared it would be over her dead body that Ramona would ever go over there again, and Ramona told Phoebe, and Phoebe told Edith, and Edith stormed the Parkers' front stoop, and Mrs. Parker served her point of view all up in Edith's face.

Ever since then, the adjacent houses had occupied different time zones.

And then they'd both ended up at Bedford. Ramona because she'd scored high on the citywide test and aced her interview, Phoebe because Edith served on several prominent City University committees.

Ramona and Phoebe had once been the same age in the same place.

"Hey, Feebs," Ramona said.

"Can I talk to you for a sec?" Phoebe asked.

"Yeah, sure." Ramona gave the nod to her AP posse. Aware of the wistful chemistry that clearly connected the two old friends, they drifted away.

Phoebe hesitated. "How's it going?"

Ramona could have offered a litany. She had applications for college, summer programs, and scholarships, with a weekend job at Connecticut Muffin to help pay for them. This afternoon she had her veterinary internship at the Tribeca Animal Hospital, plus there was the tutoring, and the new jewelry-making technique her mom was teaching her. "Pretty good," she said.

"Cool," Phoebe said. "So, it's like . . . back in November, you and Darleen. You guys made it possible for me and Claudia to, you know, get back together. I kind of think I never said thank you."

Ramona's expression was kind. "That was a messed-up situation," she admitted. Then: "You're welcome."

"But now I . . . I'm trying to get a job, you know? And my mom, she's got to sign my working papers. But, you know, the whole Robbie thing." Briefly, Phoebe glanced away. "He says the only way she'll sign is if I move back."

Ramona's arms shot out. Her hands, in their fingerless Guatemalan gloves, grabbed Phoebe at the elbows. "You *can't*," she said, grave.

"Yeah," Phoebe agreed. "I know." The first-period bell rang, and Ramona squirmed. She had never been late to class, or anywhere else, for that matter, and certainly never *last*.

"So I was wondering. If maybe you think your mom might, um, you know. Sign them for me. Or, like, go with me to the place and talk to the guy."

A security guard appeared and, one by one, shut Bedford's heavy front doors.

Oh man, Ramona thought, not unkindly. She remembered

her mess with Claudia, just a couple of months ago. How Claudia had reared up before her eyes, practically in flames, accusing her of stealing her own bag. Mrs. Parker's words from back then came back to her now. *Bullies are people who hurt.*

"I'm not sure," Ramona answered, truthfully. "I think you can definitely ask her."

"Do you think she would even *talk* to me?" Phoebe wanted to know.

"Talk to you? Why, sure, Feebs. Why *wouldn't* she?"

Phoebe shrugged. It was a standout memory, and they'd each been occupying their respective stoops when the shit went down. Edith had lobbed outraged rhetoric: *How dare you judge me.* And Mrs. Parker had smacked it back: *Oh, I'm not judging you. Because you are none of my business, and I'm glad for that. But my daughter is my business, Ms. Mendelssohn, and I have given her firm instructions to stay the hell out of your house, and I'm gonna trust that you'll respect my wishes. Now get on inside, Ramona, and do your damn algebra.*

Ramona, her head bowed, had trudged past a frozen Edith to make a beeline for her math homework, and Phoebe had watched her go. When the Parkers' door shut, Edith, her cheeks marked with their familiar, high splotches of color, had looked across the stoop to her daughter. "*Unfuckingbelievable,*" she'd said. Her voice was hurt, her shrug dismissive.

"It's like the commutative property," Phoebe now said to Ramona. "Your mom doesn't like my mom, so she doesn't like me."

"Transitive," Ramona corrected, inching away from Phoebe. "A is to B as B is to C." Bedford High School was Ramona Parker's seaworthy vessel, it was pulling away from shore, and no way she was going to miss it. Soon, another whirlwind day at Bedford would be full-steam ahead. There were four minutes to get to class. "It can't hurt to ask, right?" said Ramona.

Yes, it can, Phoebe thought, watching Ramona make a run for it.

Arriving at Hudson Plaza, Claudia fought her way against the buffeting tide of hell-bent morning commuters. Many floors up, she arrived at the padded inner lobby of Golden Fenwick Tate Stein and Lowe. The unwitting receptionist, who'd just shoved her white Reeboks into a Conway shopping bag, was currently ducked below her desk in a low struggle with a pair of navy pumps. Claudia slid past.

There was the temptation to behave in an unseemly manner. To storm Paul's office in a fury of wifely hysteria, pulling off her new black gloves as she strode, demanding an immediate solution to the outrageous inconvenience of Annie Tate. But on the heels of the disastrous surprise at the Powell, it was more important than ever for Claudia to attempt pleasantness at all times, with minty-fresh breath and plenty of concealer.

It was first thing in the morning at New York City's premier factory of corporate justice and wealth management, yet Paul's floor retained an air of fatigued activity from last night's closing. Claudia knew Paul might already be en route to Jane Street, and prayed to find him in his shirtsleeves, slipping documents into an accordion file, or whatever it was that attorneys did. Crossing through the bullpen, Claudia saw associates and paralegals of the real estate group clustered giddily around the remnants of a midnight delivery from Szechuan Delight. Here was Carter Kemp, rep tie flung over his shoulder, putting his thumb in an insulated bag to pull out an egg roll that had gone soggy. Claudia continued down the hall to Paul's corner suite.

The family snapshots and Catholic-school portraits on the secretary's otherwise empty desk followed Claudia with their eyes. She pushed forward, knowing she should slow down, square her posture, fasten her gut, but found herself growing unfortunately teary as she tumbled in to find Paul at his thirtieth-story window, running a cordless electric razor over his jaw as he stared north at the city. He could see his house from here.

"Paul." She couldn't tell whether her heart was stopping or starting. He turned. The way he looked at her, while continuing to shave, made Claudia realize she hadn't looked at herself. "Hi," she said.

Paul clicked off his razor. "What are you doing here?"

"I was in the neighborhood," she replied, falteringly. She took a step closer.

"What's wrong?" Paul went about his business, coolly returning his razor to its case and the case to his desk, in direct opposition to the heartfelt choreography Claudia had imagined. He seemed to smell the personal crisis leaching from Claudia, and intuit that it had something very bad to do with him.

"Annie knows," Claudia blurted.

Now Paul hesitated. Claudia wondered if she should use the pause to tell Paul she loved him. "How do you know?" he asked, finally. He had sunk into his tufted leather desk chair.

"I ran into her," Claudia replied. "At our place."

Paul pivoted his chair to face the window, and looked down at the bare trees of the park. He stretched out his long legs and propped his feet on the baseboard, crossing them at the ankles. His socks were a bright, devilish violet. "I told you we always needed to talk before meeting there," he said.

"I wish you'd told me we were trespassing," Claudia retorted.

Paul leaned his head back in his chair. He had a terrific

head of hair, one that would never thin. "You didn't know that?" he said, softly. "Come on, Claudia." In a sudden motion, he hunched forward with a new tautness, as though he'd spotted Annie thirty stories below.

"What are you going to tell her?" Claudia asked.

"The truth, I suppose."

"That we love each other?"

"Claudia." Paul rose from his chair. It took him only two paces to stand closely before her. To place one hand on her shoulder and the other beneath her chin, gently. She felt the urge to reach for him boldly, as a lover would, but felt the clammy void that had doused his fire. His mild touch was apologetic. Distracted by the Metro section when he was supposed to have been keeping an eye on her, he'd allowed her to tumble from the monkey bars, and while she'd gotten the wind knocked out, the playground was rubberized, and after all, she was someone else's child. "You need to go," he said.

"*That's* what I need to do?" Claudia repeated, incredulous. "*Go?*"

"Annie's probably on her way up here as we speak."

"So shouldn't we all sit down together and discuss this, like adults?"

Paul's eyes crinkled as he smiled, sadly. "'I was so much older then, I'm younger than that now,'" he quoted. "Do you know that one?"

"Oh my God," said Claudia.

Paul sat at the edge of his desk, bringing himself to eye level. He had done Outward Bound, twice, and was well familiar with the theory of "leave only footprints." But he *liked* to leave a trace. "Let the adults do their job, Claudia," he said. "Let them clean up their own mess."

The place on Montauk. The rented sedan, askew in the pebbled driveway. The slam of the screen door as they brought their bags into the big yellow kitchen. A pair of stiff drinks. Placing the grocery order for delivery from town. Egg noodles and pork chops wrapped in butcher paper, a peach pie. Paul talks to his lawyer in low tones in the den, pacing in a cabled cardigan. Much later, a walk along the beach, huddled together against the wind. "But *we* are the mess, Paul," Claudia insisted. She let the fucking tears crawl. There was only the distant hum of climate control. "I have a job interview," she added, quietly.

"Claudia," Paul said, with the tender awe of the deeply relieved. "It's over. You see that."

"*No,*" she growled.

Paul rose from the corner of his desk and dug for his wallet. He peeled off a pair of hundreds. "Here," he said.

"You want to *pay* me?" she asked. Somehow, it was what she'd always wanted. But not like this.

"I want you to take a taxi," he said. "And I want you to let me be the one to tell Bronwyn." Two hundred dollars dangled from his fingers.

"I wish I could help you," Claudia replied, as the bills lifted in the slight, manufactured breeze. "But you know how my big mouth gets me into trouble."

Annie Tate rode the uptown 1 train to Paul's office. Finding her reflection in the dark oblong window across the aisle, she was surprised to discover that her sunglasses, pushed up on her head, made her blond bob look rather *triangular*. So Annie lowered them to cover her eyes, remembering full well that Paul disdained the wearing of sunglasses inside. She realized she could now grow her hair very, very, *very* long, like the partner's wife she'd met at one of those dinners, who'd removed herself to lower Westchester to devote herself full-time to Japanese ceramics. She'd had long, rough hair like a horse's tail, part schoolgirl, part crone, the roots utterly gray, the tips frayed honeyed vestiges, her tedious monthly appointments at Garren a memory.

That poor woman, Annie had thought of her then. But now, with this morning's predawn turn of events, she seemed more like a role model, standing knee-deep on her South Salem property in Wellies, with all that hair pulled back unflatteringly in a tortoiseshell clip, tending to a fiery earthen kiln of some sort.

A woman might make art, Annie now realized, in lieu of burning the whole house down.

Despite her shawl and her coat, Annie was absolutely freezing. She glanced down and realized that while she had successfully brushed her teeth and hair, moisturized, and applied eight-hour cream to her eyelids and lips, she was still wearing her old sweatpants and her even older leather sandals.

Leather sandals, on the subway, in the dead of winter.

Scanning the car, Annie trusted that nobody noticed, and that those who did would take one look at her toes, frozen stiff but clean, pink, and groomed, and rest assured that she was not a homeless woman. The train rattled along under Fourteenth Street. She could get out at Twenty-Third, walk to Barneys, and buy a terrific pair of boots costing what other women spend on rent. But instead, Annie, having negotiated a multitude of cold, dirty puddles, flapped into the lobby of Golden Fenwick Tate Stein and Lowe with dirty feet, and the hem of her sweatpants soaked black in places. The receptionist was now fully installed and alert behind her battlement. Many times before she'd welcomed Annie, sweeping in on Ferragamos with baskets of muffins, but was now silenced by her glare as Annie stalked past. Moving quickly, the receptionist dialed Paul's direct line. He'd just pulled a fresh shirt from a tidy pastel pile, stacked in a drawer. "Your wife is on her way," the receptionist announced from the intercom.

Paul shook the shirt loose from the French hand laundry's wrapping. "She called?" he asked.

"Now. Down the *hall*," she clarified. Then: "I couldn't stop her, Mr. Tate."

Claudia came around the corner and froze. A few feet away, freshly shampooed, with a knotted plaid scarf tucked neatly into the lapels of her princess-seamed car coat and her one plain cruller in a spotted paper bag, Kelly Welch was letting herself into her office. Kelly paused and took Claudia in. The strange layered outfit that seemed part pajama, the splotchy face with its emotional nose, the cockeyed hat. Kelly tilted her head, then narrowed her eyes.

"Do you want to come in?" Kelly asked.

Claudia most definitely did not. But it was then that she heard, from around a corner, on a determined wind, the flapping of old leather sandals, followed by Carter Kemp's unseen voice, garbled with a mouthful of old, cold sesame noodles. "Hey, Mrs. Tate," Claudia was quite certain she heard Carter say. Suddenly, Kelly's office would do quite nicely.

Kelly's desk lamp was lit, casting her in an eerie spotlight and throwing her windowless territory into shadow. Despite the optimistic time of morning, the fresh sun had suddenly set behind the frisky debutante's eyes, leaving her zombified. "Close the door," Kelly said, depositing her wraps on the coatrack.

Claudia acquiesced, but hit the wall switch in self-defense. It was an insulting light, but made the office less of an interrogation cell. "Can I ask what you're doing here?" Kelly demanded.

"Absolutely," Claudia replied, then stood silently, one ear on the corridor, preparing to bolt.

"Well?" Kelly insisted.

"I said you can ask me," Claudia qualified. "I didn't say I'd tell you."

Kelly's expression darkened. "Sadly for you, you're not nearly as clever as you think you are."

"That's a relief, actually," said Claudia.

Kelly hooked a finger into the stretchy plastic spiral pushed high on the sleeve of her silk blouse. "He's done with you, isn't he?" she demanded, freeing the dangling key with the deliberate pace of a striptease. The key fit into a locked desk drawer, a file folder was removed. "That was fast," Kelly remarked as she slid the folder across her desk.

Claudia hesitated. Did Kelly have incriminating images of her afternoon delights with Paul, hot from the one-hour place on the corner of Sixth Avenue and Fourteenth Street? If that's what they were, Claudia didn't want to see them. They'd be crime scene photos, now.

Claudia approached the desk and opened the file.

Inside the folder were drawings, rendered in a familiar hand. Claudia glanced up at Kelly, letting a sigh escape. "Paul gave these to you?"

"No," Kelly replied. "I took them. They used to be a consolation prize. But now they're ammunition."

Claudia sighed. *Well*, that *fucking sucked.*

Kelly in her half-slip, furtively stuffing sketches into her monogrammed tote bag while Paul hummed in the shower. Kelly thinking, as Claudia had, that she'd bagged a Paul Tate original. Claudia following in the trail of Kelly's flowered underpants.

"Someday," Kelly was saying, "there'll be a class action lawsuit. If you actually think you're Paul Tate's first little trinket, then I feel even sorrier for you."

"And if you think Paul made those sketches," Claudia advised, "you're what my people call a *suckah*."

The folder just sat there between them.

"What's *that* supposed to mean?" Kelly demanded.

Claudia considered Kelly, the heartbroken set of her mouth that would lead to a softening of the jowls over time. Of *course*, there had been more. There would be more, *even now*. A Cecilia, or a Greta, or a Dale—a long trail of stale bread crumbs snaking around the city that Paul retraced each night to his corner bedroom in the Anselmo.

"Paul's *wife* is the painter," Claudia explained. "He steals from her. It's kind of like wearing her underwear."

"I don't understand," Kelly doubted, returning the folder to the drawer and the key to her body. "Why would he lie about *that?*"

"Because *his* art form is pussy," said Claudia, from the doorway. Then: "Door opened or closed?" She didn't linger for the answer.

Annie had hoped to storm Paul's inner sanctum, as he had sullied hers, perhaps sweeping the framed family photos from the mahogany shelves with a swipe of her forearm. Infuriatingly, Paul now emerged from his outer office just as Annie approached it, his greatcoat billowing grandly as he slid into its sleeves.

"Hi," Paul said to his wife, his voice already lowered. He ducked toward her automatically, pecking her cheek. "Let's go for a walk, okay?" He set off immediately for the elevator as Kelly Welch passed by.

"Well hello, Mrs. Tate!" Kelly chirped as she approached Annie. Annie, who'd never in her life made a rude gesture to a living soul, experimented quietly by extending her middle finger—in her pocket—to this sunny little chipmunk. "To what do we owe the honor this morning?"

"I'm sure you've fucked him, too," Annie muttered to the

girl as they passed each other. She heard an anxious, musical sound and realized she was giggling. Whatever her midnight rendezvous with Claudia had stripped from her, Annie recognized, with due respect, that the girl had bestowed something as well. It turned out, Annie realized, that she had a sharp wit, after all. It was *in* there—she'd simply mistaken it for *worrying about being a bitch*.

Annie stood her ground and waited until Paul reached the elevator bank. "So there I was at your love shack," she began, loudly. She didn't care who heard. "I mean, my studio."

When the elevator arrived Paul thrust his arm in to hold open the doors, glaring at Annie with hurt. She hesitated, then approached. His wife looked very short today. He couldn't stand when she wore her sunglasses inside. The elevator was thankfully empty. Paul stared straight ahead as the doors closed.

Annie considered the side of Paul's face as he set his jaw. From this angle, she could see not just the young man with whom she'd gotten pregnant at the Head of the Charles, but the demanding toddler. "I had a visit in the middle of the night," she continued. "From your little friend."

"And who would that be?" Paul asked.

"Claudia Silver."

Paul seemed to be methodically scrolling through every class picture Annie had ever dutifully organized in leather storage boxes. She watched her husband in deep concentration and had to marvel at his ability to pretend he didn't remember something he was actually *fucking*. The elevator arrived in the lobby of Hudson Plaza, and they stepped into the sunny atrium. Paul spotted someone he knew, and his face brightened as he raised his hand in greeting. Then, just as quickly, the hand dropped and the eyes settled into shadow.

"Bronwyn's *roommate?*" he finally asked, disbelievingly.

Paul, Annie recognized in this instant, was truly *incredible*. There was not a flinch, not a flush. Just the coolest pause, the gentlest of hesitations, then a lone sigh. "She says you're in love," Annie said.

Paul looked around the lobby, bidding an ineffable adieu. "Then she is a very deluded young lady."

"She's not a young lady." Annie's purse slid from her shoulder and she let it. "Any more than you are a gentleman."

Paul brought his eyes back. They traveled his wife of three decades and landed at her horrifying feet. "What are you *wearing?*" he asked.

Annie's incredulity was gaining momentum. "How could you be such an *idiot?*"

"I called my car," Paul said, gesturing to the world outside. "We should continue this conversation at home."

"Home," Annie sniffed, shaking her head with disbelief, "has officially been wrecked."

Moments later, having cordially greeted Tony, his driver, Paul leaned forward, and with the press of a gloved finger, slid shut the smoked window to the town car's front seat. Annie had quickly dispensed with her tight smile, removing her cold, dirty feet from their sandals and folding them under herself, Indian-style, then pivoting in her seat to face her husband matter-of-factly.

"And why have you been pretending my artwork is yours?" she asked as the car set sail up Eighth Avenue. "Why don't you make your own goddamned pictures? I can't *think* of anything so, so—" Here, she paused to consider. "No, scratch that. I can. I absolutely can."

Paul seemed absorbed by the view of the passing street. "I hear that you have questions," he said slowly. "And there has clearly been some confusion. But I can only answer them one at a time."

"*Listen* to you," Annie said. She wondered when Paul had

stopped seeing her, for clearly he was tracking the passing storefronts where once her face had been.

Paul shifted tracks. "Has Bronwyn told you the story of what's gone on over there? What Claudia and her little sister have been through? It's a terrible situation. The mother has a man living there in the house who's very bad news. The younger one."

"Phoebe?"

Paul nodded. "Phoebe. Yes. She's basically had to run for her life. She's been living with Claudia and Bronwyn. Sleeping on their *futon*. Did you know that?"

Annie shook her head. "No," she replied, sick with the pileup of extreme situations to which she'd been oblivious.

"Oh," Paul remarked, evenly. "I guess Bronwyn didn't tell you."

A florid news story came to Annie's mind, one that she'd assumed, until now, had been an urban myth, about a French housewife who, after God knows how many decades of marriage, had calmly stabbed her husband clean through the heart with a carving knife shortly after he'd complained about her roast lamb. "Somehow you've arrived at this idea that being a good father has anything to do with being a good husband," she countered. "But it doesn't, Paul. They're two entirely separate things." Annie dug in her purse.

"There's a reason that Claudia Silver has a screw loose," Paul continued, "and I have tried to be a resource to her, so that Phoebe can be declared an emancipated minor and they can start getting their lives in order. Neither of these girls has a father to speak of, Annie."

"And what's the reason *you* have a screw loose?" Annie asked, having found her hand cream. "Have you been having an affair with her?" They stared out their respective windows as Columbus Circle approached.

Paul shifted, evoking surrender as he rested his head on

the seat back and let his knees fall open. "I may have gotten too close," he said, looking squarely at Annie. "But that's only because you won't let me get close to you."

"Whatever it is that you've been doing," Annie replied, "has nothing whatever to do with me." The car had entered the serene harbor of Central Park West. Paul reached out to rest his hand on Annie's folded knee. She looked at the hand and the knee with complete removal and some relief. To look down on the scene. To see the angry toddler, dressed up in his proud man suit, and his proprietary gesture on her small frame in the car hurrying home. To consider the possibilities, from this vantage, that had once been far beyond the horizon. She could keep going, all the way to Harlem. She neither felt the entitled hand, nor fought it. "She's not your first," Annie declared, evenly.

"She's my last," said Paul.

Avenue M Studios was nestled behind a brick wall and capped with a vestigial smokestack. For some who passed by and all who worked there, the vintage production complex was a beacon among the charmless bagel shops, discount clothiers, and second-rate yeshivas of deepest Midwood. Here, enduringly, the widgets of popular entertainment were still being churned out, in this case the thirty-third year of *Hope Valley*, one of the longest-running daytime dramas on network television.

"Can I use this phone?" Claudia Silver called across the lobby to the young, slope-shouldered guard, a neighborhood *cuzine* whose lacquered hair aspired to Italian stallion while the rest of him grew pimples.

"Yeah," the lobby guard nodded. "Dial nine to get out."

The few minutes before a high-stakes job interview may not have been the ideal time to try Paul again. Plus, there was knowing better.

Claudia found herself pulling the phone to her mouth.

"Golden Fenwick Tate Stein and Lowe," the operator purred.

"Paul Tate, please." It was, Claudia realized, her motto.

"Please hold." That, too.

Across the studio lobby a door swung open, and Claudia glimpsed a tall bank of monitors illuminating an otherwise dark room as a figure emerged. She was a woman of color, that color being caramel. Her hair, relaxed and permed into a high, smooth helmet, her skin, knit ensemble, ruched ankle boots—they were all this most golden shade of brown, worthy of a ladies lunch with Claire and Denise Huxtable. The woman paused in the doorway. "When am I seeing a rough cut?" she called into the glow with a domineering warmth. "I'll be *baaahck*," she joked, then strode across the lobby. "Hey, Wayne," she said to the guard, glancing at Claudia as she passed.

After a few bars of Vivaldi, a new voice returned. "Mr. Tate is not available at the moment," Paul's secretary informed Claudia. Then, a pause, in which, according to office protocol, she should have asked if Claudia would care to leave a message. Claudia waited, but the silence persisted.

"Can I leave a message?" Claudia asked.

The secretary lowered her voice. "Listen," she said quietly. "I'm gonna do you a favor right now, okay? You should probably stop calling him."

Suddenly, Claudia's eyes were stinging, her mascara threatened. "Gotcha," she managed to say. Somehow, she floated the receiver back to its cradle. She kept her hand on it. She looked around and tried to remember what it was exactly that she was doing.

"Shelly's office is through those doors," the lobby guard miraculously reminded her, "straight down the end of the hall."

She was holding her breath, and tried to stop doing that. *In today's performance*, she decided, *the part of Claudia Silver will be played by Claudia Silver.*

Decorated with framed *Hope Valley* posters and strewn with platters of mini breakfast pastry that tormented all who entered there, Executive Producer Shelly Gerson's office was the domain of a male assistant with spiked hair, double-pierced ears, an expensive nose, pressed jeans, and a silver thumb ring.

"I don't understand why everybody is just plain bonkers," he declared. His was the bored voice from Claudia's answering machine, but in person he was a stern hive of activity, tearing about on his wheeled Aeron, hydra arms simultaneously scrambling in script cubbies, receiving casting breakdowns off the fax machine, flipping through an alphabetically organized binder of the show's sprawling contacts, and punching at the various illuminated buttons on a phone that made the ones at Georgica Films resemble Fisher-Price toys.

"Hi, I'm Claudia Silver. I've got an eleven A.M. with Shelly."

The assistant stared at Claudia blankly, formed a finger pistol, and pointed it at the phone.

"No, have her leave it," the assistant was saying, as Claudia realized, embarrassed, that he was on the phone. "By which I mean *make* her leave it, Wayne. Do you need me to come down there?" He hung up, but kept his headset on. "Actors," he sighed, scanning Claudia from crown to sole and deeming her acceptable, if not interesting. "Such desperate, desperate people. This one delivered a carnation slipper."

"Um—" Claudia hedged, still unclear to whom he was speaking.

"As in a *giant shoe*. Fashioned from *carnations.*" He scooted his chair to the fax machine and plucked a warm sheet from the tray, then pointed at Claudia and snapped his fingers impatiently.

Claudia handed him her plastic folder as he rolled back to

pluck it. *Now there's an idea*, Claudia reflected. She could have her ass done in baby's breath and left it with Paul's secretary. "Why a shoe?" she asked the assistant.

"Because we're doing yet another Cinderella story line this year, I suppose," he replied with a snort, reviewing Claudia's resumé in a single sweep. "It's absolutely *tragic*. Do they think Shelly just fell off the turnip truck? You don't get the part with *flowers*."

"What's your name?" Claudia asked, heartened by this worker bee and everything she thought he might stand for.

With this, the assistant narrowed his eyes and returned her plastic sleeve. "Hang on," he said, shoving off from his desk with the resumé as a sail and landing at the double doors of the inner office. He knocked once, rose, kicked his chair to its starting position, and disappeared inside.

"Go ahead in, Claudia," he said as he reappeared, moments later. "You get the job," he whispered as she passed, "and I'll tell you my name."

"It's on," Claudia replied.

Shelly Gerson's office, dominated by a giant, champagne-colored leather sectional sofa draped in butterscotch cashmere throws, was the perfect nook for a temper tantrum or a nap. Claudia's resumé sat in the center of a large white desk with a beveled glass top, behind which a tan leather chair was turned toward a bank of monitors showing views of the taping floor, where a hospital scene was currently being shot, as well as yesterday's final cut, a morning talk show, and a commercial for Zest deodorant soap.

"Come on in, Claudia," Shelly said. The chair pivoted and Shelly Gerson—Madame Caramel from the lobby—rose to greet her.

Claudia was horrified by her own surprise. You should never be surprised, she knew, to realize a black woman could well be your next boss. But there it was. "Thanks for having me in," she said, shaking Shelly's hand with an extra dose of nonchalant professionalism.

"I always meet with Barnard girls," Shelly said, pushing aside Claudia's resumé. Claudia assumed with a silent gulp that the stack of papers at the edge of Shelly's desk under the WOMEN IN FILM paperweight represented the competition. "Any trouble finding us here?"

"Nah. As it says on my award-winning resumé, I'm a Brooklyn girl, too."

"I got that," said Shelly, nodding at her resumé. "We stick together. Erasmus Hall, right?"

"Bedford."

"Oh, right. My husband, Arnie, went to Erasmus." It was then that Claudia noticed the framed photos, everywhere. Shelly and Arnie Gerson in snow pants with that guy who played the single dad of the smart-alecky brood on that show. Shelly and Arnie Gerson in wet suits with former child stars and in hot-air balloons with the major impresarios of disco. On all those red carpets. Arnie Gerson, always with the sunglasses and three inches shorter than Shelly Gerson, his various attempts to bridge the gap smacked down by her ubiquitous Stuart Weitzmans.

"Where did *you* go?" Claudia asked.

"Boys and Girls High."

Claudia nodded, impressed. "*Bed-Stuy, do or die*," she commented, wanting Shelly to know she was down. But Shelly, who'd finally arrived at the place where every single item in her wardrobe required dry cleaning after one wearing, dismissed the slogan with a wave of a French-manicured hand.

"Arnie lived in the same building as Barbra Streisand," she shared. Claudia, observing Shelly's talons, connected the dots.

"So you're practically related," said Claudia.

Shelly smiled. "We *are* related, in a way. We all are." She gestured to her wall of signed head shots, hung in a dense mosaic. "A lot of the entertainers you love have come through *HV*. Recognize any of them?"

Claudia scanned the gallery. "Is that Mr. Whipple?" Shelly made a face. "I'm kidding—I'm a huge fan of Anne Heche," Claudia bluffed, blessedly remembering the bit of trivia she'd gleaned from the college career counselor who'd wrangled the interview. "I think it's so cool that she played Denise *and* Diane."

"So you watch our show?"

"I'm not as current as I was in high school," by which, of course, Claudia meant *never*. "But I'm excited to catch up."

Shelly plucked Claudia's resumé from the desk. "We're telling a lot of exciting stories," she said. "Tell me yours. Georgica Films. What's that?"

"I've been the staff production assistant there for two years."

"And what sorts of films do they make over there at Georgica Films?"

"Avant-garde shorts that run between regularly scheduled programming," Claudia replied. "We call them commercials."

Shelly glanced up from the resumé, suitably amused. "And what do you do there?"

Hm, let's see, Claudia thought. *Order family-style lunch, fuck the doorman, pinch a bud, get fired.* "My boss is the executive producer, Ricky Green," she replied. "Every day is different, which is an aspect of production I really love. I basically assist in the company's creative and production process, from agency pitch all the way through client management and post."

"Do you know what the most important thing is to *me?*" Shelly asked, removing a stray no. 2 pencil from her pen jar and dropping it into the wastepaper basket under her desk.

Claudia shook her head. "*Discretion*. When you work for me, you quickly learn everything about everybody. It's quiet down here right now, but the stuff that unfolds in this office can rival our story lines. Most importantly, in here you'll learn where the actual story lines are *going*, which means where the actors' contracts are *headed*, which affects their many, many moods. Capiche?"

"I think so."

"So tell me about your boss. What's he like?"

You mean other than a seething JAP with elf boots and no recognizable skill set other than star-fuckery and restaurants? "He was great. He *is* great. I've learned a lot from Ricky and I'm grateful for the experience. But, um, my own goal is to make the move from commercial production into narrative storytelling. Plus, you know. Ordering lunch is my specialty."

Shelly smiled. "The last kid I had in here heard the same speech and then proceeded to tell me all about his boss's eating disorder." She tipped back in her chair and folded her hands behind her head. Two small, round pit stains, the size of quarters, had appeared in the thin wool jersey, an extra pair of eyes whose gaze Claudia avoided. "So tell me what you think about soaps in general."

Nothing wrong with empty calories for geriatrics and inmates, Shell, if you're into pop-culture landfill and happen to be a broke, unemployed home wrecker. "Well . . . ," Claudia began. "Soap opera. It . . . it gets a bad rap. As melodrama. It's the stuff of spoof. You know, cue Carol Burnett and Harvey Korman, trying hard not to laugh—"

"Harvey used to be Arnie's doubles partner when we lived in L.A.," Shelly interrupted.

"Very cool."

"Continue."

"But, um, what do we say about our lives, what's the shorthand we use for the inevitable complications that defy all logic? 'It's a total soap opera,' we say to our friends. When we love the wrong person. When mothers don't act like they're supposed to. When siblings emerge from long-lost trysts. When illness that doesn't appear in any medical journal alters the course of our lives." Claudia, who'd stumbled her way here, who, unlike Shelly Gerson, had the most unwieldy of plans for her future and not enough cash to pick up her dry cleaning, felt the groove and gave herself to it. She wasn't just popping shit. She was taking verbal dictation from on high, and listening to it herself. "We describe our lives as soap operas because that's what soap opera *does*," she continued. "It *illuminates* our lives, heightens the conflict we already know so that it can exist outside of ourselves, which is how we can find peace *inside*."

The more Claudia listened to herself talk, the more *Hope Valley* became something she wanted, badly. The job had come tapping on her shoulder out of nowhere. This is how destiny worked, Claudia already knew from her collision course with Paul Tate. *Destiny already exists*, she told herself, and we make our way toward it, sometimes quickly, sometimes slowly—

Claudia already *was* the second assistant to Executive Producer Shelly Gerson. It was only a matter of circumstances catching up with the inevitable—

She *had* to get this job. The only alternative to commanding these halls, wrestling these mini-muffins, speaking this language of workaday entertainment for the people, raising Phoebe in the lifestyle to which neither of them were remotely accustomed—

Was death.

"And meanwhile," Claudia was saying, continuing her aria for her rapt audience of one, "in the practical world of making a living, we're a sustaining genre. We continue when other storytelling fads disappear. We are passed down, from generation to generation. Daughters become mothers and mothers become grandmothers, anchored to our stories, sharing them with one another. We sustain the artistic life of the city"—here, she gestured to the wall of glossies that resembled, she realized, those of the dry cleaners, delis, and diners of countless New York neighborhoods—"and, for the fans who consider us family, we are folklore, we are milestone. And, you know. Like the song says. We are family—"

Deedle-eep. Deedle-eep. The timer on Shelly's bulky diver's watch sounded. *Deedle-eep.* "Sorry," Shelly fretted, tearing her eyes from Claudia to silence the alarm. "That's eleven-thirty lunch. Hang on." She leaned forward to press her intercom button.

Eleven-thirty.

Claudia, suddenly stricken, stood, remembering with horror the appointment she'd made with Ms. Krinsky to discuss Phoebe's D-plus during the teacher's lunch break, from 11:10 to twelve. Today.

The floor tipped one way, the marshmallow sofa slumped in opposition.

"Tell Tommy I'll meet him in his dressing room in ten," Shelly was saying into the intercom, "and have his agent's office holding so we can conference." Claudia reached for her bomber jacket. "You don't have to go," Shelly said to Claudia, frowning. She kept her eyes on the girl as she addressed the intercom. "I want you to give Claudia a studio tour when we're done here." She released the intercom button. "What gives, sugar?"

"I . . . I'm sorry. I have to go." Claudia slung her messenger back across her chest. "I forgot I have another appointment—"

"If it's not for a kidney transplant, you can call them, can't you? Seeing as you're in the middle of acing a job interview."

"It's basically a kidney transplant," Claudia replied. *This,*

Claudia reflected briefly, was an entirely new and different way to blow it. *Blowing It*, in fact, might do nicely as a memoir title. Claudia was at the door. "I can come back for the tour," she said, flatly, "maybe even later today." Bedford High School was twenty minutes away, and Ms. Krinsky's office hours ended ten minutes after that. No biggie. She would fly there. In her tights and cape. After stripping down in a phone booth.

Phoebe had loitered the morning away in Flatbush Junction, then positioned herself at the entrance to the subway to successfully head off Ramona at the pass. *It doesn't hurt to ask*, Ramona had claimed, and so Phoebe asked. Which was how Phoebe Goldberg and Ramona Parker now found themselves together, among the *Moxy* hopefuls at the open casting call Bronwyn had implored Phoebe to attend.

Currently, they were last on the growing queue. It started in a temporary photo studio, installed in a storefront, and ended out here in the cold, populated largely by a narrow margin of artsy Manhattan girls who were privy to opportunities like this one due to their parents' connections. Some were accompanied by their male sidekicks, club boys of lesser means and greater sartorial daring, who had their own thinly veiled schemes to eclipse their patrons and single-handedly return lower Manhattan to a kind of post-Warholian Shangri-La, starring themselves, in, perhaps, a tweed cape over hot pants. A few oddly shaped Long Island pilgrims, whose parents, unlike their Manhattan counterparts, did not consider dermatology a household line item, gave the crowd a lumpy verisimilitude. These bigger, more hesitant girls had heard the brief ad on late-night alternative radio, and wore a series of unfortunate hats at dreadful tilts.

"I can't be late for work," Ramona warned Phoebe. Her

internship at the Tribeca Animal Hospital had been won in a cutthroat application process.

"Can you hang with me until the last possible minute, then run like hell?" Phoebe asked, good-naturedly.

There was a flurry of movement at the top of the line. Bronwyn Tate was causing the minor commotion as she made her way with a Polaroid camera. At Bronwyn's side was her brand-new boss, an older chick, probably close to thirty, in combat boots, thick ribbed tights, cutoff shorts, a leather sweater, a bleached pixie cut, and a megaphone.

"Five minutes," Ramona replied.

Pixie Cut wrestled the megaphone with a buzz and a drone. "Hey, y'all!" she announced cheerfully after another few seconds. "I'm Holly Platt, editor in chief of *Moxy*, and I just want to thank you guys so much for coming out here on a freezing day! As you know, we're looking for the new face of *Moxy*, as well as other faces we can use in the pages of our supercool new magazine!" A former West Plano High cheerleader, Holly had shed her pom-poms when she'd fled north. "We are so totally psyched that so many of you have shown up!" Holly continued. "If we take your photo, it means we want to remember your cute faces—and stay in touch." At this, Holly elbowed Bronwyn, who dutifully snapped a Polaroid of a dreamy lass in a boy's suit, topped by a metallic-silver down vest and a long, striped stocking cap. "And now, my capable assistant, Bronwyn, will break it all down for you!" Holly, the self-protective, self-appointed big sister to stylish girls everywhere, dispatched the dirty work as she shoved her megaphone into Bronwyn's arms. The clipboard promptly clattered to the sidewalk, and Holly stepped over it to stroll the line. As Bronwyn stooped to retrieve it, the megaphone fell, and buzzed unpleasantly. Holly turned and frowned prettily. Bronwyn, cheeks burning, brought the megaphone to her mouth. She cleared her throat as the waiting girls, dubious, considered her.

"If I take your photo and tap you," Bronwyn began, demonstrating as she tapped the stocking-capped lass firmly on the shoulder, "it means we want to do another round of photos inside, but first you need to sign a release form." Here, Bronwyn struggled with her clipboard as she shuffled forward to catch up with her boss. She managed to free a single sheet of paper, and waved it, once, before a stiff, downtown wind came along and blew it from her hands. It skidded across Lafayette and ended its life in a dank puddle, barreled over by an H&H Bagels truck, as Holly followed the action, witheringly, with her eyes.

"If we *don't* photograph you or tap you," Bronwyn continued, "it means we, um . . ." Here, the nervous girl trailed off, looking to an unreadable Holly for more information, but none was forthcoming. "We'll be holding open casting calls again," Bronwyn faltered, scanning the vulnerable faces stretching before her, "so we want you to come back and bring your friends. For today, we're looking for a certain, um, *Moxy* je ne sais *kumquat*, but we totally don't want you to feel bad if you don't have it." Although the megaphone squawked, Bronwyn barreled ahead. *"We want you to buy* Moxy *magazine and find out how to get it!"* Keeping her back turned to her new junior editor, Holly ratified the awkward speech with a skyward poke of her thumb. It was then that Bronwyn noticed Phoebe. Her face lit with relief.

Phoebe grabbed Ramona's hand. "Seriously," she said, as Bronwyn and Holly approached. "Don't go."

"Ten minutes, tops, and that's my final offer," said Ramona.

"Hey, ladies!" Bronwyn greeted the girls, casually.

"Yo," Phoebe replied, with an easy smile that tied her height and her slouch together in an arresting package. The gap between her teeth was always a surprise, and with delighted shock, Holly Platt clocked all of it—the hair and the skin and the dusting of freckles and the moccasins.

The editor in chief tapped the two girls with her signature cheeky authority. "These two," she declared, grinning.

Claudia ran. Her ponytail flew out behind her, and every second she was about to give up, but Bedford High School's cupola, its strong white finger of reason and authority poking skyward among the crummy old apartment buildings clumped along Campus Road, beckoned.

Claudia's former small pond smelled of chalk and cafeteria. It thundered with student traffic making its way between classes. Ms. Krinsky's wavy glass office door opened, and the teacher appeared with a ziplock Baggie of baby carrots in her hand. She'd been trying to conjure Claudia Silver's face. Aggressive Jewish girls were the bedrock of the school, and the record showed that she had taught Claudia AP American History back in 1984, but Elaine Krinsky honestly wasn't sure which particular loudmouth Claudia Silver was.

"Oh!" she now exclaimed, taking in her winded former student. "I remember *you!*" She looked up and down the hall. The flood of students had dissipated quickly. "Where's your sister?" Claudia's guts tightened into a walnut as Krinksy shooed her in. "Have a seat," Krinsky said, her denim prairie skirt swirling as she crossed her legs. Claudia immediately spotted the unfamiliar man in the corner of the room. He was stout, freckled, and smiling, balding and clipped on top, with a short calico beard and a light band of perspiration framing his temples. His hands were folded in his lap, his plaid flannel shirt strained over his round belly, his jaw worked a wad of cinnamon gum, and one of his feet jittered in its New Balance running shoe. He raised a hand in greeting.

"Hey, Claudia," he said, perfectly casual. "I'm Dave

O'Malley." A decade or more Ms. Krinsky's junior, his boundless enthusiasm for the youth of New York City still got him out of bed in the morning, and he had just enjoyed a particularly tasty knish with mustard and onions.

"Dave's a social worker for Child Protective Services," Krinsky explained. So far today Elaine Krinsky had eaten only half a bagel, at 6 A.M., and she now pushed her lunch out of her sight line and leaned forward, clog dangling. "And he works here at Bedford and several other high schools in our district."

O'Malley shifted eagerly in his seat. "I wanted to talk to you and Phoebe about your living situation," he said. His accent was thick and his manner was friendly. Claudia figured his father had been a drunk cop, permanently chapped from a bitter run of K.P. duty, who'd moved the family from the Bronx to Long Island at some point, and whose regular beatings had sent his youngest son into the helping professions.

"Claudia," Krinsky asked her, "what's going on, kiddo?"

Fuck me dead, Claudia reasoned.

Upon further consideration, it occurred to her that this may have been *exactly* what Paul Tate had done.

If only there had been some way to call Phoebe, wherever it was that Phoebe was. If only Claudia could make the correct sidewalk pay phone ring precisely as Phoebe passed it, and Phoebe could duck in and answer. If only Phoebe, like Claudia, were the sort to pick up randomly ringing pay phones just to see who was there. If only they had two Campbell's soup cans strung, pocket-to-pocket, Cream of Mushroom to Chicken Noodle, by an endless filament that traversed the city. If only she hadn't had that pointless fucking exercise at *Hope Valley*, because she hadn't needed a job, because she hadn't gotten fired, and as a result, hadn't needed Paul Tate in the middle of the night, because she, in crisp shirtdress, belted cardigan, and camel-colored pumps, was already married to a rising executive in the family metals business, because nobody had ever left Europe, and she had been raised a pretty princess on some *Strasse* or other with a tiered porcelain platter of marzipan and a French tutor. It was all slightly Paul Tate's fault, and yet he was also the solution, or he once was, and the crater he left was too choked with smoke for Claudia to gauge its diameter. It was maddeningly simple to reconstruct the past so that it added up more satisfactorily. This was clearly a better use of Claudia's time than burning in the eternity of the future, or reckoning with Krinsky's goggle-eyed stare.

For her next trick, Claudia would back out of Krinsky's office. She would do what her people had been engineered to do. She would flee.

With the girl gone, Krinsky offered O'Malley her Baggie of carrots and he accepted. She sighed and pulled her lunch box close. They would call the mother next. But first she would eat her lentil salad.

Annie Tate flapped along the frozen Brooklyn side street in her old leather sandals. She was certainly *aware* of the plain row houses, several of which had been desecrated with aluminum siding and rusted awnings, and the questionable individuals hurrying between the ragged main drag on one end and the actual housing project on the other, but she was too determined to be bothered. A fat black crow pimp-rolled recklessly close to a passing gypsy cab that blared a droning beat (*La-da-deeeee la-da-daaa she's homeless*) as it lurched past.

Annie rang Edith Mendelssohn's bell. The harsh buzzer reminded her of a slaughterhouse, somehow, not that she'd ever been within one hundred miles of one, and she felt strongly that a more dignified and musical doorbell would help tremendously. Annie rang again, and was about to knock on the parlor window when the door opened, just wide enough for Edith to peer out.

182

"I'm Annie Tate," she announced into the shadows. She paused, unsure how to describe herself under the circumstances. *Your daughter is my future ex-husband's girlfriend* was just ridiculous. She opted for "My daughter Bronwyn is Claudia's roommate," instead.

Edith opened the door another inch, allowing Annie a view of the woman's large brown eyes and the pale, slender finger, unencumbered by a wedding ring. "Yes?" Edith queried, tensely.

"Do you think I could come in for a moment, Ms. Mendelssohn? There's a, um . . . situation I'm hoping we can discuss." *In which my husband's penis seems to have fallen into your daughter's vagina*, she realized with some amusement she could say if she cared to, ripped from the pages of *The Little Slut's Phrase Book*.

Edith disappeared for a moment, and as the door opened wider, it was clear she was willing. Annie stepped into the chilly foyer. Its tile had long ago lost its gleam, the light fixture was penitential. *So this,* Annie thought, *is where Claudia is from.* The girl suddenly became worthy of admiration, while at the same time her utter unsuitability was now officially cemented. Annie's disoriented spirit, right down to her sullied feet, formed a rough-hewn footbridge across which the two women carefully approached each other.

"Is there some sort of emergency?" Edith asked. Her tone was intriguing, simultaneously gamine and authoritarian.

"It depends who you ask," Annie replied. Then: "But no bloodshed."

"Do come in," Edith said stiffly. She stepped aside to open the door wider. "Tea and sympathy?" she asked.

"First one," said Annie, stepping into Edith's parlor, "and then maybe the other."

• • •

"Yup, just like that," the photographer was saying. He was a flushed, burly fellow of Nordic extraction with a halo of pale curls, a rumpled custom dress shirt, a giant camera and army pants, and Phoebe Goldberg and Ramona Parker had already forgotten his name. But they'd been tapped, snapped, and arranged by him on a white riser in front of a white backdrop, and were currently standing side by side, in a version of the pose that hadn't felt like a pose when they'd been holding hands outside.

Discovered on a SoHo sidewalk by editor Holly Platt is how the story would go, with the pesky detail of the open casting call excised for the sake of a good story.

Could you guys maybe just stand the way you were on the sidewalk? You know, holding hands. Wow, yeah, cool, thanks!

The white girl and the black girl holding hands, both of them odd looking, the white girl stunningly so and the black girl more real, bookish, and thusly exciting—it said something powerful and tender about *this exact moment*. This Exact Moment being the moving target that *Moxy* was in the business of pinning down.

Phoebe had realized quickly, and with some relief, that there wasn't much to actually *do*. Deciding to show up was the main thing, and now she was pretty much just standing there being herself. Since things seemed to be going pretty well—Phoebe could tell this was so by the rapt attention that Holly Platt and her nodding handmaidens were paying her—maybe Claudia's fucked-up-ness would prove, in time, to have been a good thing. The photographer had been at it for a while, pacing like a potbellied panther, crouching down, standing splayed. Phoebe did something with her feet, and the *Moxy* ladies vibrated. She did something else with her hip, and they froze and grabbed one another. She popped the collar of her peacoat and they cocked their collective head; she put the collar back down and they sighed, all together now, with relief. She grinned, and they gasped. At one point, the photographer had Phoebe and Ramona lie on their backs as he climbed a ladder above them. Phoebe looked up his loose shirt, like a gym teacher, and saw his round, pink belly bouncing over his belt. Snap, snap, snap. All the while, the photographer asked Phoebe and Ramona random, borderline loserish questions: "So . . . d'you guys like hip-hop?"

Still lying on her back at the foot of the ladder, Ramona turned her head to address Phoebe. The photographer snapped wildly, but it wasn't the shot they'd land on. The black girl talking to the white girl while the white girl stared straight ahead looked too worshipful, and this would be a story about how teen girls are *equals*. "I really need to go," Ramona said. "My supervisor is going to kill me, that is, if I still even have an internship."

"I can go with you and explain," Phoebe offered.

Snap snappity *snap*. This was better. The black girl and the white girl in deep *conversation*.

The photographer exclaimed, "All right, fuck. That's it. I'm done!" He threw his meaty arms in the air—"*Take* this, *Jay-sus*"—and two assistants, one lanky, the other squat, appeared at his side to remove the camera and proffer an espresso as he clattered heavily down the ladder and pushed his curls off his damp forehead. Passionate applause exploded. Phoebe got nimbly to her feet and offered Ramona her hand.

"Well, *that* was just slightly more than I had in mind," Ramona said as they stepped down from the risers. Bronwyn, beaming, hurried toward them. "Gotsta go, for reals for *reals*."

"I'll walk you to work, okay?" offered Phoebe.

"I'm *running*."

"Then I'll run with you."

Bronwyn pulled Phoebe into a tight hug as Ramona slipped her backpack over her shoulders. "My parents are taking me out tonight to Café des Artistes to celebrate my new job,"

Bronwyn said, "but seeing as we both have one, you've *got* to come. Meet us there at eight?"

Ramona, pulling on her fingerless gloves, seemed to be ignoring the fact that Bronwyn was clearly excluding her from the invitation. "Okay," Phoebe said, clocking Bronwyn's easy rudeness. "Where is it?"

Bronwyn held Phoebe at arm's length. "Sixty-Seventh between the Park and Columbus," she replied. "How *fantastic* that you've never been there before! And Holly's totally going to help you find an agent."

"I think I may already have one," Phoebe admitted, modestly. "Paolo Crespi?"

"Paolo?" Bronwyn gasped. "Oh my God, he's *huge*."

"Right on," Phoebe said. Ramona was already threading her way through the milling crowd. Phoebe was determined to stay by Ramona's side, but the Moxies were heading her way, parting the milling crowd like a pyramid of water-skiers, with Holly Platt at the tippy-top in a flowered two-piece. "Ramona!" Phoebe cried as Ramona disappeared behind the formation, her skinny braids bouncing.

"Oh, you can't go anywhere," Bronwyn admonished, grabbing Phoebe's wrist, as ten blocks north, the exact F train bearing Claudia was hurtling into the Broadway-Lafayette station. "This is just the beginning."

Annie Tate stood in the mouth of Edith Mendelssohn's parlor.

The dim room, with its torn upholstery and its rock-and-roll poster, smelled of cigarettes and incense. It was the home of a woman who cared little for housework, a helpless woman, by which Annie meant a woman who clearly did not have *help*. A woman of books, not book parties, without proper window treatments, and yet there was a peculiar style to the place—more substance than style, really. This was how a private woman lived when left to her own devices. When not trapped, and consumed, by trying to please, soothe, or entertain. This was the home of the mother of the girl for whom Paul Tate had thrown their whole life away. How many other mothers of how many other girls were peppered along the mid-Atlantic Annie could scarcely calculate, which only heightened the threadbare poignancy of this particular parlor, lacking as it did both coasters and a coffee table to put them on.

Annie was far out in a strangely peaceful sea of tiredness, past the breakers of the facts—her philandering husband, her dirty feet. She had the vague faith that she'd eventually be spit back onto shore, and that it would hurt.

"English or Chinese?" Edith asked. The question was among her favorite gauntlets.

"English, wonderful," Annie replied. She was well aware that her host was referring to the tea, and accordingly, earned a notch of Edith's estimation.

Edith nodded to the dining room table. "Please, sit." She did not offer to take Annie's duffle coat, which was fine, as the room was cold.

Annie sat and unfastened a few toggles. "You have a wonderful place," she said, as Edith set a tin of rough, seeded cookies and a chipped ceramic bowl of clementines on the table, then returned with a tea tray. While the individual elements were coarser than any Annie would have chosen, the civilized ritual gave her hope in Edith's basic womanhood. "Do you remember that old commercial?" Annie began as Edith poured. *It's ten o'clock. Do you know where your children are?*"

Edith settled in her Victorian throne and adjusted a hairpin. "I'm afraid not," she replied. "I don't have television."

From her spot at the table, Annie could see clear to the front room, where a small TV, its antennae wrapped thickly in aluminum foil, had been pushed into the corner on a green plastic milk crate. "Well," Annie observed boldly, imagining that this was where the live-in boyfriend from whom the daughters had fled must watch his baseball games, "*somebody* does."

It was then that Annie's calculations faltered.

She had decided on her announcement (*Your daughter is fucking my husband*), but how would it land? Edith was a woman with two children from two different, disappeared men. She had red lightbulbs in her ceiling fixture, for heaven's sake, and no coasters. What on earth would a woman like this care about adultery?

For all Annie knew, the news flash that Claudia and Paul were an ungodly item might earn Edith's grim *respect*.

"No television must be why Claudia's so bright," Annie praised, selecting a clementine that felt loose in its skin.

"I assure you Claudia always loved TV," Edith replied. "She made me get her that little set for her bedroom when she was a girl, to watch a program called *The Electric Company*, that, as I recall, wound her up terribly. I don't think I've seen a minute of television since she went off to school."

"Well," said Annie, "that commercial shocked me when my girls were small. To imagine a time when I wouldn't know their exact whereabouts." Annie set down her clementine and advanced along a new tack. "Edith," she began again. "Mother to mother—"

"Mrs. Tate," Edith interrupted, sounding a bit stern. Annie braced, a bird dog with a raised paw, anticipating vitriol. Then: "Can I offer you something stronger?"

Annie had been trying for some time now not to drink during the day, except that this day did not exactly count, did it, as it was the end of days. "Well, yes," she found herself saying. "I suppose that would be just fine."

From a bookshelf hollow behind three volumes of bound Judaica, Edith extracted a pint of Chivas. At the dish drainer, she removed two small glasses, and from her refrigerator's little freezer shelf, overgrown with thick frost, a blue plastic ice-cube tray. As the whiskey slid down Annie's throat, it warmed her chest and strengthened her mind. Shaming Edith with Claudia's behavior may have been an exercise in futility, but that didn't mean Annie couldn't be an emissary for good. "I want to talk to you about Phoebe," Annie declared.

"*Phoebe?*" Edith frowned. "You know her?"

"Well, yes, of course," Annie replied, despite the fact that her source of information was her future ex-husband and that she had only a vague memory of the girl from their one meeting, a month ago, on Christmas Eve. "Did you know she's been living with Claudia and Bronwyn since November?"

Edith took an efficient pull on her drink. "I've had my suspicions."

"But do you know *why?*"

Edith shrugged. "I left home at sixteen," she said, "to enroll at university. I had a borrowed suitcase, one sweater, one pair of lace-up shoes, and my collection of poetry in a brown paper bag. My mother's parting gift was a marble cake from Wertheimer's on 181st Street and a sack of Winesap apples. If I remember correctly." She took another sip and shook the ice cubes in her glass. "I'm not sure there is a particular *why* to the process of differentiation, other than a Darwinian imperative. It's much worse, I'd say, when it doesn't happen at all."

Annie set down her sweating glass on a cloth napkin, so as not to add another ring to the table, and leaned forward. "Were you running for your *life* when you left home?" she volleyed with purpose.

"Running for my life," Edith repeated, savoring the phrase. "No, Mrs. Tate. By the time I left home, we had already done that. I will say, however, that once one has escaped a burning continent, the niceties do take on a certain abstraction. I suppose one either clings to them, taking exaggerated comfort in jam pots and that sort of thing, or comes to recognize how they defile the memory of the dead." Annie stared. "Are you familiar with the Shoah, Mrs. Tate?"

"The . . . the movie?" Annie faltered.

"No," Edith countered with a withering patience, "the *actual genocide* on which it is based." The conversation was halted, and Edith sat back in the horrified silence.

Annie took a deep gulp of her drink, then broke it. "Your *boyfriend*," she pressed on, determined. She would not be shooed away by the Holocaust. "Is his name Robbie?"

"*Boyfriend?*" Edith mused bitterly. "I've always loathed that word."

"The man who lives here. With you." She indicated the old green Panasonic. "Who watches that television." She glanced around the apartment. "And smokes those cigarettes."

"Robert," Edith admitted.

Annie sat back in her seat. "Yes," she said. She sipped her drink. "This is very difficult for me to say. I am speaking to you as a mother who has problems with her own children. And as a woman. Not in judgment. But I have grave concerns about Phoebe."

"Go on."

"Robert. He . . . my understanding is . . . he is, possibly, dangerous. He is the reason Phoebe has gone to live with Claudia—and with my own daughter. To escape this situation."

"*Dangerous?*"

"He has frightened your daughter, Ms. Mendelssohn," said Annie. "Maybe worse."

Edith drank, slowly, then set down her glass. "Do you mean sexually?" she asked, finally.

"I . . . I don't have the details," Annie admitted. But as Edith dropped her head and hid her face in her hands, Annie felt the stirrings of triumph. They sat in silence, Annie sipping. From somewhere, a clock ticked. "He can't live here anymore," Annie counseled, firmly, over Edith's bent head. "You have to make him leave. Not just for your children, but for yourself. You haven't spoken to Claudia in two years. Don't you want your family back?"

"It is *she*," Edith retorted, raising her face to reveal her eyes, red rimmed and filled, "who hasn't spoken to *me*."

"A mother always speaks to her child," Annie admonished quietly. "No matter what." This is how Annie should have spoken, always. To her children, to her husband, to her own mother, and to herself, long ago, as she hesitated at the good doctor's back door in Providence, then turned and ran, all the way back to her dorm, to the pay phone in the parlor, where she had called Paul, and instead of never speaking to him again, had told him she was pregnant, with Martha. "A mother speaks to her child her whole life, and then she speaks from the grave." This is how Annie would speak, from now on. She had misunderstood the whiskey, for clearly it was fire, not lead. "If you don't believe that, down to your bones—if you don't know *how* to believe that, Edith—"

"Then *what?*" Edith cried.

The women stared at each other across the short distance of old table, Edith's desperation hanging between them. Having just recently revived her own fallow instincts, Annie was briefly mystified by the notion of growing them from seed. But, of course, it could be done. Of course, one could revive whatever was dead within. Annie was sure of it. She had to be.

"Then," Annie finally replied, "I have the number of every great therapist in New York City."

Claudia tried to shake all possible scenarios from her mind. But it was the concocting of scenarios that kept her in motion.

At three this morning Annie's directive had seemed impossible: *Either you tell Bronwyn*, she'd said, *or I will*.

But that was before Paul had destroyed their future with two words: *It's over*.

Annie had threatened to tell Bronwyn the truth; Paul had asked Claudia to refrain until he'd had his shot. At three this morning, the headline was that Paul and Claudia were the new occupants of the center of the universe, and that Claudia was soon to be Bronwyn's wicked stepmother. Now, standing in the bitter shards of all that, Claudia saw the scenario with Paul shrunken down to its essence. He was *the worst thing she had ever done*. He made Ruben Hyacinth look like Nipsey Russell. The mess with Ruben had cost her a job. Paul Tate would take with him Claudia's pretend family. She would have nothing left, that was guaranteed. But she could stop being a liar. She could tell Bronwyn in her own words what she had done. She knew that the odds Bronwyn would understand were slim. She knew that the truth, in this case, would not so much set her free as cut her loose. How could she dream of Bronwyn's eventual forgiveness if she couldn't look her in the eye right now? It seemed to Claudia that telling Bronwyn the truth was her chance to salvage the present.

Bronwyn, meanwhile, had alphabetized the release forms, filed the Polaroids for the inspiration board back at *Moxy* HQ, faxed the photographer's invoice to the accounting department, confirmed next steps for the billboards, and made dinner reservations for Holly and the rest of the senior editors at Le Zinc. She was just stepping out into the cold evening when she felt a familiar presence behind her. She turned just before Claudia was able to tap her on the shoulder.

"Claude?" Both girls, mutually startled, jumped back slightly.

"Hey!" Claudia barked, well aware that she had just struck exactly the wrong tone, defensive and alarmed. Her heart was pounding, from deep in her bowels, where it had suddenly dropped.

Bronwyn shivered and pulled her cashmere watch cap more snugly around her ears. "How did you know I was *here?*" she asked. Claudia's arrival, unexpected, in the dark, at this obscure location, did not temper Bronwyn's memory of the wee hours. Red-handed Claudia, backing away into the night, with nary a reciprocal "I love you, too," leaving Bronwyn alone in a dark hallway. That had been very strange, and so was this.

"I called your office," Claudia explained.

Bronwyn frowned. "They shouldn't be giving out that kind of information to a random caller. Not that you're random," she added, unconvincingly.

"Oh, I'm hella random." Claudia offered a cockeyed smile that hung there and dissolved.

"You just missed Phoebe," Bronwyn blurted.

Claudia's hand flew to her chest. It had been at least an hour since she'd pictured her sister. She liked the idea of Phoebe back at the apartment, listening to her *Uprising* cassette and fixing ramen noodles. "As in she was *here?*" Claudia looked up and down the sheltered run of sidewalk, strung with construction lights. "Why?"

"Claudia," Bronwyn began. "I have to tell you something."

Claudia's worry took on a whole new dimension. "Is Phoebe okay?"

"She's fine. Actually—she's great. She's . . . ," Bronwyn trailed off.

Gone forever? Eyeing the ashtrays in a social services waiting room? Married to a Rasta? Moved in with Ms. Krinsky? Claudia felt the sudden urge to shake the details out of Bronwyn, and violently, but she couldn't. Not with the grenade she had in her pocket.

"Do you want to grab a drink at Fanelli's and maybe talk

for a few minutes?" Bronwyn continued. "I have to meet my parents at Café des Artistes at eight. And actually, Phoebe's going to be there, too."

"Phoebe's coming to dinner with your *parents?*"

"She's part of the celebration."

"Me no understand." Claudia marveled at how quickly Bronwyn had jacked her ambush.

"Hence *Fanelli's*, Claude." Bronwyn took a step closer. Her expression was encouraging. She slipped her arm through Claudia's, as she had a million times before. The gesture's goodwill, the possibility of leaning, just for a minute or two, just slightly, against a warm somebody else, flooded the anxious cavity of Claudia's chest and threatened her resolve. "Don't be a stress case," Bronwyn said. "Haven't you ever heard of good news? Besides. Nothing a little hangover tomato soup won't cure."

This is, Claudia thought as they set off, their heels clicking in time, *the last day of our acquaintance.*

"How was your *Hope Valley* interview?" Bronwyn asked.

Claudia was amazed that Bronwyn could delay whatever it was she had to say until they were tucked into a cozy pub. Possibly, Claudia thought, this was the ultimate difference between WASPs and Jews. WASPs nursed their drinks. "It was okay," Claudia replied.

"What did they say?"

"It was sort of a don't-call-us-we'll-call-you situation." Claudia spotted the bright cursive of the Fanelli's sign, a block ahead. It was the first bar she and Bronwyn had frequented as actual adults. Bronwyn would probably get it in the divorce.

"I'm sure they're going to call," Bronwyn encouraged. "What did you wear?"

"This."

"Did the executive producer love that you're from Brooklyn?"

"She would've loved me more if I'd gone to Erasmus." They paused at Fanelli's front door to let a gaggle of laughing friends pour out past them.

"I may get a brandy," Bronwyn said.

Through the windows, Claudia could see the place was packed and cheerful, the bar three deep, squadrons of piping-hot baked stuffed squash and big raviolis in oily puddles of red sauce landing at the crammed tables. "What about *your* first day, Miss Moxy?" she asked Bronwyn.

"That's exactly what I want to tell you about," said Bronwyn. "Come on." She slipped her arm from Claudia's, pushed through the front door, and made her way confidently through the crowd. Bronwyn was wonderful at entrances, especially into loud, chattering watering holes. Her lanky grace, loose strands of blond hair, and persistent slimness despite the many layers, caught the admiring eye of every athletic MBA with his grip on a dark beer in the place.

Claudia drifted along in Bronwyn's wake and prayed that there wouldn't be a table. Fanelli's, she was quickly realizing, was no place to tell your best friend that you'd seen her father naked, that you'd miscalculated everything, from timing on up to intention, that yes, you'd put her out of your mind to accomplish the thing that, it turned out, didn't exist, but now her flushed, familiar face took up the entire screen, and that the only way you could do things differently was moving forward. The correct venue for that sort of thing would be a cathedral nave, or the empty private dock at the edge of a glassy lake with a gabled family manor behind, or maybe the corner of Never and Go Fuck Yourself. But here was a goddamned two-top, with its cocksucking red-checked tablecloth, right beneath the blackboard where the specials were listed with festive chalk drawings of yam fries, where all eyes would go when Bronwyn's brandy was tossed angrily in Claudia's face.

"I got Phoebe a job," Bronwyn announced as she hung her camel-hair coat on a brass hook.

"You *did?*"

"At *Moxy.* Well—she got it herself."

Claudia sat, still in her hat and jacket and messenger bag. "Wow. Is that what you wanted to tell me?"

"Yup." Bronwyn slid into her seat, tucked a strand of errant flax, and looked hopeful. "Are you mad?"

"God, no."

"Phoebe thought you would be."

"*Mad?*" Claudia marveled. "I'm *relieved.* Mama needs a new pair of utility bills."

Bronwyn gestured at Claudia's hat. "Let's park that thing."

Claudia shook her head. "I'm still cold," she said. It was true. Despite the flushed milieu, she felt chilled, feverish really. Now that she was here, facing Bronwyn, meeting her maker, paying the piper, whatever it was that was happening, and she knew that Phoebe was fine, fetching coffees for the art director or whatever it was that Bronwyn had made happen, Claudia surrendered. There was no such thing as timing. Cold sweat began to pool at the small of her back.

Bronwyn sat and reached for the red plastic breadbasket. She dug for a foil-wrapped butter square. "Don't you want to ask what the job *is?*"

"I do. And I will. But Bronwyn—" Claudia leaned across the table—it was more of a lurch, really—and grabbed her hand. Bronwyn dropped the butter. "I really, *really* need to tell you something, and if I don't say it right now I swear to you I may not ever be able to get it out." The room became a smudge. It disappeared. There was a thrum. It was Claudia's blood rushing in her ears.

"Are you pregnant with Ruben's baby?"

"*What?* No. Jesus!"

"Anything else in the world cannot be that bad," Bronwyn declared, "so just go for it."

"I . . . I've been sleeping with someone for the last few weeks." Her voice had a mind of its own. Claudia removed her body from the voice. She removed the past and the future from the present. "It was a bad idea at the time, but while it was happening, it made sense. I mean . . . it made sense to *me*." She looked down on herself speaking as though she was already floating above the bus accident in a white nightgown and freshly bathed feet with a pair of sturdy wings. "And he just dumped me."

"Oh no!" Bronwyn sympathized. "Do I know him?"

"You do." The chin that was hers was wobbling, the corners of her mouth yanked by invisible wire, but there was a time delay. She had gotten to the dire part, and Bronwyn was still amused.

"Oh my God," Bronwyn said, a smile spreading across her face. "Is it one of the associates from Daddy's office you were flirting with on Christmas Eve? Is it Carter fucking *Kemp?* What an absolute *tool*." Bronwyn raised her palm. "I hereby proclaim he no longer exists."

"No, Bronwyn. Not exactly."

The waiter, a portly fellow with a veneer of chipped cheer over a deep loathing, arrived at their table and pulled the pencil from behind his ear.

"Not *exactly?* What does *that* mean? C'mon. Tell me!" Bronwyn's laugh downshifted. "Wait. Are you *crying?*"

"What can I get you girls?" the waiter asked, invisibly.

"He's married," said Claudia.

Bronwyn gave a little gasp. "Oh no!" she exclaimed. She reached across the table and grabbed Claudia's wrist, lowering her voice. "*Quel scandale*." Then: "What's his name?"

"Paul."

"Paul?" Bronwyn repeated, confusedly.

"Your father."

Bronwyn raised her hand to the waiter. The palm should have stopped in midair, causing the world to halt and slowly reverse, but it continued to float until it landed on the young man's aproned gut. She turned her widened eyes up to him. "Go away," she said, raggedly. And then: "Please." The waiter disappeared. Bronwyn pressed her palms against the table and had it bear her weight as she stood up. The wonky table swayed, and her chair fell back with a clatter. People looked.

"Wait," said Claudia, rising in slow motion. "It's over."

"Pig," Bronwyn spat, and turned on her heels.

Suddenly, the bar erupted in cacophony. Forks and knives shrieked hideously against plates, greasy lips parted, hinged on gaping jaws—

Bronwyn was gone.

Claudia pushed through the pressing crowd, out to the cold street.

Bronwyn had grown. Her anger had made her a giant. Her long legs ate the blocks, one after the other. She would cross the NYU campus and Washington Square Park in a single stride—

Claudia ran after her. She wanted her slap. Her gut punch. A pummel. She would stand there and take it. At least a good-bye. "Bronwyn, wait!" she cried. "Please!"

Bronwyn turned, her face contorted. The girls stood there, mutually breathless. There was a rustle in a doorway, and Claudia could sense a human form shifting among piled sleeping bags and cardboard. *That might be me one day*, Claudia reasoned, and sooner rather than later. "You don't have a father," Bronwyn said in a low register, "so you think you can help yourself to *mine?*"

"I said it's over. He . . . he broke up with me." Bronwyn's

complexion had soured, and she looked ready to hurl. "Bron-wyn. I'm sorry."

"No, you're not," said Bronwyn. "You're glad. You *want* to make my family as disgusting as yours."

"That's fair."

"No. It's not fair, and you're not sorry." Bronwyn's tears and snot mingled on her cheeks and reflected the wet light of Spring Street. "And if somewhere in yourself you're thinking, *No problem. This sucks right now, but she's emotional, she's angry, maybe, in a sick way, she's even a little jealous, but she'll get over it and it will be okay?* I promise you, from the bottom of my heart. This will never, and I mean *never, ever* be okay."

"Okay," Claudia said. A passing stranger hurried discreetly into the shadows, leaving them in relative privacy. The home-less person in his cardboard yurt was silent.

"What were you *thinking?* That my father would leave my mother? They've been married for almost thirty years!"

"I—"

"No!" Bronwyn cried. "Don't you see? I don't *care*. I don't *care* what you thought." Bronwyn wiped her sleeve across her messy face and shuddered. "The thing is," she said quietly, growing composed and distant, "some people are liars and thieves, but on the inside they're good people. You're the opposite. You're a sad, pitiful person who only seems on the outside like she's good. On the inside, you're sick. You're bro-ken."

It would be useless to point out that Paul was a liar and a thief, too.

"There've been so many times that I've looked at you and wondered what's going to become of you," Bronwyn contin-ued. "But now I know. It's not going to be pretty. You want a happy ending? This is it, right here. Left on the sidewalk like the stray dog you are."

"But . . . we're roommates," Claudia croaked.

"Not anymore," Bronwyn determined. "I never, *ever* want to see you again."

Bronwyn turned, and she was gone.

Claudia stood.

After a while, the little street came back to life. A wide window rolled up to let cocktail party guests perch loudly on its sill. A Vespa bounced along.

Soon, Bronwyn Tate would be tucked into a taxi on Houston.

Soon, Phoebe Goldberg would arrive on time at an unfamiliar restaurant, not caring what she was wearing. Not having to care. She would look around for Bronwyn and Bronwyn's mother, and not spotting them, would wonder briefly if this was the wrong Café des Artistes.

Let me just stand here for one more minute, Claudia told herself, as a bright, festive Friday night in SoHo unfolded all around her.

What will become of you? Bronwyn's question, which had formed in a cloud of icy breath, was still hanging low over Claudia's head. It might stay there forever. In spring, it would form a dark cloud, and in summer it would rain.

Let me just stand here for one more minute until I figure out what will become of me.

Annie Tate bought the boots.

Extravagant, tooled Spanish leather to the knee, and a Belgian designer with an unpronounceable name. The ones she'd imagined just hours before as she'd barreled uptown far below Barneys. She'd let Edith Mendelssohn pour her one for the road—a deep one—and had made her way to the Fourteenth Street stop of the 2 train. She'd flapped to Barneys in her old leather sandals, and washed her feet in a ladies' room sink, and torn the label off a pair of cashmere kneesocks as a worried stock boy with his name, TODD, on a discreet black badge, scuttled over. As it turned out, her sweatpants *did* blouse over the top of the boots like cossacks' trousers, just as she'd imagined. She'd refused the black shopping bag and slipped her sandals into the pockets of her old duffle coat.

Now, as she entered the lobby of the Anselmo, the boots struck the marble floors with a satisfying clop. And here was Mr. Pettijohn, of the Lipizzaner posture and Shetland proportions, prancing from his podium. It was Friday night, so the doorman wore his dapper burgundy uniform with the gold brocade, as per the co-op board's request. The jacket vent strained slightly over his ass, an ass constructed high and round. An ass that, in the recent past, Annie Tate would never have admitted to having *noticed*. An ass that before all of this she would have called a *backside*.

"Good evenin', Mrs. Tate," Mr. Pettijohn greeted her, his appreciative little frown alighting instantly on her new purchase. "Now *those* boots are made for walkin'!" And then: "You got Agnes upstairs, and I got a message for you from Martha." It was their ritual of the last two-plus decades, this lobby report. Over the decades Annie had come to rely on Mr. Pettijohn for what to expect. Annie stood there, in the lobby that had once been the gleaming harbor through which, blown by a sigh of relief, she would steer herself home. She neither wanted to go upstairs to whatever fresh hell lay there, nor back out to the street where she could wander forever or possibly run into someone. "Mrs. Tate," Mr. Pettijohn asked, taking a step closer—how beautifully shot through with silver his hair had become over the years, how neatly he kept it, how curious its texture, beckoning Annie's hand—"you feeling all right, m'dear?"

My dear.

She *was* dear to him, wasn't she? Annie smiled to herself. And how *aware* he was, not just of her, but of all the Anselmo families—their comings, their goings, their thick, bound tension on the way out to a lifetime of loaded dinners, and later on, their eager dash past him, when the night had somehow righted itself and the promise of monthly lovemaking was heralded by the elevator's gleaming arrival—

"I'm absolutely *fine*, Mr. Pettijohn," Annie insisted. Still, just to *see*, just as a *foray*, she placed her hand on his shoulder.

"Mrs. Tate . . . ," Mr. Pettijohn began. The lobby had become exceptionally quiet. Even the trace hum of Central Park West traffic, able to penetrate the limestone fortress as a constant vibration, had vanished. "I got to tell you."

"Yes?" Annie asked, leaning in closer, observing his poreless complexion, his hazel eyes—truly an extraordinary color. Might Mr. Pettijohn have had a grandmother who was white? Or perhaps full Cherokee?

Mr. Pettijohn considered. He had a business to run, his own business, and it was a tricky one, in that it had so much to do with other people's.

"Martha," he said.

"Martha?" Inside her new boots, Annie rocked slightly, but it was wonderful how they held her erect.

"She ran out of here. Looked to me like she may be, you know." He lowered his voice further. Annie watched his lips move. *"Upset about somethin'."*

"Martha is upset?" Annie, whose hand was still on Mr. Pettijohn's shoulder, now applied pressure. These days, Martha called before she came over to pick up her check. "Do you have any idea *why?"* Annie asked, wondering how quickly the news of Paul's infraction had traveled, and who else on the island of Manhattan was in tears as a result. If Martha was upset because somehow she'd heard about Paul and Claudia Silver, then Annie would intercept Paul before he could snatch up the disaster and polish it, for the children's benefit, to reflect a more flattering image of himself.

Mr. Pettijohn shook his head. "She wanted me to tell you she'd be at dinner like you planned."

Annie dropped her hand from his shoulder, remembering the dinner that Paul had arranged at his favorite restaurant, in celebration of their youngest daughter's new job. She marveled that Paul's plans for dinner might still include her. The first thing Annie would do was throw away Paul's ridiculous shoe boxes filled with Grateful Dead cassette tapes. Then sell the apartment. Then move, to . . . to—

"Café des Artistes," Mr. Pettijohn reminded. "Eight o'clock."

Edith Mendelssohn placed two small dinner rolls on a dented sterling tray. She draped a snowy damask napkin over them. The rolls, their clefts dusted in flour, came, surprisingly, from a Plexiglas bakery shelf at Met Foods. The heavy napkin and the good silver from her mother's trousseau. The dents from history. When her daughters lived at home, she'd choose a fat challah from a remote Flatbush bakery and drive west with it in the passenger seat of her Karmann Ghia, a bread so full of spirit that she was tempted to secure it with a seat belt. These days, and tonight especially, Edith made Shabbat alone.

The sun had already set, and the apartment was dark, except for a splotch of brightness dumped on a useless corner of the crooked kitchenette by a clamp-on light. Edith poured a jigger of Kedem grape juice into her father's silver kiddush cup and lit the candles as her glass of whiskey melted away at her elbow. She encircled the flames with her arms, and placed her hands over her eyes. The voodoo gesture, straight from central casting, and before that, from Hester Street, and before that, from a drafty shack at the edge of a Polish shtetl, certainly had nothing whatever to do with the Shabbat dinners her mother and her mother's staff had once prepared in Berlin. Edith had learned the ritual—the waving over the candles, the closing of the eyes—from the women she'd met when Claudia was a little girl. This was back when she was trying to be good about meeting other women, Jewish American women from the Baruch faculty, women who, as tan, busty girls in white blouses, had summered with their well-fed families at ghastly Catskills hotels, eager women with recipes for kasha *varnishkes*, whatever those were, and with husbands. Edith had gamely auditioned their ultimately disappointing synagogues so that Claudia could meet a family or two. The idea had been for Claudia to get to see what it was like when there was a father, and for Edith to have someone to call when she needed help, as her own mother had left Edith behind, and visited rarely, and died.

The Sabbath ritual had true meaning for Edith. It connected her to the dead life her family once had, as mourning was the primary responsibility of survivors everywhere, while offering a hopeful glimpse of the world's creation. Week after week, the match scratched the box, the flame erupted in its penetrating whiff of sulfur to lick, then devour, the wick. Week after week, Edith closed her eyes. There, in the brief, fathomless darkness behind her lids, she pictured her mother's Shabbat table, set for eight, for twelve, for sixteen, in the sprawling Tiergarten apartment. The tasteful gold rim of the china, the cranberry tint of the beveled water goblets, the heavy sterling serving utensils in formation. Rika, the sturdy cook, entering proudly with a porcelain soup tureen leaking tendrils of savory vapor. As the Shabbats of her New York childhood came tumbling in—the little table Edith's mother had made in their dingy hotel suite, their pained, dutiful pilgrimages to the Riverside cousins, whose parents had had the foresight to leave Europe a half-generation before, how her mother had toggled between haughty pride and the anxious, driving hope of a handout—Edith would banish them with whispered prayer. "*Baruch a'tah adonai, elohanu melech ha'olam* . . ." Edith opened her eyes to confront what she herself had wrought — the clear, simple points of flame — and allowed herself to be heartened. *"V'tzivanu l'hadlik nair, shel Shabbat."* God had commanded her to light these Sabbath candles, and that was something she could *do*, goddamnit. She herself could make something, week after week, that wasn't a mess.

Edith had just begun the blessing over the wine when she heard, floating in on the winter air, a lone jangle, followed by another, then another. She'd cracked the parlor window, just an inch, wide enough to allow a warning. The familiar metallic chords that had once made her fix her hair and open a top button now quickened the pace of her heart with fear. She squeezed her eyes shut, filling the darkness with prayer. *"Boray pree ha'gafen."* *God, who has given us the fruit of the vine.* She reached for her glass, filled several times since Annie Tate's departure, with only ice cubes left. Outside, on the other side of the metal door, the lock of which Davy Locksmith had replaced only an hour before, and at considerable expense, the jangle intensified as Robbie Burns made his way through his collection of keys. How long would it take for Robbie to realize that not a single one of them would work?

Edith willed herself to offer thanks for bread. *"Ha motzi lechem min ha'aretz."*

She reminded herself that the front door was *metal*. And that she could make her way down the stairs and out the garden door and over the wonky wall fairly quickly. That as Robbie broke it down, surely Mrs. Parker would take her in. At least to allow her to call the cops. Edith's desperate arrival at her sworn enemy's door would prove Mrs. Parker correct, after all.

Who has given us the fruit of the earth. What Robbie once was to her.

But what if Mrs. Parker didn't take her in? What if she

stood by, ignoring her screams, and allowed Edith's murder, à la Kitty Genovese? Edith tore off a bit of roll and let it dissolve on her tongue, sanctifying her blessing as the buzzer started. It was a terrible shriek, really, reflecting the condition of Edith's innards. She drained the melted puddle of ice from her glass, finding a trace of whiskey in the cool water. Again and again, Robbie bore down on the buzzer. She knew what would come next.

"Edith?" Indeed, the pounding had begun. Robbie had been so insistent on being the keeper of the keys. *"Edith!"* he cried, as she took a deep breath and drifted from the dining room table, promising herself that she was safe. She crossed through the parlor and approached the window. Robbie's furious shadow danced across the lace curtain. "Edith," he warned, leaning across the stoop to angle his face to the window. "I know you're the fuck in there, now open up." There, on top of the mantel, she spotted Davy Locksmith's business card—THE KEY TO YOUR SECURITY SINCE 1976—slipped it into the front pocket of her corduroy western shirt for strength, and pushed aside the police lock with a clatter. From the little table in the chilly foyer, she plucked the envelope she'd prepared. At the mail slot, she knelt to the tiled floor. Robbie rattled, pounded, and buzzed.

The slot yielded to the pressure of Edith's fingertips. "I . . . ," she began, speaking through it, hearing the shake in her own voice. "I called Davy Locksmith."

Robbie crouched before his own side of the mail slot and lowered his voice. "Edith," he warned, as through the flap in the door, she caught glimpses of his wet teeth and tongue, "you need to open this door and cut the shit."

"Here." She slipped the envelope through the slot.

"I want to know what the fuck is going on, Edith. I need to piss, okay?"

"And do you see your bag?" Edith had packed Robbie's

duffel bag—the same one he had arrived with, three years ago—with the chamois and denim shirts and work pants and thermals and bandannas and rag wool socks with cheery red toes she had bought for him. She had folded the clothes neatly and placed a few apples and Tiger's Milk bars in the hollows, as though she were sending him off on a school trip to Bear Mountain. She wanted to open the door. She would keep it on the chain, even though his large, lanky frame hurled against it could undo Davy Locksmith's efforts in an instant. She wanted to touch Robbie Burns one more time, just a fingertip. Edith sank on her haunches. Her face crumbled, but Robbie wouldn't see it, or taunt it, because she would not open the door.

"Two hundred fucking *bucks?*" Robbie cried. Edith had been glad the bills were crisp. The door shook as he pummeled it.

"*A mother always speaks to her child,*" Annie Tate had said. "*No matter what. A mother speaks to her child her whole life, and then she speaks from the grave. If you don't believe that, down to your bones—if you don't know how to believe that, Edith—*"

Edith didn't need every great therapist in New York City. Just one would do.

She stood, wiped her face with her palms, and crossed from the chilly foyer back into her apartment, fastening the police lock behind her. At the front window, she pulled back the lace curtain. Robbie, frowning, a cigarette dangling, his aviator frames perched on his forehead, had taken a step back and was scanning the façade of the house as though preparing to scale it. "Do you have your bag?" Edith asked him through the crack in the window. He turned in the direction of the dark parlor, Edith's shadowed face a vague silhouette.

"No, Edith," Robbie replied slowly. "I do not have my fucking bag."

Ach, Edith realized. Of course, the bag containing Robbie's

Sunday best was gone. She should have known better than to leave a bag of *anything* on a stoop in a neighborhood like this, crawling as it was with unsavories like Benny Crackers. Which left Robbie Burns with the clothes on his back, two hundred dollars, and, of course, the memories.

"You crazy fucking bitch." No longer yelling, he directed himself matter-of-factly to the dark window, behind which indeed she was frozen, telling herself that Robbie Burns not only was no longer her lover, but he was no longer her problem. "You sad crazy bag of old fucking bones. You think anyone else is ever going to love you?"

Edith knew there may have been another way to go. A conversation of some sort. An accusation, a decision, an explanation. The involvement of the authorities, however one went about that sort of thing. But none of those were among Edith's fortes.

"*I* didn't even fucking love you," Robbie said.

What Edith knew were endings. This knack for the finite was, currently, her solution.

"I just loved the way you sucked my *dick*," Robbie said.

Edith closed the window.

She turned on the light.

She walked over to the poster of John Lennon, sagging inside its dusty plastic frame on the exposed brick wall. Taking it down and turning the dead man's face to the wall seemed like the next right thing to do.

There were naked girls painted on the walls. Enthusiastic white girls, all of them, kind of sporty, with boobs bigger than Phoebe's own but definitely smaller than Claudia's, playing tag among the vines, drizzling water on themselves in golden light, and generally behaving like a bunch of freaks, as a roomful of rich guys ate their stew, or whatever it was, and ignored them. Phoebe stood in the restaurant's entrance, not exactly sure of what had happened that afternoon, or of what she was doing at Café des Artistes now. She guessed it was probably true what Bronwyn and Holly had said—she was the new face of *Moxy*—but what it all meant, and what she was supposed to do next, and whether she still needed working papers or not, remained unclear. She was *definitely* sure she had no memory what Bronwyn Tate's parents even *looked* like.

"Good evening," the maitre d' said, scanning the room. "Can I help you find your parents?"

"Actually, I'm looking for somebody else's," Phoebe replied. "I'm supposed to be meeting the, um, Tates? For dinner? At, I think, eight?"

The maitre d' smiled and nodded. "Yes, of course. Mr. Tate is in the Christy Room." Phoebe followed him past chatty two-tops that flanked the long, softly lit wooden table at the restaurant's center, decorated richly with tiered pastry platters, potted flowering plants, a brass urn, piles of fresh fruit, and pots of chutney stuck with little spoons. Christmas Eve at the Tates' came back to Phoebe in a rush. *Of course*, the Tates liked this place, because it reminded them of their apartment. If Phoebe ever ate in restaurants a lot, she decided then and there, she'd eat in places that looked *nothing* like where she lived, so she could feel like she'd actually *gone* somewhere. If, she reminded herself, she ever actually *lived* anywhere.

The maitre d' paused at the entrance to the little bar. More naked girls were on the walls in here, too, but the intimate space seemed to calm their wriggling energy. In the center of the small room, an exclusive table for six had been set among the ferns, while at the bar a lone man in a tweed sports coat and jeans peeled a speckled egg, his cuff links glinting. He glanced up, slowly set the egg on a cocktail napkin, and rose from his stool.

"Phoebe." The warm way he said it, like it was the answer to a question, made her skip directly over whether or not he was Bronwyn's father and go straight to wondering what the hell Claudia had said to Bronwyn's parents about her. She had no idea what his name was, other than Mr. Tate, or whether she was supposed to shake his hand or what. Easily, she gave him a grin. Her smile, as she had now learned, seemed to change people. It did one thing to her face, and something else entirely to the face of the person looking.

"Paul Tate," he said, taking Phoebe's hand in both of his own.

"Yeah," said Phoebe. "Hey."

"But please call me Paul."

"Okay," Phoebe agreed, doubting she would ever do that. She figured she'd avoid calling him anything at all.

"We're the first ones here," Paul said to Phoebe. Using just his fingertips against the small of her back, he steered her, lightly, to the bar. Phoebe found herself on a bar stool, with her peacoat unbuttoned, facing her host. "What would you like?" Paul asked. Scanning the display of gemlike bottles, she wondered briefly if she should remind him she was sixteen.

"How about a kir royale?" Paul suggested before Phoebe could answer, effortlessly securing the bartender's attention. "It's the perfect first cocktail of young ladies everywhere." If you counted Colt 45, Boone's Apple Farm, Coors Light, Violet Crumble, Owsley blotter and pretty much endless Baggies of dusty shake, then this was most definitely *not* Phoebe's first cocktail. Didn't Mr. Tate remember serving minors in his own living room?

"I expected you to arrive with Bronwyn," Paul continued. "She said the two of you are going to be working together."

"I guess." Phoebe shrugged. "I think it's more like I'm going to be working *for* her, but I'm not really sure, you know, how it all works."

"Either way," Paul affirmed, "congratulations are in order." The champagne cork popped on cue, and the flute was filled.

"Bronwyn had some stuff to do after the shoot," Phoebe said. "So I came up on my own."

"I'm impressed," Paul remarked. "Navigating Manhattan on your own. Given that your family lives in Brooklyn."

"You know they let us out, right?" said Phoebe.

Paul chuckled.

"I'm looking for my sister," Claudia explained to the approaching maitre d' before he had the chance to inquire. "She's meeting the Tates." Claudia knew better than to include herself in the coterie, and headed for the Christy Room. "Don't you worry your pretty little head," she said over her shoulder. "I know where they live."

Paul sipped his Manhattan as the bartender set down Phoebe's kir, with its snaking ribbon of pink, and plunked in a fresh raspberry. "Bronwyn tells me you're very talented," Paul was saying to Phoebe, "and that you're going to be the face of her new magazine."

"I guess." Phoebe shrugged. "Yeah."

"Are you looking forward to it?"

"I . . . I'm not sure," she admitted. "I think I probably have to *do* it first, and then see how I feel."

"Wise approach," Paul praised, as Claudia took a tight turn around the prominent wooden table staged with abundant fresh fruit displays in the middle of the main dining room. She grabbed a Bosc pear. She knew she'd never eat at this restaurant again.

The freckled bridge of Phoebe's nose banged against the rim of her glass as she took an awkward sip of her kir. "There's paperwork stuff that isn't really worked out yet," she admitted to Paul.

Paul leaned in to Phoebe and lowered his voice. "Tilt

your chin as you lift the glass," he instructed. Phoebe did, and things went better. "*There* you go," he encouraged softly. Then: "Are they giving you a contract?"

"Yeah, um . . . I don't know. But I think I need working papers, and I don't have those yet, so. I need to get my mom to sign, and she's not that psyched on it." Phoebe sighed. "It's kind of complicated."

"Yes," Paul said. "You know, I may be able to help you. Sort out this business with the working papers."

"Right on."

"I'm an attorney at Golden Fenwick Tate." He shifted on his stool, fishing a slim leather case from the inside pocket of his blazer, and removed a business card. "A senior partner." He held out the card in his fingertips. "I want you to call me."

It was then that Phoebe's champagne glass exploded. It shot off the side of the bar, having been nailed by the pear Claudia hurled from the doorway of the Christy Room. The pear continued on its reckless, bobbling trajectory to take down a bottle of Goldschlager's. "Jesus!" the bartender cried.

Fuck, thought Claudia, noticing the Valentine's Day menu handwritten on the mirror as she calmly approached the bar. She'd been aiming for Paul, and briefly regretted never having let Darleen Parker coach her in stickball.

"Hello, Paul, Phoebe." Claudia glanced at the bartender, now dashing about with a wet rag and a betrayed expression. "Those flakes are actual gold, you know," she remarked of the glinting cinnamon schnapps, studded with broken glass and spreading everywhere.

"Claudia," Paul warned, unruffled. The alarmed maitre d' now appeared in the doorway with Annie, Martha, and Agnes Tate. Paul raised a hand to both welcome and halt the group's advance. "I've got this," he declared. His announcement seemed unlikely to all.

Annie, who'd freshened up, downed a quick vodka, and

changed into a belted wool-jersey turtleneck dress, to flaunt the new, million-dollar boots, certainly had no desire to see her husband now, or perhaps ever. She had no interest in enduring a last supper at their former neighborhood haunt. But it would be unfair for Paul's gross mishandling—or, *handling*, more like, HA!—to deprive their youngest girl her due. She took one look at Claudia and closed her eyes. Agnes fixated on her mother's pained expression.

"Daddy!" Martha cried, bursting into tears as she headed for the bar.

"Let's go, Feebs," Claudia said to Phoebe.

"*Excuse* me?" Phoebe crossed one very long leg over the other, tethering herself to her stool. She looked at Bronwyn's mother and a fully formed picture came to her mind. Annie Tate, by her side, at Image Model Management. Having signed her working papers. Ramona Parker had promised her: *It didn't hurt to ask.*

"Claudia," Paul said quietly, "you should *go.*" He was relieved to have his family there, and frightened of them. He wanted to embrace them, to beg them, but not to see their facial expressions. He was unspeakably glad to have finally been found out, after teetering for years on an invisible mountain at the end of the line built from stray bobby pins, restaurant matchbooks from remote neighborhoods, and invented business meetings. Bold and brave, tethered by faith, but with his back turned, he would rappel from that mountain and hit bottom in a verdant valley called forgiveness. The worst was a girl called Claudia Silver. The worst was over.

Claudia braced herself for Paul's inevitable shooing gesture. She wanted it to be that everything between them had happened long ago, to other people. The girl who had pictured the beach wedding with the rowboat full of beers was her enemy now. She was dead, but her cheeks still burned.

"Susan Curry-Baum *died*," Martha announced plaintively,

picking up one of her father's large hands in both of her own as she glanced between her parents, fairly oblivious to Phoebe's presence. Paul had no earthly idea who Susan Curry-Baum *was*, but he was desperately grateful for his oldest daughter's touch. Annie opened her eyes to find Agnes pointed at her, unnervingly, and took a step into the intimate dining room to escape her middle daughter's ungodly stare.

"We're going," Claudia said to Phoebe. "Put your jacket on."

Phoebe hooked her ankle around a leg of the stool. "It's on," she replied, defiant.

"Then button it."

"You don't need to leave," Martha said, seeing Phoebe for the first time. "This is Bronwyn's dinner, after all."

"Where *is* she?" Agnes asked, suspicious.

Annie glanced at Claudia, then back to Paul. "Running late, I imagine," she said, darkly.

"You're a *liar*," Phoebe declared loudly, accusing Claudia as her eyes filled. The Tate women were now staring at Claudia, as Paul looked away. "You lied to *me*."

"Yup," Claudia concurred. "Let's take it outside."

"What the hell is going *on?*" Agnes demanded, dialed in to the room's palpable frequency.

Claudia knew she was supposed to vanish, taking her charge with her, but her rage was moving faster than her big feet possibly could. It was the sight of the Tates, knitting together before her eyes. Why did some families knot, and others unravel?

"Claudia," Annie explained matter-of-factly to her frozen daughters, "is Daddy's girlfriend."

Phoebe's eyes widened as Bronwyn Tate now appeared, unsteadily, on the threshold, borne on an insurmountable wave of shock, confusion, betrayal, disgust, sorrow, humiliation, and judgment. Her eyes were red rimmed. Her pale lips, devoid of the signature red lipstick, disappeared into her wan face. The sight of her father at the bar with Claudia nearby caused Bronwyn's shoulders to sag, as though her camel-hair coat had become unbearably heavy. Somehow, her father's handsomeness made it all worse.

Claudia gripped Phoebe's upper arm. "*Now* let's go," she said to her sister, bringing the stunned girl to her feet as she yanked. With the physical strength that she rarely flaunted, Phoebe yanked back.

"Does anybody have a cigarette?" Bronwyn asked, as Phoebe bolted past her. Claudia paused, torn. She wanted to catch her sister, quickly, and manage the younger girl's resistance with her thirty-pound advantage, and she also wanted the last word with Bronwyn.

"Please," Claudia said to Bronwyn, quietly, pausing at her side on the way out. Bronwyn, after all, was now Phoebe's colleague. Phoebe and Bronwyn would work together, seeing each other more often than Claudia would see either of them. Stonily, Bronwyn stared straight ahead. "Look after my sister," said Claudia. Then: "Thank you."

Phoebe hadn't made it far along Sixty-Seventh Street before Claudia grabbed her elbow and spun her around. The sisters stared at each other. The knobs of Phoebe's wrists jutted from her sleeves as she folded her arms tightly. A faint drift of sparse flakes had appeared in the damp air.

"Is that *true?*" Phoebe demanded. "Are you, like, *sleeping* with that old preppy guy?"

"No . . . ," Claudia faltered. Then: "Not anymore."

"Since when?"

"Recently."

"What the fuck is *wrong* with you?" Phoebe cried. Her body jolted with exasperation.

Claudia sighed. "I'll explain at home. Let's go, okay?"

"*Home?*" Phoebe scoffed. "No. I'm not going with you."

"Meaning what?"

"Meaning you are not my mother."

"Come on, Feebs."

"No! I'm serious. You are not my mother. You are not the boss of me."

"I don't want to be your mother," Claudia muttered. "Believe me."

"Thanks a lot."

"Jesus Christ!" Claudia cried.

Then, silence.

They stood on the sidewalk. Nobody walked past or stared, or came in or out. The snow suspended gently between the sisters, mingling with their breath before vanishing on the ground. "That's so fucked up," Phoebe said finally, her red eyes refusing to spill. "That's so . . . *Mom*."

"Yeah, well. I get to be fucked up, too, okay?" said Claudia. "It isn't just for breakfast anymore."

"What does *that* mean?"

"It's a commercial for orange juice," Claudia explained.

Phoebe pressed her hands to her face. "Sorry," she said, from behind them.

"You have no reason to be."

"Not *me*," Phoebe said. "*You*. You *are*, and you *should* be."

Claudia hesitated. She wanted to tell Phoebe that if she was capable of turning a phrase like that, then she really had no business getting a D-plus on a *Huckleberry Finn* paper. "I am," she said. "Sorry."

"Okay." Phoebe sighed. "I'll see you around."

Claudia grimaced. "See me *around*? The fuck is *that*?" She grabbed for her sister. "We're not *dating*, Feebs—"

It was then that Phoebe, with an actual growl, flung herself at Claudia's shoulders, pushing her. Claudia stumbled back. The fierce, final look on Phoebe's face, coupled with the unexpected gesture and animal noise, startled Claudia out of giving chase. As Claudia watched Phoebe lope away toward Lincoln Center, she let herself hallucinate, vividly. Phoebe's pivot, her sprint back. But with every passing second, Phoebe was swallowed further by the city.

"Claudia Silver is your *girlfriend?*" Agnes repeated. She couldn't help but smirk—the idea was that bonkers. At the same time, given that over the years she'd abandoned a graduate degree, psychoanalysis, Big Sisters of New York, and a massive floor loom that had forced her mother's baby grand piano into storage for months and left marks in the carpet while producing not so much as a doily, it was a relief to consider that her father might be a bigger disappointment than herself.

The consommé had cooled at the table, and only Agnes had taken a seat. She held a skinny breadstick in her fingers like a cigarette, taking occasional nibbles and tipping the imaginary ash as the cracker shrunk. Martha had fled to the bathroom.

"No," said Paul, from his spot at the bar. "She's not." His voice was firm but his face was in motion, flushed and wobbling. He ducked his chin to his chest and reached for his youngest daughter: Bronwyn had steadied herself against the next bar stool. Bronwyn watched her father's hand approaching. It was fascinating to briefly consider his hand on the body of her ex-best friend, then gag on the image.

Annie had caught the bartender's eye moments before he'd had the good sense to disappear, warning the wait staff to hold off on delivering menus for the time being. She'd just downed a vodka, neat, and now she was standing. That's all she knew.

"If Mommy hadn't caught you, how long would you have kept on with Claudia?" Bronwyn asked, snatching her hand away.

"Bronwyn . . ." Paul's voice held an unmistakable, weary plea. "Mommy didn't catch me." He lifted his eyes and searched, vainly, for his wife's. "I . . . wanted it to stop. I . . ." His voice broke, and a strange, lone sob flew from his chest. He remembered the drive to the beach in the old, vaguely rusted Town & Country station wagon, listening to the radio and singing along with Bronwyn, or trying to (*Drove my Chevy to the levee but the levee was dry*), then the walk over the dunes, the bent, slatted fences sloped low among the sharp grass, Bronwyn high on his shoulders, his hands gripping her ankles, the heels of her red sandals bouncing against him. He dropped his head in his hands.

Martha returned from the bathroom, blowing her nose in a wad of toilet paper, to find her sisters staring at their broken father. Determined, she crossed to Paul and placed her hands on his shaking shoulders. Paul reached for his oldest daughter, but did not look up.

Finally, Paul spoke. "I have a problem," he said.

Bronwyn considered her mother's vacant face. She was tempted to rail at Annie—*How could you?* or alternatively, *Why couldn't you?*—even though Annie's particular fault in the hideous matter of Claudia Silver was hard to define. But in regard to Paul, Bronwyn wanted something violent and ineffable. She could not tolerate his vulnerability; she'd need to grow herself bigger. She wanted to give his malfeasance a run for its money. Something that neither of her sisters had ever tried before. Something far beyond a hand in a cookie jar, a married boyfriend, a touch of anorexia, or an Edgartown holding cell.

What was so totally *maddening* about Paul's obscenity was that it was *impossible* to best.

"Someday, when I get married," Bronwyn said, "I'm going to have—" Here, Bronwyn paused. "I'm going to have *Agnes* walk me down the aisle," she decided. "I'm not even going to *invite* you." At the moment it was the worst thing she could think of. Agnes, smoking the last of her breadstick, wasn't sure whether to be flattered or offended.

"Okay," Paul said, quietly.

Annie, more regal and serene than ever, glanced at her husband with the same look she'd worn as she handed Claudia Silver a spare blanket, just last night. *Factual*, was the best way Paul could explain it to himself. She was looking at him *factually*, from what seemed like a great and unfamiliar distance, as though he were over here, and she were far away, over there. His wife had begun a new thought process, a relentless, audible connecting of the dots, like the manic clicking of knitting needles. Paul was grateful, in a way, to know what he was in for.

He would endure a season of punishment before they could get on with it.

"We're going to the funeral," Annie declared, with a new, steely tone. "It's the right thing to do."

"Funeral?" Paul repeated, dazed. "Who died?"

Martha sighed, gently. "I told you, Daddy. Susan Curry-Baum."

"Married Michael's wife," Agnes explained.

"What did you call him?" Martha demanded.

Annie made eye contact with the bartender and raised her index finger. There would not be an overnight departure for a new life under her maiden name. Instead, they would make a handsome entrance, with their good coats and their square posture, except for Agnes. They would occupy a pew. They would ride out the storm in the sturdy ritual.

The Tates *needed* Susan Curry-Baum's funeral.

They were mourners now, too.

Claudia Silver hesitated on the sidewalk in front of Caffe Reggio. She'd removed her notebook from her messenger bag and now hugged it to her chest, contemplating the rivulets of condensation trailing along the plate-glass window. Comparing them to tears would be a little much.

And yet.

Home is a place—she was sure she'd botched the quote, coined by some patrician white guy of American letters or other—*that when you go there, they have to take you in.* The truth was she had no such conviction, and never had. Not about Edith's, which had once been her *house*. Not about her apartment with Bronwyn, which had been her *place*—and especially not now.

So she had *pretended* herself several homes. The Tates had been one, and college before that. And this particular café, where not that long ago Claudia would rent a few square feet of sticky West Village real estate by the hour, for the price of a painstakingly nursed Americano and a slice of Italian cheesecake.

She'd once sat here, nightly, glue stick in hand, free-associating into her fat journal, bound in black, making a collage of the bits and pieces that she'd gathered on her travels through life. Not sure where all of the scribblings and pastings would take her, but understanding them as sketches, preparations for something. Maybe for her eventual life as a member of the creative professional class.

Claudia exhaled to the count of seven, as her college therapist had once counseled her to do, squared herself, and ducked in.

At ten o'clock on a Friday night, the café was crowded and steamy. She scanned for a table, not remotely sure she'd stay. Faces glanced up, one or two vaguely familiar, but many new ones. Claudia considered ordering the linzer torte as a symbol of her determined break with the past. She had no idea how much money was in her wallet, or if it would be enough.

It was then that a dark, curly head, bent over a notebook of its own, lifted, and a round face rose up. The dark eyes that immediately found Claudia's flashed surprise, hope, and fear in semaphore.

Oh, for fuck's sake, she thought.

Moving very slowly, so as not to enrage her, Garth Kahn raised a mitt. He refrained from even waggling his thick fingers, and showed no teeth. Here, Claudia considered, was the perfect opportunity to ricochet herself down Macdougal Street, and from there, into sweet oblivion. But instead, pressing her notebook even more closely to her chest, she gestured, with a small shrug, in Garth's direction. It was a request to approach. He nodded.

Claudia threaded through the tables. Garth watched her, his expression neutralizing. "Hey," she said, arriving before him.

"Hey yourself." Garth was working on a pot of tea and a plate of pignoli cookies. His cheeks had grown pinker with her approach. His big silver parka occupied the extra chair at his little table.

"How are you?" Claudia asked.

"Wary," Garth replied. "And yourself?"

"I'm okay."

Garth's hair had grown up and out since they'd last seen each other, and a thin headband pushed it back from his forehead, creating a halo effect. "You don't look super-okay, to be honest," Garth admitted.

"Good to know."

"Let me rephrase that," said Garth. "You're a beautiful girl who looks like she's having a shitty day." Claudia shook her head, dismissing his ditty. It was so awful, somehow, how Garth insisted on seeing her. "It's what my mother would call a Jewish compliment," he explained.

"Got it." Claudia glanced back at the door, confirming its exact location for her pending escape.

"Do you want to sit down?"

"No. I—" In an instant, Claudia dropped her notebook to the table, snatched up Garth's parka, and clutched it like a silver shield as she slid into the extra chair. "I want to tell you, Garth." She paused. *Goya.* That's how Garth looked. *Goya-esque*, Moorish. He just needed a lute, a velvet doublet, and a disturbingly human spider monkey on his shoulder and he'd be good to go. It was something, really, how Garth climbed right into her eyes. "I . . . I'm really sorry," Claudia said. "For being such an asshole. On more than one occasion. But especially for hitting you. That's so fucked up." She sank against the scrolled metal back of the chair. "I . . ." Her voice strained, breaking, but she pushed through. "*I'm* actually pretty fucked up."

Garth gently removed his jacket from Claudia's grip and draped it behind his chair. "I felt like, you know, Joan Crawford for a second," he said. "It would've been cool if you'd kissed me afterward, but whatever. To be honest, the not-returning my phone calls after Fela Kuti was worse." Garth smiled, with teeth this time, a little sadly. He pushed his plate of cookies in Claudia's direction.

Claudia paused, considering uncomfortably that other people remembered the things she said and did. Too warm, she now removed her fur hat. The gesture provided a spontaneous air of deep humility. "So," she hesitated, "do you want to accept my apology?"

Garth Kahn's hips pumped up and down, his sturdy thighs groaning through his jeans. Claudia's legs splayed, flanking Garth—she had no idea where to put them. When he'd offered her a ride back to Park Slope, Claudia pictured a Datsun. Now she focused on maintaining her perch on the back of Garth's bike, and wished, as Garth worked hard to get them over the Brooklyn Bridge, that she wasn't so heavy.

Garth was standing up, leaning over the handlebars, the wind off the East River tossing his dark curls. He'd given Claudia his helmet and clamped her fur hat into the rack behind the seat. At the top of the bridge, the dark hill turned in their favor, and the bike soared into Brooklyn. READ GOD'S WORD THE HOLY BIBLE DAILY, commanded the sign on the side of the Watchtower Building, while unknowable Queens sparkled in the distance.

"You okay?" Garth bellowed into the swift wind.

"Yeah!" Claudia called back, realizing, to her own surprise, that she was smiling.

Meanwhile, under the river and through the walls of an improbably engineered tunnel, Phoebe Goldberg, tucked into the orange plastic corner seat of a crowded Brooklyn-bound F train, suddenly felt hungry, like she could go for a chicken-flavor ramen or a Swiss Miss. She got off at Bergen, hoping there'd be no reason to see Edith or Robbie on an utterly shuttered Smith Street. Soon, she stood at the foot of the Parker's stoop, just twenty feet and a lifetime west of Edith Mendelssohn's.

The Parkers' steps offered choice selections of the neighborhood's windswept grit: straw wrappers, a mangled flyer from Peking Garden with a boot print, the cellophane off a box of butts. The Parker's front door featured a stale Christmas wreath, and the parlor window glowed with unseen evening activity. Edith's place was dark. Her stoop had been swept by Robbie Burns twice that morning and once more before he set out on his last ambivalent stroll to a church basement before coming back to a new set of locks. Edith's front door featured a mezuzah and a water-stained sign, written in fountain pen, laminated with clear packing tape and hung from the doorknob with red yarn: *Absolutely No Menus*. But it was the Parkers' front stoop that Phoebe now ascended.

Darleen Parker answered the door in her Knicks warm-ups and giant teddy-bear slippers.

"What's up?" said Phoebe, casually. She could have thrown her arms around Darleen and clung for dear life, but instead she jammed her hands deeper into the pockets of her peacoat and raised her shoulders to her ears.

"Oh man," Darleen chuckled, as Mrs. Parker appeared, her Rite Aid readers tucked into her twisted and coiled hair. "You got some *witchy-ass* timing. We was just talking about you."

Phoebe glanced over at Edith's darkened building. "Oh yeah?" She hadn't figured on Mrs. Parker being home. She'd wanted Darleen to herself. Then: "Hi, Mrs. Parker."

"Hello, Phoebe," said Mrs. Parker, looking like her next word for sure would be *good-bye*. Accordingly, Phoebe quickly began to map her next stop. It was too late to land on the doorstep of anybody she went to school with. It was too cold to wait out the night on a bench in Cobble Hill Park. *This*, she realized, picturing the white building near the West Side Highway with the porthole windows, *is why they invented Covenant House*. A wind kicked up, rattling the rusty aluminum awnings slung up and down the block.

"We need to talk, Phoebe," said Mrs. Parker. "Can you come on in for a minute?" Phoebe hesitated. There was something about Mrs. Parker's tone. But she stepped inside. The foyer, with its enduring kids' art, inspirational plaques, and Afrocentric crucifix, opened directly on the Parkers' tidy world. Unlike Edith Mendelssohn's building, the Parkers' place had never been officially subdivided into apartments, although it had seen a steady parade of boarders over the years. Phoebe saw the chubby chintz sofa under its bright afghan, and met the rich aroma of Mrs. Parker's Crock-Pot as it wafted out to greet her, along with the *Quiet Storm*. Darleen had disappeared, and Ramona was several flights upstairs, reading Cheever in bed.

"Ramona got a talking-to at work today," said Mrs. Parker. They were still in the foyer, as there'd been no further invitation. "Do you know why?"

"No," Phoebe answered.

"She was *late*," explained Mrs. Parker, evenly.

"Shit," said Phoebe, silently considering that of all the harsh consequences in the world, a talking-to didn't really sound like one.

"You know *why* Ramona was late?" Mrs. Parker pressed.

"Yeah."

"Well, I'm gonna tell you about it anyway," Mrs. Parker declared, folding her arms high on her chest. "She was late 'cause she was messing around with you at a photo shoot, holding hands, lying on the floor. With Punky Brewster and friends taking notes. Ring a bell?"

"Yeah."

"You heard of the Venus Hottentot, right?" Mrs. Parker asked.

"No."

"*Oy vey*," Mrs. Parker sighed, then shifted gears. "Then let me tell you about my daughter Ramona. Ramona is not about style. She doesn't have to be. That's because Ramona's about substance. She works hard every day to accomplish goals of *substance*. She's going to be a veterinarian. And to get there, she puts her back into it, every day. And I *know* you know that." Phoebe nodded. "So why would you do anything to knock her off her game?"

"Did she get fired?" Phoebe asked.

"That's not the point," said Mrs. Parker.

"I know, but I'm still asking."

"No," said Mrs. Parker, after regarding the girl with growing benevolence, "she did not get fired."

"I . . . I just wanted her to come with me," Phoebe admitted. "It was like this kind of random job interview, I guess. And I didn't want to go alone."

Mrs. Parker shook her head. "The thing is," she said, "is that girls like Ramona can't *afford* a talking-to. That's the thing you've got to understand. Ramona's going to work twice as hard her whole life, and she can't *never* get a talking-to. Four hundred years of slavery means you two aren't the same. You know that, right?"

Phoebe slowly unhooked her shoulders from her ears and allowed her full height. Then: "No."

"*Excuse* me?"

"I . . . I don't know that me and Ramona are not the same," Phoebe declared. "I don't see it like that. At *all.*"

Mrs. Parker leaned against the door frame and cocked her head. "You don't see it like that," she marveled.

"No."

"Go on and tell me how you see it, then."

Phoebe's throat constricted. It wasn't just that she was hungry and cold, but that she was tired. Deeply so. And unable to picture how and when she'd ever be able to rest. She could lie down, right on the Parkers' stoop, with the Peking Garden flyer for a duvet, and never get up. Instead, she raised her voice. "The way I see it," Phoebe said, "is that we're, you know. *Equals.*"

Mrs. Parker gave a mild snort. "Well, that's not how the world sees it, I'm afraid."

"Then the world," Phoebe countered, "is wack." Silently, she conceded that what she and Ramona had in common was possibly outweighed by what Ramona had that she didn't.

"That's right," Mrs. Parker agreed. "The world is wack. Which is why I'd appreciate it if in the future you'd avoid any damn thing that keeps my baby girl from getting her slice."

Phoebe suddenly gave up trying not to cry. "Mrs. Parker?" she said. Hot tears and snot came next, but she refused to hide her face in her hands. "I need help."

"Your mama know you're here?" asked Mrs. Parker.

"*No*," sobbed Phoebe.

"You eat dinner?" Mrs. Parker asked, steering Phoebe toward her bright kitchen. Later on, she would sit up with Phoebe, and she would listen.

Claudia hesitated in the doorway of her apartment, thrusting her arm against Garth's chest in the futile manner of a suburban mother stopped short at a red light. "Is something wrong?" Garth asked, the warmth of his body spilling out as he unzipped his big silver parka. Claudia just looked at Garth, unable to imagine ever breaking it down for him. She knew Bronwyn wouldn't be there, but as their steps echoed down the hallway with a wrong sort of hollow, it occurred to Claudia that Bronwyn might be *gone*. Even the dust bunnies seemed bewildered.

"So when does your roommate usually land?" Garth asked at the kitchen sink. He filled an empty Bonne Maman jar with tap water and drank deeply.

"I have a feeling she's not my roommate anymore," Claudia replied, taking the jar from him.

"You know the one about another door opens, right?" Garth offered, unhelpfully. "I love that one." He reached out and put his hands on Claudia's shoulders. "You're tense," he said. Garth's touch was solid. Claudia nodded, keeping the empty jar to her lips. Gently, he took the glass and set it down.

"I'm kind of screwed," Claudia said, but it came out as a whisper. "I mean, not really, I guess." She tried for a casual shrug. "It just, you know, kind of feels like that at the moment." Garth's expression was unbearably kind, but she let him look at her. "I'm fine," she said, unconvincingly.

"Do you know how to roast a chicken?" Garth asked.

"... *What?*"

Keeping his mitts on her shoulders, Garth stepped closer to Claudia. He had very thick, very dark lashes, and his lips were dark, too. Actual red lips. "Roast chicken is sort of like the grandfather of all dishes. It's cheap, and you can eat it for days, then make stock from the carcass. And while it's cooking, it fills your place with the best smell. I could teach you."

Claudia nodded. *Fuck it*, she thought, and let roll the few tears she'd been holding back.

Garth ran his thumb along her jawline to wipe the tears that had gathered. He opened his arms, and Claudia stepped in.

Phoebe Goldberg slept the night on the trundle bed in Ramona's room under a pile of patchwork quilts. On Saturday morning, Mrs. Parker fixed oatmeal and turkey bacon and cling peaches in syrup. She offered to accompany Phoebe on the long march next door to see Edith, and even to have a word with Edith; Phoebe demurred. Mrs. Parker promised there would be a solution, and she had some ideas. But what she couldn't do was pretend to be Phoebe's mother for the sake of the working papers.

Phoebe took a deep breath, and she rang Edith's buzzer.

Silence. Footsteps. The lace curtain. The police lock.

"Phoebe," said Edith, as she opened the door. She looked more exhausted than usual, but a current of gentle relief enlivened her features.

"Mother," Phoebe replied. Edith's invitation was silent. She offered it by opening the door wider. Phoebe jammed her hands more deeply into her peacoat pockets. "Is Robbie here?"

"No," Edith replied. "He's not."

Phoebe stepped into Edith's chilly foyer. The door to Edith's apartment was ajar, and Phoebe glimpsed the exposed brick wall, empty of the poster that had hung there for six years. "Where's John Lennon?" she asked.

"He's headed off to Goodwill," Edith replied, as Phoebe followed her into the living room. Edith nodded at a pile stacked in the seat of the shredded wing chair. Lynyrd Skynyrd albums, most of a carton of Pall Malls, a large lighter shaped like a skull, a pair of barely worn Rockports, and a variety of mismatched sweats. A pair of bulging Met Foods shopping bags flanked the chair. "As soon as I can find Benny Crackers to help me schlep."

Phoebe's heart had begun to pound. She didn't want to come in any further. She didn't want to sit, and when Edith inevitably offered her tea, she planned to say no. She took a shallow breath and felt the words about to tumble. "When I was over here the other day," she found herself saying, "I asked you to sign my working papers and you freaked."

Edith's jaw momentarily tensed. "Would you like a cup of tea?" she asked.

Phoebe shook her head emphatically, and continued. "There's only one reason I'm back today," she said quietly. "And that's because you need to do it. You need to do it because it's not right for you not to." Phoebe's heart galloped wildly in her ribs, but her voice managed to stay astride. "It's not right for you to let fucked-up shit happen on the one hand, but then also keep me from getting a job where I could make my own money and maybe do some cool things." She took another breath. "And, you know. Start my life."

"Your life," Edith recounted, "started in the year of Our Lord nineteen-hundred-and-seventy-seven. I know. I was there. With no drugs."

"That's not what I mean." Phoebe looked her mother

directly in the eye. "What I mean is start my life without *you*."

"Exactly what variety of fucked-up shit, as you call it," Edith scoffed, so as to defend her fear, "have I let happen?"

Phoebe took a step closer, allowing herself to loom over her mother, in the manner of her memory. "Do you really have no idea what his deal is?"

Edith backed away another step and dropped to the edge of the futon sofa. Phoebe lowered her voice further. "At night," she said, "he comes downstairs to tuck me in, like he did when I was a kid. While you are right upstairs. And . . . he sits at the edge of the bed." Her voice had begun to shake, but she let it. "And do you know what he tells me?" Edith's face contorted. Phoebe did not look away. "He tells me I'm driving him crazy, because I'm teasing him, and . . . and . . . he wants to fuck me. He tells me that one day, he's going to do it, too. And it's not going to be his fault. And then he puts his hand right here."

Phoebe thrust her outstretched palm toward her mother, and placed it high on Edith's chest, pushing her back against the futon. Phoebe looked down at the terrain of her mother's frightened face. The pale olive complexion, barely lined. The bare lips with their waxy, plain–Chap Stick sheen. The new gray in her arched brows. "He held me down, Mother," she said. Phoebe spread her fingers, so that the tips reached the base of Edith's throat, and she pressed. "He held me down like this." Phoebe's breath had steadied. She could easily encircle Edith's slender throat with her hands. Edith blinked, wildly. "And then he kissed me, Mother," Phoebe said. "Not just one time."

There, thought Phoebe. She pressed her hand against Edith's chest one more time, hard, for emphasis, and stood up. Edith remained frozen. Joyful shouts sped past outside on stolen bikes. The kitchen clock ticked.

For a long time Phoebe had figured that not saying anything about Robbie meant she wouldn't think about it, so maybe it wasn't happening. But saying something, as it turned out, wasn't as impossible as she'd thought. In fact, she'd already done it, which meant it was over. Dust motes danced along the Saturday-morning sunbeams that had found their way into Edith's living room. Phoebe saw her story as it hung in the air between her mother and herself. There was a difference between what had happened and who she was.

"He's gone," Edith announced quietly. She was looking down at her feet in their boiled-wool clogs.

Phoebe hesitated. She looked around the apartment and landed at the pile on the chair.

"Robert," Edith said, as though it were necessary to clarify. "I . . . called Davy Locksmith—" But her breath now ran out in a sob. Edith closed her eyes. She reached her hand out for Phoebe, but it simply hung there as Phoebe stared, and so she dropped it. "I may not have known the details," Edith said finally, opening her eyes. In a slow, pained motion, she stood. "But I came to understand he's very bad news."

"You did?" Phoebe asked. "How?"

Edith crossed to the fireplace and, from the mantel, plucked a small paper bag from Hector's Hardware. She reached inside. "It was brought to my attention," she replied softly. She handed Phoebe an old tooled-leather key chain shaped like a strawberry, from which a freshly cut key now dangled.

Claudia Silver awoke that same morning in her futon bed to the shriek of the buzzer.

She was alone.

She pulled a pillow into a full-body embrace, and let herself remember what it had felt like, last night, to be in Garth's arms. Standing in the kitchen. At first, not moving. Half-dead. Both halves. Then, feeling the return of her breath. And Garth's breathing, moving against hers, until they were breathing together. The realization that even after humping them both on a five-mile, mostly uphill bike ride, he smelled good up close. Piney. That the phrase *in Garth's arms* didn't cause an equal and opposite reaction.

That she had changed her mind.

Changed her mind about changing her mind.

Garth hadn't stayed, and Claudia hadn't asked him to.

"I'd rather come back too soon than stay too long," he'd said, having kissed her exactly once, tenderly, with his plump red lips.

When the buzzer shrieked again, Claudia sat up.

A white guy with dreads and his burly Dominican sidekick stood at the top of the stoop, wearing canvas coveralls and winter hats. Behind them, a large truck puffed at the curb. NICE JEWISH BOY MOVERS. It was freezing out, and the breath of the men and the truck rose visibly into the air.

"What's up?" Claudia asked, shivering in her bare feet and pulling the hood of her sweatshirt over her head. She was glad she'd pulled it on over her long johns.

"Yeah, good morning," said White Guy. "We're moving Brenda Tate."

"Bronwyn?" Claudia asked.

"Her, too."

"Damn," said Claudia, stepping aside to let Dominican Sidekick bounce a hand truck into the foyer.

"What kind of name is that?" White Guy asked.

Claudia shrugged. "Money," she said, as they followed her into the apartment.

"She got a lot of stuff?"

"You tell me," said Claudia, gesturing to the contents of the living room. The sofa and the coffee table, the rocking chair and the Mexican throw, the Murano glass paperweights and the heavy ashtray, the beautiful books and the bargello throw pillows. "None of this shit is mine," she acknowledged. It was then that she saw, in the corner of the brick-and-plank étagère, a blinking red eye.

"Excuse me for a sec, gentlemen," Claudia said, approaching the answering machine. "Actually"—she turned and crossed her arms, eager to don a bra—could you give me maybe five minutes so I can get dressed?"

"Yeah, of course." White Guy gave a chivalrous tip of his hat as Dominican Sidekick blew his nose extravagantly into a bandanna. "We'll start with the boxes."

"Cool, thanks," said Claudia. She turned, and she pressed PLAY.

"Claudia Silver?" said the nasal voice, far less bored than the last time she'd heard it. *"This is your old friend from* Hope Valley, *and I think you may recall that I promised you if you got the job, I'd tell you my name. Well, it's Josh. Josh Spinelli. And I'm calling on behalf of Shelly Gerson, who I am quite happy to say is your new boss. That is, if you can start here on Monday. Give us a call back right away. And welcome to the family. Oh—and make sure to practice exemplary dental hygiene. Because we're sharing an office."*

Claudia stood, and she stared at the answering machine, which also belonged to Bronwyn, along with the portable phone, the microwave, and every dish in the place. She hit PLAY again.

Soon thereafter, Claudia dressed, and stepped outside into the bright January morning, leaving Nice Jewish Boy Movers to do their thing. On the corner of Seventh Avenue and Seventh Street, she stepped into the phone booth. It was a bustling Saturday morning on the avenue, and it was just a phone booth. She dropped a quarter into the slot and dialed from memory. The phone rang and rang before it was answered. Claudia's voice found itself speaking.

"Mother?" she said. "This is Claudia."

Two hours and thirty-six minutes later, Claudia arrived at the sprawling marble palace she'd visited often as a child, and took the stairs easily, without deference. She knew, somehow, *exactly* how one would live in the Frick Collection. Not in a *From the Mixed-Up Files of Mrs. Basil E. Frankweiler* way, but *actually*. She had always known. *How* she would awaken upstairs. The first, early morning view of her pale-blue ceiling, from the middle of a bed so high she leapt slightly, each night, to claim it. *How* she would watch Cook prepare the farina, and *how* Cook would scold her for dumping in too much sugar, and later on, *how* she would dress for lessons, then later, tennis. What was this knowledge doing in her muscle memory, and who had put it there?

Her grandmother.

Who had brought her here when she'd visited from Europe. They would stand before the big, gentle Renoir depicting three darling, fuzzy blonds, a mother and her two matching children, with muff and doll, strolling the Tuileries. "It is you and Phoebe and Mother," Grandmother teased. But it was a wistful tease. As though they *had* been this trio of little princesses. As though, by universal law, having been princesses *then* meant they would never get to be JAPs *now*.

But the big blond in the Renoir, Claudia now realized as, for the first time, she read its plaque, wasn't the mother, after all.

She was the *governess*.

The mother was somewhere else entirely.

So there was that.

Claudia knew the pale entrance to the Garden Court was just a few feet away, at the end of a dim hall. She knew the

234

central pool, and its quiet fountain, would cast the space in a cool, greenish light. A grand, human terrarium, with Claudia and her long-lost mother as tough little turtles, outlasting time—

Goddamn. Claudia was frightened to see her mother now.

If, in fact, Edith Mendelssohn would show.

The feet, in their black cowboy boots, didn't walk themselves.

Claudia pushed them, one after the other.

At the center of the Garden Court, a lone tourist, strung with a heavy camera, formed a breathing statue near the fountain. Claudia scanned the marble benches for Edith, then spotted, tucked into the alcove window that offered a clear view to the living room, the burgundy velvet hem of her mother's best coat, with its curlicue brocade and gray acrylic trim, and the legs sticking out below, in bulky mukluks, with ankles crossed. It occurred to Claudia now that Edith was probably as nervous as she was. That Mr. Frick's house had been chosen as their meeting place to avoid a public scene, while at the same time, choreographing a tasteful one.

We're all just people, Claudia told herself, several times, as she approached her mother.

"Hello," she said, upon her arrival.

"Claudia." It had been more than two years.

So much had happened in that time, but at the moment Claudia wasn't sure exactly what. She made herself look at her mother for clues. Edith's hair was piled higher and more precariously than ever before, so it must have been longer, and there were a few bright threads of white among the rich brown. But also, she looked the same. There was something about Edith that never got older. She had kept her gloves on.

"It was good of you to call," Edith said.

"Thanks," Claudia replied.

"How have you been?"

"Okay."

"Would you like to sit down?" Edith inquired, gesturing to the space next to her. Claudia wasn't sure, but she sat next to her mother on the bench and unzipped her bomber jacket a few inches. The slice of neon orange lining comforted her. Reminded her of Ruben Hyacinth. Of her very own trail of wreckage, awaiting its monogram. "Anything new to report?" Edith asked.

Claudia leaned back against Mr. Frick's living room window, as though she were *in* it, back from her tour of the Continent, and making a formal presentation, before a roaring fire, with sherry and savories arranged on a low, inlaid table, to a distant mother, who, as a rule, farmed out the messy details to others. "I, um, just broke up with somebody," she said. "And my roommate moved out. *Is* moving out. As we speak."

"And these individuals are one and the same?"

"No. Two different people." Claudia briefly considered displaying her affair with Paul Tate as a badge of womanhood, then rejected the idea just as quickly. "They know each other, though," she allowed.

"Ah." Edith, too, considered and rejected the idea of announcing her own new singleton status. She didn't want Claudia to think the end of Robbie Burns had anything remotely to do with her availability for a rapprochement.

"I have a new job," Claudia ventured.

"Mazel tov," said Edith. "May I ask?"

Claudia hesitated. *I've just received the Cocksucking Chair in American Letters from Princeton*, she considered replying. "I'm going to be working on *Hope Valley*," she replied instead. Then, before Edith could offer her guess as to what that was: "It's a soap opera."

Despite it all, Edith frowned. "A soap opera," she repeated. Then, silence.

This is weird, Claudia thought. This mother and child reunion was more of a *vacuum*. She decided, as an experiment, to hold her tongue. Having picked up the phone in the first place—or maybe it was the phone that picked her—she'd let Edith make the next move.

They sat. The fountain burbled. The greenish light lay over the room like linen. One tourist strolled off, to be replaced by a graying pair, appropriately foreign and clothed in loden. Claudia felt the pounding of her heart recede.

Finally, Edith spoke. "When we lived together," she said, as though they, too, had been roommates, assigned to the dorm by the big Dean of Student Life in the sky, "I know you found fault with my housekeeping. Dismay is perhaps a better word." She stared straight ahead.

What Edith said was true. "I . . . I'm sorry about that," Claudia offered, unsure how to reply.

"The point is, when I was a child, my mother had a staff. And once we came here"—she indicated the marble walls with a sweep of a gloved hand, but Claudia assumed she meant New York City—"she no longer did, and she never learned. And neither, I suppose, did I. I don't expect you to understand, Claudia, but the wretchedness our lives became during the war, and after . . . it was also what held us together. My mother and I. It wasn't that I couldn't picture doing things differently, a different way of life. But doing any better than *she* had . . ."

Edith trailed off, and in the brief silence that followed, Claudia, for the first time in her life, did the math.

Claudia had never been good at math, and so she counted carefully.

She was twenty-four. And Edith, twenty-eight years old when she'd become a mother, had been born in 1942. The same year *they had left.*

Claudia ran the numbers again, and suddenly realized.

Edith had never actually *lived* with her own mother's staff.

She'd been born, and then they'd gone.

What Edith had lived with, as a girl, was her own mother's *memories* of how things had been. These tenacious ghosts of the good old days were actually the ghosts of her *mother's* ghosts. Great-great-grand-ghosts. Thin and bound, like paper. Claudia glanced over her shoulder at Mr. Frick's preserved living room, the cold fireplace behind a velvet cordon. *You could hurl the book on the fire*, Claudia figured, but it would help to have a working fireplace.

Edith turned to face her. "Doing any better than my mother did," she concluded, "felt like a *betrayal*. So when it came to housekeeping, and perhaps a few other areas, I suppose I never did."

Only a few? Claudia could have asked. But instead, she kept very still. Edith had never been one for information. But here, in marble captivity, the nervous bird had hopped its way into her palm.

Edith stared out at the fountain. "You're a child at home with your mother," she said, "and then, quite suddenly, all that is over." She removed a tortoiseshell hairpin, and plunged it back into her mane. "One is wrenched. Booted. From everything. That's how it was for me. And how it was for my mother. She had lived with her own parents into adulthood, and one day the war came, a war that hadn't had a thing to do with them until it did, and suddenly they were in cars, headed for Marseilles, for any ship that would get them out of there." Edith looked at Claudia. "We are *booted*, Claudia. By *history*. And we find ourselves on ships." Edith glanced across the courtyard. "Ah," she said. "There she is."

Claudia followed her mother's gaze. Phoebe had emerged from the dim corridor into the pale light. Moving slowly, Phoebe removed her hand from deep in her peacoat pocket and raised it in hesitant greeting.

Claudia looked at her tall, beautiful sister and imagined her mother as a girl of sixteen, in a shirtwaist dress straining at the placket, and pumps and ankle socks, stepping into an uptown hairdresser's to cut off her braids. Claudia imagined her mother starting from scratch. Making it up as she went along, gathering marmalade and teapots and bus routes and hairpins along the way. Gathering whatever she could and storing it all in the basement.

Claudia waved back at Phoebe.

By the time Monday morning rolled around, a pair of girls would tower over the corner of Broadway and Houston on a giant billboard. One tall, one short, one white, one black, one with glasses, one with a liar's gap, no dads, both scrawny, looking wise, a pair of scrappers, true-blue. Folks would stop and stare; Ricky Green would eat his heart out and suffer indigestion. It was an ad for *Moxy* magazine, and it would stick. It would say something that made people feel good about young people. About the young people they'd once been. About New York City.

Annie Tate would be en route to meet the realtor about new studio space on the Bowery. She had an idea in mind for a monumental sculpture. It would be an enormous welded-steel bobby pin, visible in all seasons from the New York State Thruway as it thrust up from the rolling lawns of Storm King sculpture park. She had no earthly idea how one welded steel, at least, not yet. But she knew what she would call it: *Je Sais*. Paul Tate would take a leave of absence from work. He would grow a beard, gain thirty pounds, let go of the lease on the Jane Street apartment, lose the weight with help from a bulky, streetwise personal trainer, the kind of guy around whom he would ordinarily have watched his wallet, and finally confess during a workout that it was *he* who wanted to design a new kitchen, with an island and a wine fridge, as the old one depressed him. Darleen Parker, not one to leave Brooklyn, would be neither bothered nor impressed by her sister's starring role on a poster and the sensation it was creating. But as soon as Ramona matriculated at the College of Veterinary Medicine on a full-tuition scholarship, a Cornell hoodie became her new uniform. Martha Tate would move to Northern California and place Married Michael on her annual holiday-card mailing list, cruelly forcing him, in his dotage, to face the image of her three golden children and venture capitalist husband. Bronwyn Tate would get a promotion and within the decade rule the mastheads of midtown; eventually, she'd marry at the Pierre, her father walking her down the aisle. Agnes Tate would register for philosophy classes at the New School (Myth and Politics and Hegel's Phenomenology of Spirit) and wake up on time. Ruben Hyacinth, admiring himself in a dorm bathroom mirror on the morning of his fortieth birthday, would notice with alarm a new, turkey-wattle looseness to his throat and throw a cold look over his shoulder at the flushed and snoring NYU senior whose name he couldn't remember. Edith Mendelssohn would answer the door to Dave O'Malley, from Child Protective Services. She would assure him with all sincerity that things were better now. Appreciatively, she would scan his stout, muscular physique, that of a high school wrestler gone to seeded bagels, and offer him a cup of tea and a slice of banana bread. He would accept.

Claudia Silver wouldn't see the billboard until later that week, when she and Garth emerged from the subway, holding hands. But then her jaw would drop. To see Phoebe Goldberg and Ramona Parker towering over lower Manhattan, dignified and stunning, almost as tall as the Twin Towers behind them. The girls and the buildings, guarding the city as they reminded all who gazed upon them to look neither down, nor back, but *out*.

Here at the Frick, Claudia watched Phoebe approach. She shoved over on the marble bench to make room. "Mother?" Claudia asked Edith.

"Yes?" Edith replied.

"Do you . . . want to have a relationship with me?"

Gently, Edith Mendelssohn placed her gloved hand on her older daughter's bare one. "I do," she said.

Claudia was grateful for her mother's touch, and also for the glove that protected them both. She couldn't remember the last time they'd all been together. But as of now, all of that would simply have to be left behind, in the past.

Acknowledgments

I offer heartfelt thanks to my early readers for the generosity of their time, the wisdom of their comments, the practical assistance they provided, and their encouragement: Dede Gardner, Shade Grant, Ellie Hannibal, Chris Pavone, Karen J. Revis, and Elle Triedman.

To Lauren Graham, Julia Hirsch, Lili Krakowski, Liza Mills, Claudine Ohayon, and Fran Wasley, my deepest gratitude for unconditional and tireless support over many years.

My gratitude to Marian Ryan for her expert stewardship of the manuscript, and to Will Amato for the gorgeous website.

Gail Lerner and Molly Luetkemeyer deserve special recognition for devotion, encouragement, keen creative insight, and unshakable faith far beyond the call of duty.

Thank you, Adrienne Brodeur, for your editorial brilliance and advocacy, patient guidance, and for helping me to envision this book long before it was one.

To Betsy Lerner, for reaching out, holding on, digging in, and naming our baby, I owe this new chapter.

To my beloved John Crooks and Clyde Crooks, my love, admiration, and appreciation. You make me the luckiest gal in town.